The Other Room

About the author

Gillian Kersley published a biography of Sarah Grand with Virago in 1983. Titled *Darling Madame, Sarah Grand & Devoted Friend* it deals with the late nineteenth-century New Woman novelist, Sarah Grand, who coined that famous phrase demanding social and sexual equality for women.

'A fascinating, marvellously documented portrait ... reads like a novel.' Professor Elaine Showalter

The Other Room

by

Gillian Kersley

To my long-suffering daughters Katherine and Caroline and my late husband, and to my sister Alison who kindly typed it all, I dedicate this novel.

Published under licence by Brown Dog Books and
The Self Publishing Partnership
7 Green Park Station, Bath BA1 1JB

www.selfpublishingpartnership.co.uk

ISBN printed book: 978-1-903056-63-9
ISBN e-book: 978-1-903056-64-6

Cover design by Kevin Rylands

Printed and bound by CPI Group (UK) Ltd, Croydon CR0 4YY

Preface

'It probably started a couple of years ago.' Sally pushed a shard of glass off the carpet to join the debris in the fireplace. 'Not that we noticed then, of course. You don't, if you see what I mean. People you've known forever, they don't change. You don't exactly go around recording odd behaviour, particularly in the family.'

She wasn't going to look at the policeman. Was he blaming her or something? Why did she have to do the talking? Mark was being an absolute wimp, just sitting there sobbing like a drowning man or a blocked drain, or a man drowning in a blocked drain, slurping, gurgling, wet. But she knew better than to rely on him. Dad was doing his usual thing when anyone misbehaved, pacing up and down as if measuring the length of the big bay windows, rattling the change in his pockets, not at all pleased to have a stranger in on the scene. Granny and Aunt Fay were sitting like mice for a change, good as mice with their paws up. Even Granny had nothing to say.

'I mean,' she added, to be helpful, 'this family's pretty screwed up anyway. Come to think of it, it's amazing we're all here now.'

She wished she wasn't. But the policeman – Marsdon? Marston? – had been eyeing her up and she quite fancied him. They were the only two alive in this dead room, the only ones sane in this mad house. He must think they were all potty. Quite a hunky man, what she could see of him. Wasted on this kind of work – none of her friends would approve. He was probably only learning the job and got sent off on all the weird calls instead of a proper detective.

Sergeant Marsden had been in the Force all of eighteen months and had been thinking his talents wasted questioning delinquents and drunks and filling in forms all day long. Start at the bottom. Learn the ropes. Okay, but by now he had hoped to glimpse light and colour, a script worthy of TV. All right, he was the most junior in the department, but even his bosses seemed to cruise through the days with more pen pushing than crime solving. If he'd gone into Business Studies instead of English at the Polytechnic he'd be on the way to running Selfridges or ICI by now.

This case – well, it wasn't typical, but really it wasn't a case. Not drunks or juvenile delinquents, at least, just a batty old bird. Quite off her rocker, really. Something for the Social Services perhaps, if the doctor couldn't cope. That would be the simplest way to deal with it on the form. You can't have murder without a body and he hadn't before heard of a suspect who insisted on being taken in for killing someone nobody had heard of.

It wasn't that they were shielding her. He was sure of that. They were all genuinely shocked, in a good old middle-class way. Tut, tut – pull yourself together, dear! He had even heard someone telling her to snap out of it and stop being so silly. They obviously hadn't a clue, and he believed them.

It was a bit like a stage set for something out of Chekhov, this gloomy old house with dark passages and noisy floors, way out in the country with a long drive full of potholes. And this big lounge full of antiques, little tables with bowls of flowers, profound chairs, boring paintings no one notices and this huge mirror over the fireplace which someone must have bashed with the candlestick. Exhibit A. The cracked mirror gave a funny effect to the whole place. It dominated the room because you could see everything, all over again, with a greenish tinge from the glass, completely distorted now by zigzags of fractured silver. Quite interesting if you were a painter. Each bit not quite fitting with the next. Picasso, wasn't it?

Sergeant Marsden twisted his neck, tilted his head, so that an ear moved across a crack to join an eye, and then he noticed the girl's head to the side of his in unharmed reflection, watching him. A good looker! Bags of personality, you could tell from the way she had taken over. Lots of wavy blonde hair right down over her shoulders, and great big tits. She was looking him over just as he had checked on her – well, that was only natural really. They seemed to be the only people aware of what was going on.

The suspect (culprit? patient?) had stopped yakking on about guilt and reparation and was lolling in the big leather chair beside the fire like a dummy, staring into space. At least she was quiet now. With luck the doctor would arrive soon and he could sum up and hand over and leave them to it. He hadn't read up on insanity, didn't even know if it was supposed to be part of the course. None of them seemed to know how to cope with her, but the husband looked like the type who could take command. It didn't seem fair to keep on at the daughter, and the son was obviously shattered. Marsden stepped over the fragments of glass to join the man who was glaring out of the window now.

'Were you with her when she phoned the station, sir? Can you tell me if she said anything before that which you could understand?'

Mr Bryant looked at him as if he were the loony one. 'Of course I could understand what she was saying, Sergeant. As I told the officer on duty, this is all a storm in a teacup and I'm sure we can sort it out. If she hadn't insisted, there would have been no need to get you involved. I'm sorry about that. What I suggest now –'

'But when did it all begin, sir?'

'When she woke up this morning. She was perfectly all right, as far as I know, before that. All she needs is a little rest. She's overtired, that's all. And I would most humbly suggest –'

'But you must admit she really does think she's killed someone.'

'My dear chap,' Mr Bryant's smile, intended to draw them together, didn't reach his eyes, 'you probably haven't much experience yet of, er, women of a certain age? No reason you should. Indeed, no reason you should. They can be a little irrational, you know. Don't worry about it.'

'But she seems so sure –'

'Don't worry about it! She'll be right as rain tomorrow. If you'd been married as long as I have –'

'But does she normally do this?' That he could not believe. If she did, why were they all acting so stunned? 'Has she done this before?'

'Well, not exactly, of course. But she does get rather emotional about things – gets them out of proportion, you know. Women are like that. Don't worry about it. I do suggest –'

Sally watched them standing like silhouettes against the grey light from the window, like puppets made of black card, hands going up and down, chins nodding, half turning to look back furtively to where her mother sat in the wing chair beside the fireplace. She had been quiet for a while and looked quite normal, but she was starting up again, plucking at her skirt, moaning, staring at the sofa where Granny and Aunt Fay huddled together in one of their few moments of unity.

'Where have they taken him?' Mother cried yet again.

'Taken *whom*, dear?' Granny asked, ungumming her brightly drawn lips and leaning forward as if she expected some sense now.

'Sir Roger … Monsieur Duclos … Before you take me away I must see his body!'

That again. Sally felt the hairs at the back of her scalp tingle and a chill run down her backbone. It was quite terrifying to hear Mother talking like an imbecile with a silly pseudo French accent, to see her behaving like a stranger. Terrifying! At first she'd thought it was some joke – well, the tears were real enough, but it was just as if she was hamming it up. Calling Dad Hugo and going on and on about having killed this Monsieur Duclos. Honestly! And then on and on about Sir Roger as if she were auditioning to play Lady Macbeth and Juliet at the same time. And when Granny came in and she curtsied and called her 'Duchess' – well, that was really over the top!

The policeman cleared his throat and came back to scrunch glass into the hearthrug. 'Take it easy, Mrs Bryant,' he said. 'It's all right. If you'll just be calm –'

Mother laughed apologetically to Granny. 'Perhaps you could explain, M'lady that I'm not Mrs Bryant? I do indeed apologise. This gentleman is behaving very strangely. I cannot understand –'

'It's okay, Ma'am,' Marsden cut in. 'Don't you worry yourself about that. We've got the doctor coming and he'll fix you up. You just sit tight, okay?'

'Oh – the doctor is still here?' For the first time Mother looked almost happy and jumped from her chair. 'Then it was he who removed the body! Where did he take it? I must see him before we leave.'

'You'll see him very soon,' Marsden soothed her, looking at his watch and wondering why the hell he hadn't arrived yet. 'Don't fret. Perhaps it might be a good idea to have a cuppa, eh?'

Aunt Fay bathed him in her biggest, roundest smile and bustled out, but Sally could not bear to leave the room.

'Come and sit down, Mother.' She laid her arm awkwardly across her mother's shoulders and tried to lead her back to the chair.

Mother shook herself free and giggled again with a shy glance towards Granny. 'Pray, stop this nonsense, girl! I have no child!

I fear I shall never have a child now that Sir Roger is dead. But indeed, in Bridewell I am sure 'tis all for the best.'

They all exchanged significant looks and Mark hiccupped.

'Constance, that's really enough!' said her husband. 'Come upstairs and have a little rest. Sally will bring you some tea and the doctor can see you up there.' He approached her with the firm step and eye of someone dealing with a chained Alsatian.

'If you would prefer that, Hugo,' she smiled sweetly. 'Naturally I will do as you wish.' And with a curtsy to Granny and a nod to the policeman she followed him through the door.

Marsden tried not to look relieved. No one here needed him to sum up, and the doctor should arrive any minute. That was what she wanted. It had quite obviously been a false alarm, whatever the lady said. No crime had been committed that he could see, and it wasn't his job to reason why or to apportion blame. All that talk about her lover, and bashing the brains out of a Frenchman – most embarrassing for her husband! No wonder he was a bit put out. Perhaps she was play-acting, as Mr Bryant implied? If it was for real, it couldn't have started this morning and taken them all by surprise. People don't go mad just-like-that, surely? You'd have thought someone would have noticed something before this, wouldn't you?

Chapter 1

Connie sat in the high-backed wing chair, her usual place in the drawing room, fingers woven on her knee like a Chinese puzzle, but loosely threaded to show that she was completely at ease. Her head stood at a strange angle where it had come to rest after a gesture of conciliation, and the smile on the lower half of her face was equally out of date, petrified. Any movement, like rearranging her lips to match the expression in her eyes, might goad Sally to exasperation or, worse, implore sympathy and bring them both to tears. A Mother's life is one of Sacrifice and Pain. She saw nothing even remotely amusing in her present situation and little, viewed from this distance, that could be called fun during two decades of marriage. The fun part had been swamped and discoloured in retrospect by all the detail of responsibility and trying to do the right thing. It had been too much for her; it was too much for her. Having coped for years and years with maintaining (as in motorcycle maintenance) a happy healthy family against all the odds of sibling rivalry and accidents and illness – quite dreadful squabbles amongst the children, blood and even broken bones to be bandaged and rushed to Casualty, terrifying temperatures, aches and rashes – now you would think the worst would be over and a mother could sit back and enjoy a little peace. She had expected that. Vaguely, to be accurate, she had feared it. What would she do when the children no longer needed her and fluttered from her grasp? A cold and empty nest. Cold and empty parents, bereft, in search of a new role. But now that fear seemed to be postponed, indefinitely, for ever, and she was beginning to understand 'once a mother always a mother'. The only change could be an increased concern, if that were possible, and a heightened sense of her own inadequacy. Anything she said or did nowadays was bound to be wrong, any choice automatically a miscalculation. The realisation had turned her from a cheerful incompetent to a ditherer.

'For heaven's sake, Mother!' Sally swung away, clenching her hands in the pockets of Tim's leather jacket, making ugly faces at the garden through the only windowpane which did not distort the view. 'What's so special about eleven o'clock? Or midnight, even? I haven't turned into a pumpkin, have I? I wish you'd just get off my back – both of you.'

'But darling...' All the sensible arguments had drifted out of Connie's mind. A list, she should make a list. An agenda. Stick to the point. Nothing she could say would impress Sally. She had given up trying to explain what must seem like parental whims; Sally knew the explanations and would argue anyway. It would be simpler to say nothing. Just sit there and allow her mind to become an empty screen disconnected from the mains. Pull the plug. Switch off. Let everyone else do the thinking and the fighting. The word and the image of the pumpkin bounced at her in the void. Sally was putting on weight. Could she possibly be pregnant?

'You just don't have enough to do, either of you. So you spend all your time fussing about me and Mark. It's silly. It drives us mad. We're perfectly all right!' That in itself was silly. Neither of them was perfectly all right. That was pretty obvious, but what else was there to say?

Sally jerked her head to peer through the next pane, one of the original eighteenth-century glass, as crystal clear as its neighbour but with a tracery of hills which distorted the lime trees like a fairground mirror. If she moved a fraction to the left the spinney advanced, to the right and it jumped away. As children she and Mark had discovered the effect of these wavy lines and had counted their way round the house, numbering the old panes in a notebook. Mark had taken the front of the house overlooking the drive and the paddock, complaining as always that she had tricked him, given him the short straw (he had been a baby then as he was still), too slow to realise that she was bound to win with the pretty side. The broad bay of the drawing room contained thirty-five flawed old panes and only one replacement, but those in the corresponding curve of the library, where Granny now lived, were almost all new. Aunt Fay's room above had modern glass, too. Sally had decided there must have been a fire in that part of the house, shattering the windows; Mark had disagreed, because the shutters and panelling remained. Mother had simply said that it was not surprising to break a few windows over two centuries and she was amazed so many were original.

A dusky pink blob wavered at the edge of the spinney and suddenly shone shocking pink in the sunlight on the lawn. Aunt Fay trailing Old Man's Beard and rosehips, returning from a nature walk. She would never lose the schoolmistressy habit of collecting Things of Interest; her room was impenetrable, stacked to the cornice with books and fossils, jars and vases of decaying vegetation. Her pink sweater swung comfortably, full of unrestrained bosom, as she strode towards the house. Diversion! It must be nearly teatime.

'– are you?' Mother had been wittering on, indirectly complaining about Tim. It was almost more maddening having to delve through what she said to find its meaning than to be lectured by Dad who came straight out with it, calling Tim a lout and a layabout and a lot of other even less flattering names. If only Mother would cut out this plaintive, hopeless tone. She was becoming so boring and lifeless, no fun at all. Grey. Everything about her was greying, hair and clothes and speech, so that soon you wouldn't notice her at all. Even Aunt Fay, who really had the monopoly on being a bore, tried to be part of the human race. She wore jolly, or jolly awful, colours and at least was enthusiastic about her pet subjects. And Granny could either be thoroughly nasty or cunningly sweet; certainly her eccentric makeup, however embarrassing that might be, showed some spirit. Mother's recent neutrality was beyond a joke. Neutral. Neuter. What she needed was something like a passionate affair to brighten her up, but who with?

'Am I what?' Sally asked in her coldest, most put-upon voice. This stupid conversation had lasted long enough and Mother should know better than to pry. 'Look, honestly, Mum, as long as I don't wake you up and I get to school on time, what business is it of anyone else? It doesn't affect you. None of my friends get all this hassle and I can tell you they're much worse than me. Just lay off, all right?'

'But that's not the point.' Connie could see Aunt Fay looming across the lawn with yet another tribute from the fields. Damn.

'Listen darling, it's for your own good. There's no way that you can study sensibly if you are out all night, and this has got to stop. It's not necessary. Saturday night, perhaps, but not during the week. Daddy and I have discussed it and –'

'You just don't understand.' Sally's face had closed, all the generous features drawing together, narrowing. 'It's not like that any more. I'm almost seventeen and lots of my friends aren't even at school any more. They're completely free. It's just not worth it for a few silly exams. I wish I'd left with the rest of them. Okay, so you want me to stay in the salt mines, so you must let me get on with it my own way – right? If you'll simply –'

Aunt Fay's face, magnified as she peered through a lower pane, her grin distorted through a ripple. Three smart taps against the glass. A wider grin and then a pantomime of raising a cup, smacking her lips, tilting her head like a huge, coy bird.

Connie waved without smiling. 'Darling, it's not a bargaining matter,' she continued to Sally. 'I'm just preparing you. Daddy will talk to you when he comes back from his walk. No – listen a minute. There is a compromise. You can always ask your friends here during the week, of course. It won't be too bad, you'll see. Truly, darling, it will be much more sensible and it won't do you any harm. You'll see.'

She smiled now, a silly weak pleading grimace, she could feel it. Hugh would approach the problem quite differently, no doubt, and it would end in tears and mutiny, threats, more tears, impasse. She hoped that her compromise would help them both, otherwise Hugh would make himself ill with rage and would never give way, and Sally could easily refuse to agree or refuse to work or refuse to go to school. They were both so strong, so pig-headed, so bent on winning an argument. All this year they had clashed like medieval armies, like battering rams, like foot soldiers thwacking axes on shields of steel; the house had echoed with the noise which rang and reverberated in her ears even when she tried to dull them with her hands or escape out into the rain or the dark.

All year, since Hugh came home to enforced retirement and sat about with time to notice what was wrong with the family. All year, while Sally grew into this strange truculent pseudo-adult who argued and refused to accept and resented. Both were filled with resentment; each was crammed full of emotions and warring strengths and weakness, love, hatred and imagined slight. Crash! Bang! The house had become a battlefield and no one was spared. The weak to the wall.

'Can I entice anyone?' Aunt Fay at the door with her infuriating bad timing and ceaseless good nature; despite her good intentions, a catalyst which had managed to create some of the most furious of the onslaughts.

'Such a beautiful afternoon. I thought we might even take tea in the garden. I've taken the liberty,' a phrase which always turned Hugh's eye red, really incandescent, and raised a sneer from Granny, her sister, 'and set a table under the limes. It's simply too lovely to be cooped up indoors. I've persuaded Edith and have now come for you!' A roguish smile. 'Seed cake, too, made this morning – can you resist?'

Sally could. She hated Aunt Fay's seed cakes but realised, or assumed, that caraway seeds were all she could afford. An impoverished spinster great-aunt, downtrodden by Granny, could only make seed cake, had nothing else to offer and so must be rewarded for the effort. If only she could rise to chocolate, or even coffee.

If only, Connie thought wearily, she could be entrusted with proper food. No one needs cake. Everyone demands breakfast and lunch and dinner. But Aunt Fay had shied away from serious cooking: 'Oh, I could not presume – I *would* not presume! I shall not impose at all. Just a little nothing, a frivolity when you are not using the kitchen, Constance dear.' As if Connie were a good wife and mother who enjoyed rubbing flour and eggs into each other and shunting trays in and out of the oven.

'Would you care,' Connie had suggested one day early last year after Aunt Fay had arrived from her precarious retirement at Bexhill-on-Sea, 'to do an evening meal? Just for the four of us, when the children are out? I really don't want to hog the kitchen and I'm sure –'

'Constance dear, I would not presume! I could not possibly begin to compete!' Aunt Fay wobbling and swinging, ducking her head and then (a gesture which still convulsed the children) yanking her pink or canary jersey down as far as it would reach over her hips until her bosom slumped even further and she looked like an overstuffed tailor's dummy.

'That's lovely, Aunt Fay,' said Sally. 'If you've enticed Granny out, too.' She made a face at her mother, who tried to ignore it. 'Come on, Mum, because I've got to get changed. It's Saturday, remember? Okay? The maid's night out, remember? I'll see the boss in the morning, all right? Don't wait up!'

Exeunt Sally and Aunt Fay, leaving Connie to link her hands together again and then to leap up and pace the room. At the mirror over the fireplace she stopped. I didn't set a time, she thought. I said nothing about time. That silly, piteous face stared back at her. Hugh will be furious. If Sally was sensible and came home early he would be pleased and perhaps… But I didn't and it's too late now. If I go up now – Oh *Mother*! and she will stay out late on purpose. I can't cope with either of them. They are better off without my interfering. Fight their own battles.

The chimney-piece below the mirror, typical of the Adam School, was carved, fluted, scrolled and decorated, with urns and a frieze tablet representing Aurora galloping off in a chariot pulled by two fat horses. The original hob grate had always belched smoke when the wind changed to the north, bronzing the chariot between countless coats of white paint. Connie ran her finger along Aurora's thigh, glanced at the film of soot and wiped it down her skirt following the same curve. The last thing she wanted was tea in the garden with her mother-in-law and her sister, pretending all was well and happy, listening for Hugh's return, Sally's departure. She straightened the ornaments on the mantelpiece and stared into the mirror, past herself, into a room slightly blurred, faintly green, surrounded by carved and gilded wood.

Framed and set back like this the drawing room always pleased her with an elegance and order it lacked when she turned around.

Often she had stood there, strangely at peace, reflecting on past owners, past wives, past scenes of joy and sorrow enacted in that same arena. A dumpy Victorian matron in bombazine and coiled hair might so have paused to prink and pat and glance at buttoned sofas, antimacassars, potted plants. Or a Regency buck might have peered, when no one was looking, to check his neck cloth and a chiselled profile. Or, in the brand new house, the mistress could well have traced Aurora's outline with a fingertip and admired powder and patch and lovely young shoulders while her handsome husband pressed sapphires against her white skin. Removed in time and space, Connie could escape the twentieth century as easily as she could lose herself in a novel. Life is how you see it, more than how you are forced to live it. The living may be unsatisfactory, but there is always space to dream.

'Constance!' her mother-in-law's voice strong, annoyed, drifting in from the garden. The company of Aunt Fay palled quickly out of doors away from distractions.

'I'm coming,' she said, knowing only the room could hear. 'Hey ho! Off to duty! No, don't disturb yourselves, please, I pray you.' She smiled graciously into the mirror. 'I will not be away for long.'

Chapter 2

Connie's week followed a pattern, coloured in her mind from dark to light, growing paler and more pleasant towards the weekend when, from habit, a holiday atmosphere took over. T.G.I.F. Memories of the working week. Thank God It's Friday, even if only to pack produce for the Women's Institute stall. Habits are difficult to shake. Monday was bound to be awful, the weekend some kind of highlight. Now that for Hugh every day was a Sunday, someone had to impose order, and they competed daily to appear the best occupied. Each morning Hugh read *The Times*, holding a biro to make it look official, starring paragraphs of interest and circling possible jobs. Each afternoon he marched the dog across the fields for exactly two hours (vital exercise without which neither of them could survive) or visited the reference library to continue his research into the pedigree of his family, the Bryants, (a paper chase now revealing unimagined delights: a hanging, a disinheritance, even a title). Between these activities he killed things in the garden, spraying ground elder and nettles in the spinney, greenfly on the roses, blackfly on the beans, daisies in the lawn; policing the boundaries with his gun occasionally to shoot a squirrel or a rabbit or a pigeon, searching with a can of white powder for ants, with a spade for moles. Or he would sit at the bureau in the drawing room covering pages with figures, adding, subtracting, dividing, and would tell his wife yet again that the house must be sold.

'Nonsense!' Edith would reply when this conversation lapped into a mealtime. 'Your father,' pointedly to Hugh, 'would not wish it.' As the house had been bought by her deceased husband when he returned from the War to shelter his family while he exploded things on Salisbury Plain, she had a point. The Brigadier would not like to see his wife moved to a sheltered home in Bath. She knew that. 'We can economise,' she said, gesturing vaguely with her glass of wine. 'Now that the horses have gone and the children have grown up we can live more cheaply. It's only the five of us, after all,' implying the laying-off of a retinue of servants, 'with Mark away, too.' Mention of Mark was normally enough to close the conversation.

Aunt Fay, whose pension covered her keep and most of the drink bill, would eat or knit in silence, knowing how fortunate she was to be included.

'At least we know that if the worst comes to the worst we *can* sell,' Connie would add. 'And then there will be plenty of money.'

They had believed that two years ago, after Hugh's father died and they had sold the Coach House to the Fosters. A nice little nest egg in exchange for the family nest, a simple move across the stable yard to share the Hall with his mother. Connie had been cautiously delighted. It suited everyone. A new family now enjoyed the converted buildings where Mark and Sally had been brought up; Hugh was now master of the estate, and also heir to its liabilities. Too much of the nest egg had been blown on patching the roof. 'Plenty of money' was a myth.

'And in the meantime?' Hugh would ask. Money doesn't grow on trees, you know. The interest from his golden handshake, and the remains of the egg, only paid the bills by constant juggling and the use of his credit card to postpone the day of reckoning. Hugh would prefer a simpler establishment with a new roof and double glazing. In the meantime, however, the juggling and the paying filled a lot of his spare time.

Connie's attempts to be usefully employed were more haphazard and she drifted through the week pegging all the little household chores around Tuesdays and Thursdays. She too had tried the job hunt, her confidence swiftly shattered by a total lack of response. No one wanted a middle-aged secretary rusty from years of neglect and unable to write 'Word Processor' or anything contemporary on her curriculum vitae. Only one company had bothered to reply.

'You don't have to work.' Hugh had said kindly. 'And I'd rather you didn't, anyway.' No one would accuse him of being kept by a woman; he despised any man who was. Pin money, of course. Connie could make no more than that. A waste of time, set against tax.

On Tuesday mornings Connie took the bus to Bath, collected a group of tourists from the Abbey churchyard and led them for two hours round the city. Her friend Lettice had been a guide for years and long before Hugh was forced to retire had suggested Connie took the Tourist Board course.

'You'd find it interesting,' Lettice had said, sliding one shiny knee over the other, her skirt hitched high. 'And not difficult as you're always reading historical novels.'

'I couldn't possibly!' Connie could never look or act like Lettice, could never enthuse about Georgian architecture even to her family, let alone to a tourist. 'Not possibly!'

But Lettice, who did not believe in failure and had already decided Connie should be rescued from a morbid obsession with the family, had cajoled and encouraged her through the course, shepherded her round the sights, quizzed and lectured her on details and dates and enrolled her with The Bath Belles as she termed her elderly, mostly male, colleagues. After several weeks of sleepless Monday nights and terror the next day, Connie now accepted Tuesday mornings as part of her pattern, middling-dark in colour, felt confident enough to throw in jokes like 'In summertime you can't see the Woods for the trees!' (pause) and enjoyed the sense of purpose of the day.

Not only the purpose. A competing tour company, nicknamed The Beaux by Lettice, assembled their flock nearby and set off slightly earlier than The Belles. All their guides, according to Lettice, were prime examples of masculine beauty – 'Not a load of pensioned-off schoolmasters and frustrated RSMs like ours' – and Tuesday's beau was, in Connie's untutored opinion, no exception. Something about the way he ducked his head and smiled shyly at his assortment of tourists drew a response from her; she identified with his efforts to please the group, with the need to get everyone on his side and the fear that some might not like him or might not appreciate his stories. A good tourist guide, she thought, has no such sensibilities. This man, like her, sweated blood to get it right and it showed. He never carried an umbrella – he looked as if he could not afford one despite his expensive uniform anorak. When it rained, as it frequently did on a Tuesday, he would turn his face exultant to the heavens and the façade of the Abbey, pointing out the angels climbing ladders to the Heavenly Host. To Connie he had a mystical quality, he seemed inspired, saint-like, and he also somehow made her feel that if he could cope, so could she.

'Oh, Roger,' said Lettice. 'He's a strange one, a sort of recluse I reckon. You don't get him joining the gang for a drink after a lecture.' (They had trained in the same year). 'Rather reserved, but quite a dish, don't you think? Those bedroom eyes and the little-boy-lost look – wowee! Tain't natural – a lecher manqué, I'd say!' And Lettice should know; she evaluated everyone on looks and sexual potential and had years of experience putting the two together. No one escaped her net and she spent her spare time practising with a local Marriage Bureau. 'I guess all the girls have tried to save him, but no dice,' she reflected. 'Not surprising, he's got a stunning wife.'

Connie had not been interested in the wife. Roger had presented himself as a handsome subject for daydreams and already she had allotted him a heroic role. By the time he noticed her, with a long grey gaze, she feared she had fallen in love, and Tuesday mornings had assumed piquancy as much as purpose.

Her only other set occupation took her into town again on Thursdays, to meet her son. Highlight or lowlight, these excursions were solitary, ignored by all but Sally, not for discussion. Mark's name arose only in moments of stress, as a weapon or as proof of failure, anyone's failure. They had all failed Mark, or failed with Mark. They shared the stigma of having son, grandson, nephew, withdrawn from anything they could understand as society and they reacted to this by ignoring him.

Soft, spoilt, bewildered and the elder child, he had become a hanger-on to the strongest gang in the school, happy to be used and included, drawn by an alternative security. When his best friend changed his name to Baz and ran away before the 'A' level examinations to join a squat in a derelict house in town, Mark visited them daily on his way home from school. When Baz and two others tired of the harassment in town and decided to build a bender by the river, Mark helped with scouring the rubbish tips for sacks and soft furnishings and passed a happy summer constructing a similar playhouse for himself. When his father settled back at home with nothing to do all day but criticise his habits, his interests, his friends, his dress, Mark had taken two sleeping bags and an alarm clock and left. 'Opting out,' he had told Sally with a newly acquired brevity. 'No point arguing. Keep Mum from visiting, just say I'm okay, right?'

Hugh had visited. The next day, warning Connie to keep out of it, he had driven off with Sally and a spurt of gravel down the drive. They returned within the hour, Sally weeping, banished to her room, Hugh rigid with anger to fill his killer spray and attack the entire spinney. When he came into the house again he ignored Connie's anxiety and settled to dismantling the spray. 'Just in time, that,' he told her over his shoulder. 'If it doesn't rain tonight, I'm hoping I've got the lot. Any later and they'll have stopped growing, gone dormant for the winter. This can be put away now until next Spring.'

It had rained, of course, that evening at drinks time, before Edith and Aunt Fay joined them. 'I think,' said Hugh, peering through a doubly distorting window-pane, 'there was just enough time for it to have taken. An awful waste of money if not.'

'What happened with Mark?' Connie demanded. Now that he had a whisky in his hand and no excuse to escape her, it seemed safe to ask. In her bedroom Sally had merely shaken her head.

Hugh had turned from the darkening garden, lit the lamps on each table and prodded at the grate. 'Isn't it time we had a fire?' he asked. 'Nearly winter. Aren't you cold?' He had moved a cushion and sat himself in the centre of the sofa, crossed his ankles and twirled his glass. 'Mark will come to heel, don't you worry,' he said. Then, 'Impudent puppy, he should be horsewhipped!'

'But what happened?' Connie could hear her voice climbing.

'He's no son of mine. Until he apologises, he's out, he doesn't exist. And that's enough on it. Sally becoming hysterical too, but luckily she's got more sense. I told them both, this nonsense has got to stop. Thoroughly spoilt, both of them. Nothing but take, take, take – and aided and abetted by you. Well, they've met their match now, I can tell you. High time I took over, I blame myself. No more hand-outs, no more mollycoddling. If he wants to live in filth and squalor, then let him. He can learn the hard way. He'll come down to earth pretty quick, you'll see, when he's cold and wet. You'll see. Then he'll come crawling back – and then, well, I'll think about it. He's got a lot to learn, that boy. My God, he's got a lot to learn!'

Aunt Fay had asked Sally, when she arrived for dinner still red-eyed and sullen with the required apology to her father. Hugh had intervened with, 'We will not discuss Mark, if you don't mind. He'll come to me first. I want no busybody do-gooders interfering. This is between him and me. For too long I have sat back and allowed you women to run the show – and look what you have produced! You'll now leave him to me.'

'It's about time,' said Edith. 'A bit of discipline did no one any harm. Mark was becoming quite uncouth. No, really, I must agree with Hugh. You've been too soft on them, Constance. I didn't like the look of that friend of his one little bit, did you, Fay? A nasty piece of work, I thought. I remember saying to you, not so long ago. Is he staying with that boy? Well, I don't like the sound of that.'

He'll come back to heel.' Hugh helped himself to potatoes and passed the dish to Sally. 'You'll see.'

But he did not, and it was now a year later.

On alternate Thursdays Mark collected his DHSS cheque and met his mother for coffee nearby. Only twice had she visited the benders. Sally had escorted her soon after the clash with his father and again when Mark had flu in the Spring. The journey had frightened Connie as much as the commune beside the river, but in a way she applauded their arrangements. Once she had seen how he was coping and had heard his enthusiasm and commitment to parroted but strangely attractive ideals, she had been persuaded to meet him in town and allow Sally to keep a check on his lifestyle. The last thing anyone wants, her children explained, is a mother fussing about. Mark was old enough to draw the dole, old enough to decide how he wanted to live, old enough to take care of himself. He would prove to his father who was right. And there was nothing, she knew, that she could do about it except to nurse the fireball which lay in the crater of Mark's absence. The lack of Mark shaded half her vision to grey, day and night, day after day; concern about his health and happiness and the battered shape of her family darkened all the view.

Two days after Hugh's visit, Connie had met Sally from school and driven to the end of a cart track at the city boundary. Carrying bags of tinned soup and a cooked chicken, they had followed the track, ducking brambles and avoiding puddles until they reached a sagged wire fence beside the railway line. Sally helped her mother over the fence. 'We've got to get under that bridge,' she pointed. 'It's not far but you must listen. It's the 125s to London, they come round that bend. You listen and if you can't hear anything you run. But watch out for the loose stones.' Beside the line ran a string of concrete blocks, balanced a few inches from the rail, narrowing under the bridge. 'I don't think I can hear anything. Follow me – and don't stop!'

Coats flapping, hearts pounding, they had raced along the pathway through the bridge and had thrown themselves onto another sag in the fence. A north-easterly wind bit their ears and noses, froze Connie's glasses to her cheeks trapping little pools of tears which she feared would rise to blind her, drown her like a deep-sea diver in a leaking mask. But Sally had pulled her over the fence before she could turn against the chill, unstick the glasses and smear cheeks and lenses with her glove. Mark would think she was crying. 'Wait!' she called, groping for Sally, fumbling for a tissue. The bridge stood behind them, when she could see again;

the lines gleamed, wicked snakes curving instantly into thicket hiding a danger that could strike at any moment. She and Sally were giggling, stupid with excitement that they had survived. After that nothing could be feared, except the return trip.

The clearing below the railway line filled a curve in the river. At the right time of year Corot would have painted the scene, any of the Impressionists. Connie could imagine clumps of primroses, mosses, ferns, a riverbank for nymphs and shepherds, stippled bathers, dappled sunlight. Even that day, dressed in shades of grey under a sky of steel, the river brown and swollen near flooding, she could see a harmony of shape to encourage the amateur to bring out a sketching board. A charcoal day. A day for a faint stub of burnt wood on dirty paper. Mud and leaves lay like refuse where the primroses would grow and the only colour in this wilderness, too blue and green for nature, covered three giant molehills half-way to the river. The benders, draped in tarpaulin, were no more remarkable in this setting than a hiker in his anorak or a horse in a New Zealand rug, a patched crinoline skirt in a deserted ballroom.

'Hi! Mark! Baz!' called Sally. 'Come on Mother, it's this one. The door's round this side out of the wind. You have to take your shoes off as you go in. We're lucky there's a frost because it can be very muddy.'

She had ducked through a canvas flap and then another, removing her boots, and they stood on a strip of grey haircord in a room clearly lit through a band of corrugated plastic at floor level, furnished with an empty cauldron and the front seat of a car. Very primitive, Connie thought. And chilly. Impossible. He can't possibly stay here. But to be fair she admired the lack of wind and the structure of branches laced together with binder twine, the polythene sheets under the tarpaulin for insulation.

'What are you doing here, Mum?' Mark had emerged through

a flap to their left, no scruffier than when she last saw him, apart from the beginnings of a beard. 'I thought – Jesus, Sals, you promised!' His eyes accused Sally and then returned to his mother. 'Well, what d'you think?'

'Darling, you can't possibly –' What could she say?

'Hang about. Come into the parlour, but you'll have to ignore the mess. If you'd let me know … I'm not quite straight yet, not up to the standard of the others. Oh Mum, you're too soon!' His voice wobbled between pride and despair, her little boy, uncertain, unsure. She wanted to scoop him up, praise him, hug him, tell him it was all over now and take him home for a hot bath and supper in pyjamas beside the nursery fire. 'I wanted you to see it right. It's going to be right very soon. You'll see I can manage. You'll love it. It's going to be brill. And really hot, you know. In the summer holidays it was too hot in here, believe it. I had to hook up the sides. Honest!'

They had groped their way through a curtain into a room slightly larger than the antechamber but with most of the floor space occupied by a mattress and a cast-iron stove.

'Arabian Nights!' Connie exclaimed, bent on enthusiasm, taking in a patchwork of bits of carpets and rugs draped over ceiling and walls like an oriental bazaar. 'Darling, you have been clever!' A complete Victorian window of leaded lights and coloured glass brought out the reds and blues of a Turkey carpet as if lit by footlights on a stage. They fell onto the mattress.

'It's all off junk heaps, you know.' Mark was watching her as if she were reading his school report, rubbing his hands together, pleading. 'And it's nowhere near finished of course. I'm going to make shelves and lots more things. But it's completely watertight. We got that sorted out in the summer. And it's really warm, even when the fire goes out.' He reached for a branch behind the stove, snapped it and poked through the little door. 'Isn't the fire good? I can boil a kettle on top and this little saucepan just fits inside.'

'That looks very dangerous.' Connie could not help the concern in her voice. 'Darling, you can't –'

'No honestly, it's perfectly all right. Everyone's checked. Baz helped me build the chimney. It's no problem. Honestly.'

'You didn't see, Mother,' Sally joined in. 'It's crazy but it works. See there? It curls round outside like the ones on the tops of toadstools in fairy stories.'

'Yes,' said Connie.

'And anyway, we're surrounded by water. And if the worst comes to the worst there's enough drinking water in that can to douse the stove. There's a spring half a mile down the line. You know, it's really hard work just surviving! We're always fetching wood or water or something. No time to sit about in daytime. Always something to do.' He was still pleading and justifying, half child, half adult. 'You'll see, Mum. I promise you it'll be all right.'

He made coffee and they passed the mug between them. Connie shed her coat, pushing it to the back of the sleeping bags to give herself the opportunity to examine the mattress.

'How do you keep the water out?' she asked, testing the floor with the palm of her hand. 'I mean all the rain must flow across this area to the river, and when there's snow,' she had to play the game, had to check his plans, hoping without hope that he would mention coming home before then. 'If it snows – how will you keep the carpets dry?' Please God, let something bring him home! A damp mattress seemed as bad as a fire.

'A ditch!' Mark was triumphant, he had an answer to anything. 'I've dug a ditch all around. It drains away. We've got it all sussed. Honest. And the floor's up on boards and a plastic groundsheet – you can feel how warm it is.'

Connie could not, but above that the room felt as dry as a house. 'You know you can come home any time,' was all she could say. 'Any time, darling. We want you home. I mean it.'

Mark had made a furtive expression at his sister. 'I like it here, Mum. Honest. So stop fussing. I can manage. I'll see you in town, okay? We see Sals and Tim often. You'll know what's going on.' He had grown up and would prove it.

A year later was proof of a kind. His conversation on Thursdays often frightened her, but she felt powerless to draw him back across the chasm and into harmony with his father. Hugh never mentioned him, nor referred to her Thursday errands, but she suspected he made his own trips along the riverbank and knew as well as she how their son fared. Paternal love, she was forced to admit, took a different form from hers.

* * * * * * *

Under the lime trees at the edge of the lawn nearest the library windows late September sunshine slanted onto a table laid with a pink linen cloth and embroidered napkins, a silver tea service and the seed cake. Edith sat in a wicker chair behind the table tapping a finger and watching the corner of the drive over her glasses. Aunt Fay rearranged the china on the trolley yet again to prevent herself from reaching for the knife. They had both seen Sally sneak off to the road, they could both see Constance in the drawing room; Hugh should be home by now.

'I should pour,' said Edith. 'There's no need for us all to have stewed tea. Let them eat cake.' The smile, which nowadays emphasised a firm jaw more than the pretty scarlet mouth, never reached her eyes. Aunt Fay knew that smile as a private pleasure, a reflex to some hidden thought, not put on for sharing. Edith would make no such effort for her sister. 'Constance!' she called.

'I believe,' Aunt Fay busied herself with the tea strainer, 'that Sally has gone to catch the 4.30. It's Saturday, of course, and she will be meeting Timothy.'

'That,' said Edith with evident pleasure, gesturing for her cup to remain on the table, 'will not please Hugh at all! I overheard him telling Constance that she was to be confined to quarters.' She sighed and dismissed the offer of cake. 'Really, Constance is the limit!'

Chapter 3

In the stable yard between Hallatrow Hall and its outbuildings, Emily Foster was grooming her pony. The Fosters lived in Hallatrow Coach House. One of the reasons why her father had taken a mortgage and invested in this elegant address was to give his little girl all the advantages of a Country background, the other was a shrewd idea that such a property could only appreciate in value, whatever happened to the Hall. An Estate Agent should know such things and Lewis Foster was well on the road to becoming more than a seller of mere dwellings. Senior partners die or move on and he had long ago seen the potential in his chosen career. Starting at the bottom as clerk and general dogsbody he had nowhere to go but up, and he had chosen well. Now at the age of thirty-five, with a clever wife and cute little daughter, he was well established on the ladder of success, several rungs up and the sky's the limit. When Hallatrow Coach House had come on the market – 'sympathetic conversion of 18th Century coach house … a comfortable family home within easy drive of Bath … must be viewed!' – he had managed to convince the Bryants before it was advertised that his family would be unobtrusive, circumspect, ideal neighbours, and he had bought the place with a gentleman's agreement to use of the paddock and stable buildings. Somehow that had been the clincher. He had revelled in the idea of a 'gentleman's agreement' and they, or at least Mrs B, had seemed pathetically pleased that he would carry on the horsey associations of the place. Not good business – he had seen Mr B evaluating what he might otherwise have gained in possible rents – but the ladies had obviously been swayed by his assurance and his nice manners. And it had turned out very well, for both parties.

The pony had arrived decked in pink ribbons for Emily's seventh birthday. Plump from a hay meadow and now even plumper after grazing his way through the summer paddock, Pickle was Emily's best friend.

Lewis Foster had been amply repaid for the outlay. Throughout the summer evenings and much of the weekends he had stood in the paddock with Pickle circling him on the end of a clothes line. It was Mrs B who had seen him plodding about holding the ring of the snaffle and had shown him how to use a lunging rein. It was she, too, who had come out to correct Emily's position and to demonstrate how to pick a hoof. Handy having her kitchen window overlooking the yard. He had wondered if he could suggest a little remuneration in exchange for her giving Emily lessons, but Annie had said definitely no. Annie was difficult with other women, which was funny when you knew she was a feminist – not one of those Greenham Common women, of course, but with strong views about mothers working and what was fair play and what you should eat. He had been attracted to her before he realised all this, and although he was happy to be fed on vegetables and opinions he would certainly not allow her to neglect Emily and take a job. His mother had had to work and his childhood had been deprived, something he preferred to forget. Look at Mrs B – she didn't work. He wanted a nice home like hers, with all the trimmings. 'You can learn a lot from Mrs B' he told her, but she didn't seem to want to. Annie had her own ideas and he had to admit she was a good wife. He was lucky in his family, he considered as he watched his little daughter reaching on tiptoe to brush Pickle's flank: Annie was like one of those paintings of a lady standing on a shell wearing nothing much more than her long hair, and Emily was like a fairy and bright as a button. Sitting on the mounting block in the yard, resting from the afternoon's session in the paddock, he hugged his knees and a huge warm feeling which threatened to explode inside him. Such a lovely day, such a lovable, happy little girl; everything going just right. And all, really, due to him.

Hugh and the dog had also returned from the fields invigorated, in harmony, at peace with their worlds. 'Seed cake! Yes, please!' he said. 'Indian summer,' he added, nodding to his mother, 'It was glorious up on the hill. A perfect day for a long walk.'

Edith made her mouth-only smile and flexed her fingers on the arm of her chair to show arthritis, irritation, inability ever again to enjoy a long walk, and said, 'I'm sure, dear.'

'Poor old Sheba looks exhausted!' cried Aunt Fay sawing through her cake. 'She'll sleep well tonight, won't you, my sweetie? We were beginning to despair of you, Hugh. I'm afraid the tea's –'

'The tea,' said Edith with relish, 'will be undrinkable, but we tried. No, don't bother, Fay.' She caught a movement near the house and peered over her glasses. 'At last!' Constance deserved the full body of anger which had been accumulating, fighting its passage through her internal tract, bile bubbling and battling into the bloodstream. It was not fair, nobody cared. She and Aunt Fay had been sitting there, waiting for someone to condescend to join them for tea, helpless, old, impotent, while Hugh enjoyed his long walk, Constance titivated before the drawing-room mirror – yes, she knew what her daughter-in-law was up to! And Sally sloped off to some rendezvous with that undesirable young man who wore an earring. She knew, all right! That she had difficulty (and pain) in moving did not mean she was senile. They were all behaving as if she were blind or stupid or did not exist. And meanwhile the children were getting quite out of hand. 'Finally!' she added as her daughter-in-law arrived.

'I'm sorry, Aunt Fay,' Connie accepted her cup, 'but I had to sort out Emily who was combing Pickle's tail from a very dangerous position.'

'It might be better for all concerned,' said Edith, 'if you put more effort into sorting out your own daughter.'

Hugh chewed his cake, noting a more than usually liberal hand with the caraway seeds and deliberating whether to add a mouthful of the thin grey tea to wash it down. 'Where is Sally? I'm going to have a talk with her.'

'Sally has already gone into town.' Edith felt better, in control again. 'Without a word. We had expected her for tea, Fay had asked her. But not a word.' A little snort, a toss of the lilac rinse, a quirking of the brow to imply 'what can you expect?' 'We don't mind, of course, but it would have been good manners just to have said goodbye. At least.'

Hugh looked at his wife. He had tried the tea and the mixture in his mouth now resembled damp cement in a concrete mixer, the flavour of the seeds released and strengthened by the liquid.

'She had already arranged to meet Tim,' Connie explained. 'I did talk to her and she understands, but today is Saturday. She said she would see you in the morning.'

Hugh swallowed the lot in one gulp and pushed himself up from his deckchair. 'How very good of her!' Hugh employed sarcasm only when he was furious. His eyes twitched and jumped. 'There is obviously no point in discussing anything with you. We had agreed, in case you don't remember, that Sally will remain at home for a change and for once will do as she's told. Was that too much to ask? Obviously yes. Yet again you defy me and allow her to go gadding about Bath like a bitch on heat. What support do I get? You have no control over her whatsoever. Well, now I'll take over. You have had your chance. I shall wait up for her tonight and make it completely clear how she will behave while she is under my roof, take it or leave it. And you will not interfere.' He strode towards the house with Sheba, head lowered, one pace behind.

'You must have known that would happen,' said Edith. 'Really Constance, I can't help but agree with Hugh. He's been a saint, putting up with that child's behaviour. I'm surprised you don't appear to have noticed. A girl of seventeen is vulnerable. She needs guidance and control. She not only needs it but would welcome it, if you want my opinion. True Christian values, you've been very lax. It's about time someone tells her what's what.'

Aunt Fay was pushing the crumbs of her cake back towards the whole as if they were wayward children. Connie watched the fingers, half expecting her to mould the recalcitrant pieces into figures. Aunt Fay was not allowed an opinion, but Connie half hoped she would express herself by modelling her sister in cake crumbs and lancing the result with the pin of her cameo brooch.

'It's not for me to tell you your duty,' Edith continued. 'But I'd have thought you should go to Hugh now and sort out some plan of campaign.' Edith was not stupid. She knew about bargaining and the problems of entrenched positions from her years of marriage to the Brigadier. She had not lived near Hugh for most of his life without knowing when he was on the lip of a trench. 'You don't want Sally going the way of Mark, do you?'

Connie had been studying the dregs in her teacup, concentrating on the film of milk which seemed to float above the murky depths. She could trust her mother-in-law to mention the unmentionable; she had seen it coming. All Connie's married life Edith had proved her ability to sum up any situation and present it in its worst light. She knew his mother had warned Hugh against marrying her. Hugh had laughed comfortably about it. 'You're too modern, darling,' he had said. 'Youthful competition, you know.

She thinks you'll be unreliable.' Hugh could cope with his mother by ignoring her. Hugh coped with most problems by ignoring them. Until now. She, Connie, had been the one who had fussed about the children and agonised about their quarrels and their ailments while Hugh laughed and told her not to be silly. She had been the one to worry about discipline and results and good behaviour while he came home from the office benign, detached, and more interested in the football or cricket results. He had maddened her by seeming not to care; now his involvement terrified her. The only answer seemed to be a reversal of roles. She could not compete with him. Now she would try to leave him to the children and she would be the one to ignore his mother's gibes. But that left her without any role and with all the fears and uncertainties as before. Something must fill the gap. She gathered cups and plates onto the trolley, avoiding Edith's gaze, wishing she had some spirited reply. 'I'll take this in. It's high time I got on with supper,' she said.

As she pushed the trolley along the terrace she could feel Edith's eyes like a laser on her back and wondered why modern trolleys were so low, forcing anyone of any height into an undignified, cringing position. The ancient vehicle that this replaced had been breast-high with enough shelf space to carry an entire meal, built in the Edwardian era to be manoeuvred by a little maid. Both must have been designed by a man.

' – a sticky end,' she heard Edith announcing with the satisfaction reserved for dire results. Whose sticky end? 'An unhealthy interest in that Foster child,' Edith continued as Connie paused to negotiate a worn flagstone. 'And I don't entirely trust young Mr Foster. Insinuating.'

Connie clattered the trolley to safety round the corner of the house and in through the scullery door, laughing, pretending to laugh, making laughing noises with the air in her lungs, at such need for a scapegoat. As if she would even consider Lewis Foster!

From the beginning Edith had mistrusted her, she knew that from Hugh, always asking loaded questions about their male friends and looking smugly disbelieving. If she had been a raving beauty, a sex symbol, she could have understood this, but with her skinny, mousy looks it was quite absurd. More likely, Connie had long ago concluded, Edith had given the Brigadier a run for his money during their own marriage and because of that assumed the worst for her son. Before her flesh spread and settled into old age she had been a remarkable woman – countless photographs in silver frames, removed now from the piano to her own quarters in the library, attested to this. Pictures ranging from oxidised sepia portraits through family snapshots to Polyfotos and beyond showed the same drooping eyelids and tilted nose and the enchantingly drawn mouth which nowadays, in technicolour, gave the face more than a hint of caricature. These good features had somehow bypassed her son, who took after the Brigadier with the Bryant blunt head, all rectangles and lugubrious lines; but fortunately they had emerged in contemporary style in both Sally and Mark, broader, softer, with fuller lips. That mouth, Lettice had said when she was helping Connie move into the Hall, must have some history. Lettice admitted she found Connie's mother-in-law fascinating. 'Quite a raver in her time she must have been, believe me! And someone evidently told her she looked great in drag, or in some way pushed the pancake makeup. There aren't many women of her age who would dare go around like that! I give her full marks.' Perhaps Edith had guilty memories of her own behaviour, to assume her son's wife would be 'unreliable'.

'She doesn't understand you, darling,' Hugh had comforted her. 'You should be flattered.' She wasn't sure how to take that, but sometimes wondered if perhaps Edith had a point. Most of her life she had dreamed of a hero, quite unlike Hugh, who would gallop past on a chestnut horse gathering her up, all flowing skirts and trailing hair, to bear her away to his castle or hilltop or lair. But none of their acquaintance was like that. Certainly not Lewis Foster.

Hugh was in the kitchen scraping mud from his shoes with a fruit knife. 'What's so funny then?' he asked. 'I meant what I said. Sally's got to come to heel. If something's not done now she'll be as bad as Mark and I'm not having that, whatever you say. Insubordination!' The word echoed in his head and made him pause, fruit knife raised. His father, also a reasonable man, had used that word sometime in Hugh's youth. Could it have referred to him? Unlikely. Discipline when he was a lad had been a different kettle of fish. You knew your place and if you forgot it the reminder was swift and painful. The Brigadier had used a hunting crop. Some of that would have done Mark no harm. The beauty of it struck him now – a few strokes and it was all over. No need to sulk for months in an igloo in a muddy field. No confusion over who was in control. Afterwards you shook hands and that was that. He missed Mark; he missed the idea of Mark his son. He liked the idea of Mark in his igloo no more than Connie did, but he was damned if he would discuss it with her and let himself in for all her arguing. Women who want something never let up. There was no honourable end to this nonsense except for Mark to call a truce. It wasn't for him to make the move. If only he had taken a firm line earlier, instead of giving way to Connie's wishy-washy ideals and emotional blackmail. Spare the rod and spoil the child. How right that was! But it was not too late for Sally. She was an intelligent child, doing well at school and, they said, should go on to university and do even better. She would understand. It was for her own good. 'Sally knows which side her bread is buttered,' he added.

'Does she?' Connie's laughter had died and she was standing

over the trolley thinking that the silver should be polished. The sugar basin showed thumb prints as well as tarnish on its smooth surfaces. 'Darling, go gently with her. Of course she'll understand that she needs more time to work, but out-and-out vetoes will only make her defensive. Bear in mind that her chums all seem to be given a free hand. In the Sixth Form they're supposed to learn responsibility. It's quite a sensible idea, as a middle ground between absolute school and absolute freedom, for them to learn to handle it. It *is* a good idea before they are turned loose into the world. She has to learn –'

'Exactly.' Hugh washed the cakes of mud from the sink and polished the fruit knife. 'She has to learn that there are ways and ways of behaving and that there are some things up with which, like Churchill, I will not put! That's all. That's all I'm going to say. Take it or leave it.'

'But gently!' Connie knew there was no hope. The 'take it or leave it' sounded like the ultimatum given Mark. If Sally rebelled, even slightly, he would insist on 'take it or leave it' – and she could imagine Sally's reaction. With Sally's spirit there could be no choice; she had been surprised about Mark.

'Of course.' Hugh dismissed her fears. 'Don't worry. I'll sort her out when she comes in. Now I'm going to have a bath before Aunt Fay takes all the water. Don't worry! You'll see.'

'Couldn't you,' she could hear her voice pleading, though he would consider it whining, 'wait till tomorrow? It's so much easier in daylight. You'll both be happier in daytime. Why wait up? You'll be tired. You'll both be tired.' And Sally might come home late.

'What time did you tell her to be back?' He asked it quite gently, but as if he ran a whiplash through his fingers. He knew. He had not been married to her all these years without knowing where she failed.

'I didn't.' Almost she was tempted, just to keep him happy.

Silence. Worse than a reaction. And then, worse than the silence, 'I see.'

He replaced the fruit knife in the drawer, collected his shoes, checked that the sink was tidy and walked to the kitchen door with the tread of a hangman. At the door he turned. Quite kindly he said, 'You are you own worst enemy, Constance. You know that. You have set Sally up. She won't be back at any reasonable time, and you know that. It's you who have done it. You have given her the licence to do as she wishes. Not only did you not pass on my instructions and make her wait for me, you have left her the freedom (as you'd call it) to defy me. You have both defied me.' His voice was horribly pleasant. 'I won't waste my time telling you what I think about that. I'll leave the bath in for you and will see you at dinner. But be under no illusion, I will wait up for Sally and when she does come in I'll talk to her, then and there, whatever the time.' He closed the kitchen door, something he knew she hated.

Sheba whined, padded over and scratched at the paint which already bore her mark. Connie threw open the window over the sink instead and clattered everything off the trolley under the running tap. To hell with polishing the silver! Outside Lewis Foster waved.

'Come over and have a drink,' he called. He knew the Bryants started drinking whisky at six, but seldom managed to entice Mrs B. He and Annie had only been entertained at the Hall on special occasions like Christmas and Easter or when the Hunt met in their drive, but he persevered, knowing how Mrs B liked Emily and was interested in her progress. He still hoped that she and Annie would hit it off, that the day would dawn when Annie would say 'The Bryants are coming to dinner' or, better still, 'We're dining at the Hall'. 'Mr Bryant too, of course, if he can spare the time.'

'I'd love to,' Mrs B replied with that lovely gracious smile. 'As soon as I've sorted things out here.'

That gave him time to rush the hoover over the lounge floor and tuck Annie's books and embroidery behind the settee. Annie would not change into something pretty, but he shooed Emily into a bath and dressed himself in a new Viyella shirt and his cavalry twills. Just enough time to have the ice and water on the drinks trolley and some peanuts in a pretty saucer.

'What a nice idea!' said Connie, noting as she always did an alien smell and feel to the house she still considered her own. Funny furniture stood in clusters on her carpet and the same buttermilk walls held etchings of some kind which she could not quite interpret without rudely removing her glasses and peering. The broad basic hearth which Hugh had built to burn tree trunks now contained a gas coal-effect fireplace with, on the mantelpiece, a glass and brass clock with an obtrusive pendulum.

'Come on in!' Lewis was rubbing his hands. 'Now, it's ice and water, isn't it? With your whisky.' He selected a glass, held it to the light, measured a double-double tot in the bubble plugged into the bottle. 'Teacher's all right?' He had noticed that the Bryants drank Teacher's.

'Oh, that's marvellous! We only have Teacher's for high days and holidays. The rest of the time it's the cheapest we can get, I'm afraid.' She laughed, made her way to the window (still the green silk curtains, the linings must be in shreds) and appraised the view (unchanged, and the blackberry hedge looked untouched). 'Do you pick blackberries?' she asked and had to laugh again, it sounded so pedantic.

'Blackberries?' What blackberries? Should one? 'Not often,' he temporised. 'Have you got some?' And he brought her drink and the dish of nuts to stand beside her at the window. Their shoulders were just about level, his tan-and-cream check Viyella and her subtle greeny-grey cotton. The hand she reached for her glass showed a map of blue veins in creamy skin; an aristocratic hand, you could tell, with a touch as cold as ice. Poor circulation, he remembered his mother saying about the Vicar.

'That hedge in particular,' she said. 'The one that gets all the sun. I used to make jars and jars of blackberry jelly. The children loved it on everything.' She smiled mistily and he thought what a perfect mother she must have been – must be – knowing all about horses and blackberry jelly and economising with the whisky.

'No, we haven't picked *them*,' he said. 'Perhaps it's too late now? Been rather busy with Emily's riding and such like.'

'Of course,' said Connie. 'Tell me how it's going. Did you find that Pony Club manual useful?'

'She can tell you herself!' Lewis' face lit with pride as his daughter trotted in wearing teddy-bear slippers and dressing gown and her white gold hair, dressed like a circus pony, flying from the top of her head.

'Daddy, Daddy – oh!' she paused for effect, huge eyes wide. Had it been rehearsed? 'Mrs Bwy-ant!'

'Well, Emily,' said Connie. Perhaps Sally had been as theatrical at that age, though she doubted it. 'How's your new school? How's Pickle?'

'Oh, school's lovely, and Pickle –' Emily rounded the sofa and reached up for a peanut, 'he's being a very good boy, he's doing exactly what he's told, isn't he, Daddy? We can gallop now – we *did* gallop today! But Daddy wants me to trot all the time.' A more or less perfect *moue* with dimples and rolling eye. Men! Well, really!

'That's the most difficult thing,' Connie sympathised. 'Once you can trot properly you'll find everything else is easy. You must keep at it. He's looking very well.'

'Oh, he *is*! But Mummy says he's too fat.'

'That will wear off in the winter,' Connie was saying as Annie joined them, quite as dramatic with her red hair dressed like her daughter's to make a waterfall down to her shoulders.

'Sorry, but I had to finish in the kitchen,' she said, striding her bare feet and stone-washed jeans to the drinks trolley. Annie was always a surprise, the hair like a torch, which she seemed to do nothing to control, the translucent skin that by comparison gave an unearthly pallor, the cat-green eyes.

Connie felt wafts of cat-caution and disregard. Annie's space was not to be invaded. How did she cope with Lewis' too obvious wish to be a part of the whole, the Hall, the Bryant clan? The Coach House was too close for such comfort, which was why Connie had avoided more than the essential invitations across the stable yard. If Lewis Foster had his way it would be much deeper than 'Mrs B' and an exchange of drinks, he would be brushing up on idiotic copycat details and everyone would feel like tin soldiers on display. 'I've only thrown a casserole in the oven,' Connie said. 'And I must get back soon to do the rest.'

More than a casserole? Lewis' expression implied as he took her glass. Annie looked bored. 'It must be handy having a teenager. I can't wait till Emily can scrub potatoes as well as she brushes Pickle.' She flopped onto a beanbag and wriggled until it took her shape. 'That's what we have children for,' she told Emily. 'Then you can get me out being useful in the yard. Fair shares.'

Lewis' laughter brayed like a donkey. He wanted to make his joke about the woman's lot but was not sure if Mrs B might not be on Annie's side. 'Your Sally must be a great help,' was all he said.

'Yes,' said Connie, gulping her second, barely diluted, Teacher's.

'Emily will be just like her when she's older.' He ruffled his daughter's ponytail.

Annie's cat-lynx eyes were on Connie. 'I was joking,' she said. 'I know what hell my mother went through when I was an adolescent. But they say the menopause is worse,' she added, the eyes narrowing, intrusive.

'Oh really?' Connie regretted her impulse to cross the yard alone and wondered if Hugh had seen her note on the kitchen table. Much as she feared and distrusted him at the moment, she wanted his protection against Annie's green searchlights. If he joined her, too, Annie's attention might take his mind off Sally.

As if on cue he arrived, very clean and almost as smooth as Lewis with an almost identical shirt. While he was moving across the room, complimenting the Fosters and being welcomed, Connie watched the shirts, comparing the men inside them: their fussy little host and her big solid husband, the pressed pleats and creases on Lewis's extended sleeve, the well-worn moulding of Hugh's, the stiff folds of Lewis' polyester cravat, the way Hugh's comfortably filled the gap. Regency buck and country gentleman, or a matter of age and usage?

'Great, great! So glad you could make it!' Lewis decanted whisky into a glass and Hugh settled himself on a stool beside Annie who paraded her tightly clad legs and continued her explanation that once in a beanbag one cannot rise to greetings. Connie and Lewis sat on the sofa to watch them.

'I couldn't possibly get the hang of those sacks of marbles' Hugh said. He had already told Connie that nothing would induce him to try.

'Me neither!' said Lewis. 'Don't like the look of them, too. Not in the lounge.' They don't go with good furniture, he was always telling Annie, they look all scruffy in here, drag the place down.

'You don't know what you're missing,' said Annie, wriggling deeper with hips and shoulders, pointing her breasts towards Hugh so that they threatened to burst through her blouse. Her space glowed with colour and vitality, reds and golds and milky flesh, the only light in the room. 'When you've got it right it's a great experience, all enveloping, womb-like. I'll give you a lesson if you like.'

This show-off side to Annie Lewis had never liked, even when it was directed at him. Rather vulgar and unnecessary and not at all the way to behave with the Bryants. He frowned as Emily fetched the other beanbag and threw herself on to it yelling 'Look at me!'

'That's enough, Em,' he said. 'You take the nuts to Mr Bryant while I freshen Mrs B's glass.'

'Oh no, really,' Connie began to protest.

'Can't sit there waiting for it to hatch! And then I can join you. Want another, Annie?' He normally allowed her two of the single tots unless it was a special occasion, though sometimes, if he wasn't concentrating or if it was the night for sex, the bubble would blip into the next digit and pour a double. Annie always allowed at least one extra blip. Each tot, he had explained, cost nearly a pound. You had to look at it that way. Of course with the Bryants that didn't matter, but still.

'I'll get my own,' she replied, 'when Hugh's ready,' and made her eyes long and thin and mean like she did if he was fumbling and fussing and not quite managing in bed.

He fixed Mrs B a double and measured a single for himself so that Annie could see. Annie wasn't watching and was making an exhibition of herself showing Mr B how to organise the beanbag. Her yellow blouse, he noticed, was unbuttoned far too low so that anyone could see what was inside. He also saw, as he carried the glasses back to the settee, that Mr B had noticed too. He glanced upwards at Mrs B as he handed her drink but she, bless her, was talking to Emily about not giving Pickle too many pony nuts.

'Didn't I tell you?' He had thought that himself. 'Mrs Bryant knows about these things, Em. You listen to her and you'll learn what to do. We were wondering,' he continued, slipping an arm around his little girl and feeling the fragile bones through her teddy-bear dressing gown, smelling the Boots baby powder and the shampoo, all so clean and responsive, 'We didn't know when exactly we should bring Pickle in to the stables for the nights. Now that the frosts are beginning. We don't want him catching cold. Or should he have one of those canvas covers?'

Mrs B was ignoring Annie's antics. 'Oh, Pickle's fine as he is. He's better off outside. These ponies are tough and used to the weather. Certainly he won't need a rug and you'd only bring him in to keep him clean and dry for a special ride next day. He'd –'

Annie was at the drinks trolley adjusting her yellow blouse. Lewis could count the number of blips in the whisky bubble as if it were bugged. Mrs B was not concentrating on Pickle but watching her husband watching Annie, and allowed her words to trail off. She leaned towards Lewis he feared to protest, but instead bathed him in her most beautiful smile and looked surprisingly pleased. 'I really must get back,' she almost whispered. 'Don't disturb yourself, I insist. There's no hurry for Hugh. Thank you so much for the drinks, I feel much better now.'

As she left, with a kind word to Emily, he stared after her. She had really enjoyed herself. He had made her feel better. Was she ill? He thought over what she had said. Poor woman, the Hall was a big house to run and she wasn't that strong like Annie. Mr B probably made demands on her. He could imagine. He wished he had said something to show he understood. Anything he could do to help. Any time.

Emily trotted back and climbed on his knee for a cuddle, thumb in mouth, fairy hair tickling her chin. They sat in peace watching Annie chatting to Mr B and Mr B enjoying his whisky.

Chapter 4

After dinner Edith invited Aunt Fay to watch television with her in the library, a Saturday evening ritual always politely offered and graciously accepted. Other nights Edith would yawn and sigh about boredom but would dismiss her sister to her upper room and watch whatever appeared on BBC 1 from her bed. During the week she refused to watch commercials; on Saturdays she allowed Aunt Fay to choose and then criticised and complained throughout. On Saturdays they dressed for dinner as if it were a party – all that effort would be wasted on an early night. Sometimes her invitation included her son and daughter-in-law. But not tonight.

'Quite disgraceful!' she said to Aunt Fay as the library door closed. 'Shall we have the fire?'

Aunt Fay arranged the electric bar so that it faced Edith's chair and fetched the brandy decanter and two small glasses to the table beside it. 'Yes dear,' she agreed. It was not for her to comment. 'Would you like that detective serial or would you prefer the news? In which case –'

'Both of them! *Both* of them inebriated – anyone could tell. You noticed? And Hugh a quarter of an hour late, too. I've had my doubts of course, for some time, about Constance and that young man. But Hugh! She's undoubtedly a tart – all that red hair and the way she flaunts her body. Proximity,' she added after a moment of staring at Benedict Cumberbatch. 'Temptation right on his doorstep. Difficult for a man to resist.'

'They only went there for a drink,' said Aunt Fay.

'A drink!' The famous Bryant snort which accompanied any

revelation of human frailty. 'I'll say! *She* went over there on the dot of six and he was there by six thirty. And we didn't eat till nearly half past eight. A great deal more than one drink, I can assure you. And Constance hadn't even changed!' She dwelt on that solecism through the weather report. 'Hardly coherent, either of them.'

'Oh, my dear, I don't think you can quite say that.' Aunt Fay switched channels and the room filled with gunfire.

'I most certainly can!' Edith raised her chin and glared at her sister. 'The way she was trying to entice him up to bed, whilst we were having our coffee – quite disgusting! I don't know what's come over her, I really don't. When she knew he wants to wait up for Sally. Well good luck to them both, sitting it out in the drawing room! If you ask me, I think they're so intoxicated they don't know what they're doing.'

'He said he would take Sheba for a walk,' Aunt Fay reminded her, to be fair.

'And that's all the proof we need!' Triumphantly. 'Who in his right mind takes a dog for a walk in the country in the dark, I'd like to know?' She appeared to give all her attention to a young man with yellow hair and a leather jacket who was inching his way round the bonnet of a red car. Aunt Fay leaned forward, having seen the other young man with black hair and a polo-neck sweater now crouching behind the car. The music warned that someone would get hurt.

'You know,' said Edith as the music reached its climax in a hail of bullets and the yellow hair slithered prettily down the red car door. 'It's quite possible he's using Sheba as a blind. He could well have an assignation with that doxy next door.'

The neatness of this idea silenced her while she reached for the decanter, poured the two glasses and waved one at her sister.

'I don't really think so, dear.' Aunt Fay could see several obstacles. 'Not in his own back yard, so to speak, and with both families looking on. It wouldn't be nice.'

'Hmm,' said Edith. If it had been Constance they were discussing she would have pursued the argument, but some kind of blood-loyalty returned her attention to the screen. 'What on earth is going on here? Really, these thrillers are desperately dull.'

The drawing room next door, with heavy wine-brown curtains drawn all round the bay and the beginnings of a fire licking coals in the grate, gave an impression of warmth and ease. In a corner of the sofa Hugh rustled the paper as if he were reading it; in her wing chair, with her feet curled up under her skirt, Connie was working her way through a paragraph in *Devil's Cub*. She had reached for that over *Northanger Abbey*, *Humphry Clinker*, or *Tom Jones* as she would pick a soft centre over a nut, nougat or toffee, not because it was irresistible but because it made no demands. If she could not lose herself in a Georgette Heyer novel, there must be something wrong. Heyer was like aspirin, a panacea to all ills, needing no swallowing or gagging or effort. Any of the Heyer novels taken at random from the shelf offered this barbiturate escape. Almost immediately it would take effect and Connie could lose herself, find herself carried to some exalted world where irrepressible merriment and cool reserve met in a minuet and a young lady wore armazine skirts or worked muslin with a tiffany sash and the provoking male with the cruel regard and the laced and scented coat was at first disdainful, then diverted, and then the keen eyes became intent and he drawled 'I'll never rest till I've got you. Never, do you understand?' and he caught her in his arms so fiercely that the breath was almost crushed out of her, and she yielded, carried away half swooning on the tide of his passion.

But not today. Connie was reading words, not even prettily turned phrases, whilst behind them she saw Sally happily chatting with Tim in a smoke- and noise-filled bar and then returning to a cold, implacable father. And before her the provoked male without a trace of keen amusement or irony or gentle disregard was rattling the pages of *The Times* like Madam Defarge's needles. There was nothing she could do. Too late to simper and swing her coquelicot ribbons, to peep through languorous lashes, to falter or to swoon. His Grace would not be amused or swayed. There was no escaping Harsh Reality.

'I'm going out,' he said.

'And you may be a long time?' She thought that quite funny, but it sounded desperate. 'Don't lose Sheba in the dark. I'll wait up for you.'

'Don't be a little martyr, I meant what I said. You'd be more sensible if you went to bed.'

'Ah, but...' she said, airy and profound, perhaps disdainful, perhaps provocative; more likely provoking. 'But darling,' she tried a seductive voice, which only sounded like pleading. 'Darling, how about us *both* going to bed, like together? You know, like a loving couple? Like –' If only she could calm him down, delay his confrontation with Sally. Surely sex could be a distraction at least – even, if instigated by her for a change, would cheer him up, take his mind off the children?

'Don't be so silly,' he told her as he folded the paper and switched off all the lights but the one beside her. He closed the drawing-room door, shutting her in, locking her out, as he called Sheba to heel and slammed through the kitchen.

'The Marquis of Vidal had not expected to enjoy his interview with Avon, but it turned out to be more unpleasant than he was prepared for. To begin with, His Grace was writing at his desk when Vidal was ushered into the room, and although the lackey quite loudly announced his lordship, his fine hand continued to travel across the paper, and he neither looked up nor betrayed by even the smallest sign that he had heard the announcement.'

Devil's Cub was Connie's favourite, and by now she knew the Duke of Avon and his son quite as intimately, she felt, as the Duchess and Mary Challoner who, after several more misunderstandings and misadventures and another couple of hundred pages, would reap the rewards of True Love. In *These Old Shades*, the previous volume, which she had read first at the age of thirteen, Connie had lived for weeks as Avon's page and protégé and, ultimately, wife. In this one she already admired the Cub, his son, but was torn by memories of her infatuation with the Duke. Vidal stood at the fireplace, dressed with unusual care in buff breeches of impeccable cut and a coat of azure cloth with silver buttons, but it was His Grace who still held Connie's attention with his faintly disdainful glance and his sardonic smile.

'I suppose I should count myself honoured that you have been able to visit me,' said His Grace gently … After a moment's uncomfortable silence the Duke continued: 'Your presence in England is extremely – shall we say enlivening? – Vidal. But I believe I shall survive the loss of it.'

Connie spread the book on the arm of her chair, untucked her feet from the skirts of her grey gown and ran impetuously to light all the lamps in the room. 'A fig for you!' She snapped her fingers at the window and paused, catching sight of herself in the mirror over the fireplace.

Without her glasses, which she seldom wore in the house, anything more than a couple of feet away lost definition and merged with the background. All the objects were there in their different planes but softened, delicately painted. In the mirror, framed by swags of gilded flowers and fruit and foliage and occupying most of the wall above the mantelpiece, those objects stood further removed, fainter, less real. Peering into this canvas from the middle of the room she could only recognise herself because she knew she was there. The pale face showed no features, the hair might well be dressed in powdered curls and threaded by a blue riband, the grey blouse and skirt blurred to become a gown of silk brocade with underskirts and a hoop.

* * * * * * *

In the expanse of the mirror she can easily make out the man at the bureau behind her, his fine hand shaking back a lace ruffle while he awaits the arrival of his son, the lean countenance turned from her, the hint of steel in eye and pose.

'Don't be too hard on him,' she whispers, with a disarming smile.

'The puppy must come to heel,' His Grace replies, sounding just like Hugh. 'Marcus must leave England until he has learned how to behave.' He is smiling at her with kindness and an understanding that a mother might be concerned about such things which are not her concern. 'Marcus must learn and I do not want you bothering your pretty little head over this. He has overstepped the mark with this duel and I shall deal with him. Now, my dear, pray return to our guests and leave this to me.'

The fire spits and she drops her gaze from the mirror, past Aurora, to the grate. The spell is broken and with it her ready acceptance of anything the gentleman might say.

She felt the pain of being dismissed by this gentleman quite as fiercely as when Hugh had driven off to the bender with Sally, telling her to keep out of it. The man at the bureau wavered and faded to the same greenish distance as the rest of the mirror furniture. She held on to the image of him as she would the last wisp of a dream on waking, willing him to remain. This other-Hugh, this Hugo as she named him, would deal more kindly with Marcus if only she could keep him there in this other-room. If she could force herself to accept his guidance, give up her own will in the belief that Hugo knew best, she could change the whole course of what happened last year. Transported, removed from her possible control, the fate of Mark might be transformed. It only required faith in the man to hold him. Such a small step. While she almost floated in that greenish hinterland, part of neither world, she fought against her instincts. Sink, sink into silken skirts and pretty smiles and good behaviour, forget autonomy, equality and the need to interfere and argue; trust the man.

Hugo, posed in blue cloth coat and breeches, one leg elegantly extended, one hand arrested mid-gesture, hesitated, sometimes crystal clear, sometimes indistinct.

If only she could believe in Hugo and become his captivating, adorable wife – Polly? – and if Mark could be simply and briefly despatched to France 'to learn how to behave', then Sally might be saved the inquisition tonight and the probability of rebellion, and the family would be reunited under benign rule. She, Polly, could see to that and undo the harm Connie had begun. Sally – Sarah? – alone would charm her father. Hugo, left alone without interference, would deal fairly with both his children.

She stared now into the mirror, searching. Hugo, with a graceful, languid wave of the hand, swam back into focus and dismissed her.

'But not Sarah too – you won't despatch Sarah too?' she wails, to remind him that there is more than one interview and that, although captivating and adorable and acquiescent, she, Polly, is still there.

Sarah is silly and flighty and very young and Hugo has discovered the traffic of letters between her and young Sir Timothy, but surely Sarah will have more sensibility than to blacken the family name? Surely she will listen to her father, will not dare defy him and continue the liaison?

'Sarah will obey.' The words are Hugh's but the tone is altogether different. The obstinacy is there but tempered by a gentleness Hugo would use towards his wife. Beneath the sound of the words, however, lies all the violence and determination she knows so well. 'When she returns from the ball I will talk to her. Now leave me, please, my dear Polly.' He returns to his letter.

Polly gets up and wanders to the mirror with heavy step and leans her face close to the glass, so close now that she cannot see her curls, the riband, the blue-grey gown, and the room is frosted by her breath. The sense of fear and anguish at being separated from her son fades into the realisation that he has been abroad a year and will soon be home, the duel forgotten, his father forgiving. The colours in the room brighten, the last roses in their silver bowl on the sofa table glowing as if in the sunlight. She smiles against the glass. She can almost hear Marcus' step in the hall, the throwing open of doors. He must soon be home from France. She feels the heat of the fire through her skirts and swings gracefully away from the mirror, swirling the brocade behind her. She will hide in the wing chair while Hugo interviews Sarah. Mousy quiet she will watch and listen.

No sooner has she settled herself, feet drawn up, pressed back and lost in the high leather angles of the chair, than Sarah dances into the room breathtakingly beautiful in apple-green cambric embroidered with garlands of rosebuds, her fair hair in ringlets.

'Oh Papa,' she cries. 'I am so happy!'

How can he spoil that? Polly, from her vantage, knows it all. If Hugo shows the slightest insensitivity, if he demands, insists, then

Sarah may defy him and elope with young Sir Timothy. Would she? No. For all her high spirits, Sarah would never disobey her father. Hugo will deal with her sternly but wisely. A few tears there will be, a prettily stamped foot perhaps, but the interview will end in agreement, order, and common sense will be restored. Polly trusts her husband.

'You see, my dear!' Hugo, now definitely in focus, with disarming smile and a long, careless stride, arrives later at the fireside. 'You had no reason to worry. I can deal with the children – see how Sarah has agreed to continue at Madame Blanche's seminary and to put all idea of that fortune hunter out of her mind. And Marcus returns next week. You will find him vastly improved. There is nothing for you to fear.'

She can rise now, from the cover of the wing chair, radiant, her pleasure reflected in his eyes. Her handsome husband with the saturnine smile and the elusive charm. 'Why, oh why, did I doubt you?' she cries.

'Come.' He draws her into his embrace. 'You look fagged to death, my dear.' And he escorts her to the door.

'I am tired, Hugo,' she replies in a small voice with a backwards glance at the mirror. 'So very tired.'

In their bedroom upstairs Connie dropped her clothes where she stood, not even bothering with cleansing cream or toothpaste. The bed felt cold and wide and empty.

'Vastly improved,' she echoed as she switched on the electric blanket. 'Nothing to fear.' And she buried her head in the pillow.

* * * * * * *

'Have you any idea,' Hugh demanded in the kitchen next morning, 'what the hell you were up to last night? I came back to all the lights blazing, and the fire with no guard. All the doors open and your clothes just littered about. You hadn't even taken your face off. Or put on your nightie. Fantastic! Just look at you!'

She couldn't, but was not impressed by the sight of him unshaven and in his pyjamas. At least she had dressed and cleaned her teeth and made the coffee.

'Have some orange juice,' she said, 'and don't shout. I didn't hear you come in.'

'You wouldn't have heard the last trump!' He knocked back the juice and sank onto the chair opposite her across the scrubbed table. 'You must have been plastered.'

'Me?' she said, remembering that he had stayed longer at the Fosters and had taken the dog for a quite unnecessary walk. 'Was Sheba all right? Where did you go?'

Sheba, unencumbered by hangover, seemed livelier than both of them and had already taken herself off across the paddock.

'Around and about,' he replied. 'She thoroughly enjoyed it. Lots of strange things to chase.'

'And then?' She wanted to cut straight to Sally, but hadn't the strength.

'Then sensibly I got into my pyjamas – which entirely escaped you – and waited downstairs for Sally.' He paused for her question. 'She came in at five o'clock. A.M.'

'In the hall? Wasn't that rather chilly?'

'In the drawing room. And yes, it was.'

Connie poured coffee, waiting.

'Funnily enough,' he said, 'we came to an agreement.'

Connie slumped back in her chair and stared at the milk jug, counting its facets but not seeing it as a whole. Heavy cut glass, rather ugly, hobnail cut with a blunt knife, a quaint lopsided jug. Agreement. Who agreeing with whom? At that time in the morning. She caught a glimpse of Hugo seated at the bureau, one elegantly clad leg extended, his head turned so that he could quiz his daughter; Sarah defiant. 'An agreement?'

'As I've told you countless times, without you fussing around I can deal with the children perfectly well. We understand each other. They can understand me, funnily enough. If you're not there.'

She repressed memories of his dealing with Mark, bit back an obvious retort. Hugo would not be so blunt. Nor would he wear a camel dressing gown with a frayed cuff. Hugo would be arrayed in frogged velvet to match his casually tied locks. Perhaps if she dressed Hugh more elegantly? Perhaps it was all her fault. Perhaps he did know best. He had sat up all night to talk to his daughter. 'Will you not watch one hour with me?' Her husband was the saint who put up with all her imperfections. She failed him as she failed the children.

Hugh drained his cup and sat there obliquely reading the headlines, torn between desire to get into the ritual of *The Sunday Times* and enjoyment of tormenting his wife.

'It was about time someone pulled her up,' he said. 'I'm amazed at what you have been allowing her to do. Five o'clock in the morning at her age! It's incredible. And you had no idea.' He allowed the enormity of that to sink in while he refilled their cups. 'We discussed all that.'

Connie could imagine the discussion: Hugh owlish with sleep, Sally tired but defensive; Hugh awakening to imagination and fury, Sally becoming sullen. How could that lead to agreement? When Sally made that familiar mule of a face there was no way for her mother to penetrate it. But Hugh could.

'Funnily enough, she understood my concern. I think she quite appreciated it. Children actually like discipline, you know. There are ways to show you love someone other than by letting them do exactly what they like. Anyway,' his hand reached for the Business News, 'we have agreed that she will stay at home during the week from now on and go out only on Friday and Saturday evenings, as long as she has arranged the timings with me beforehand. If that is once overstepped she will not be allowed out at all. That's more than fair, don't you think?'

Connie could by then imagine the bargaining, the two armies drawn up, Putin and Obama on either side of the table. 'I'll trade you one extra evening for a time limit.' Had they discussed the timing of the time limits? She foresaw instant breakdown of agreement.

'That's lovely, darling,' she said, 'that you agreed so easily.'

She saw the satisfaction on his face: he didn't doubt it, had none of her qualms. Would the agreement last through next weekend? Hugh thought he was dealing with a Sarah, not Sally. Connie feared she knew Sally better. All he had accomplished was a postponement. Wearily she cradled her coffee cup, watching him disappear behind the paper. Where had she gone wrong that she could assume Sally would not accept Hugh's terms but at the same time know that Hugo had won with Sarah? Was it the century of the father or their liberal training that made Sally and Mark feel free to do as they wished and their parents powerless, or unwilling, to stop them?

Much later, when the papers had been shared and scattered across the table, Sally breezed in to finish the coffee. The Paisley pyjama trousers, deliberately patched in strange places and torn at knee and hem, she wore below a crumpled shirt and a sweater Hugh had consigned to Oxfam; her favourite dress, guaranteed to disgust adults.

'I won't be in for lunch, Mother,' she said from behind her

father, flicking the collar of his dressing gown and blowing at the top of his head. 'Do you know your bald patch is *growing*?' Mock horror and a pantomime of ruffling Hugh's hair while he reached back to grab her, an indulgent expression rounding his cheeks. She had become his little girl again, his naughty little daughter, amused and amusing. 'Mark's cooking us all a curry – believe it!'

Connie tried. That dangerous little stove with its fairy-tale chimney snaking through the canvas roof. Mostly she tried not to think of Mark cooking anything and at the same time tried to believe he made himself lots of healthy, warm meals. Each Thursday she checked anxiously on all she could see of him – his face now wreathed in a full beard – to see if he had lost weight or showed any sign of needing maternal care. 'Give him my love,' was all she could say.

'They're useless on Saturdays now that the hunting's begun,' said Sally, taking the cups and saucers to the sink. 'They're becoming really boring with the 'Antis', always at some Meet or other. I don't approve, for what that's worth, and we have endless 'discussions' about it. Of course he hates me mentioning that he used to hunt, it absolutely ruins his image with the rest of them, but they're getting used to it! You know, they're forming quite a coven down there, hatching plots and spells and things. It's becoming a crusade.' She was washing up with a dutiful daughter technique.

'Well you can't go out looking like that.' Hugh had noticed.

'Oh Daddy, you should see the others,' she laughed. 'I'll be the snazziest dressed of the lot. Bye for now – and don't wait up! Don't worry, I was only joking!'

Chapter 5

A dinner party given by Lettice was always interesting. She threw her guests together rather like her food, richly but at random, and usually created a strong mixture. A bank manager, an MFH, an underemployed Latin tutor and a redundant salesman appeared to have little in common. The choice had certainly not been influenced by their wives.

'I'm asking you,' Lettice had told Connie, 'expressly to control Sylvia Benefield, Roger's wife. She's far too glamorous and rather snooty with it – and I've discovered she's quite a well-known interior decorator to boot. Puts us all in the shade! She needs someone around who won't be impressed, know what I mean?'

'Me?' cried Connie. 'How do you know I won't be impressed?' She had never seen herself in that light.

'Well, now that I've told you, you won't show it, will you? That's all. I can't rely on Ginger, who will make a great thing of sitting with her knees apart and booming away about hounds and horses, and poor Mrs Gibson – I had to ask them because he's been so sweet about my overdraft – will be knocked speechless.'

'You think I won't?' The responsibility of talking, with her legs crossed, to this paragon alarmed her. 'Really, Letty, you're asking too much. If only you hadn't told me.'

'Forewarned is forearmed, darling,' Lettice informed her. 'You can practise on your mother-in-law, you handle her beautifully.' They had both giggled at that. 'And anyway it's high time you were introduced to Roger. I think he's fed up with Sylvia and the marriage is on the rocks.'

Sally had given all her support and a lot of advice. 'Nonsense, Mum, Lettice is quite right. Wear your slinky black trousers and that silk shirt and I'll do your eyes and we'll put your hair up – that woman won't be able to compete!'

'You will not go in trousers,' said Hugh. 'This is a dinner party, not a transvestite parade. You've got a perfectly good frock and I won't have my wife looking like a teenage tart. And if Sally makes your eyes anything like hers you'll just have to scrub it off again.'

Sally winked an encrusted eyelid; it was Friday and she was dressed to meet Tim, all in black and with her hair teased into a Struwelpeter mop around a white face and panda eyes. The 'timing' had been agreed, with reluctance on both sides, as midnight. Sally had made her remark again about pumpkins, but had given in, knowing that Saturday was more important: if They were to be out to dinner tomorrow he would have to be more lenient.

On Saturday evening Sally assisted and encouraged. The dress was grey crepe but even Sally approved its swingy line and would have borrowed it if she wasn't so into black. She offered strings of necklaces but agreed that her mother looked more sophisticated without, and they compromised on hooking the hair back with combs rather than something that might fall down. The eyes were a compromise, too – 'I'd feel exhausted from the start carrying all that mascara!' Connie said. 'It's not me.' Sally made herself late painting blue and grey eye shadow and was proud of the result.

'Twelve-thirty,' said Hugh yet again, not noticing. 'You'll be in, Sally.'

Sally had narrowed her eyes, witchlike, at her mother.

'You can bring Tim home for a coffee,' Connie offered.

'Only in the kitchen,' said Hugh. 'I don't want you and that layabout loose in the house.'

'You make us sound like a herd of buffalo!' complained Sally.

'And I can't see why we can't go in by the fire. But still.' She kissed her mother and made the mean look at her father. 'Have a jolly time with the lovely lady, and give my love to Lettice. And behave yourselves, mind!'

Lettice lived in Bath in a 'little Georgian gem', one of Wood's lesser houses, down a pedestrian precinct where no car could park and it was always raining. Lettice was the only person unaffected by this because she had taken a slice off the end of her back garden and her Mini nestled there under a canopy of wisteria.

'Dinner with Lettice,' Hugh grumbled as they fought their way along the street with his umbrella braced against the wind, 'is a nightmare. Makes one think twice about accepting. She should only entertain in the summer.'

'Wouldn't make much difference.' Connie clutched his arm and huddled close, keeping her eyes on the cracks between the paving stones. 'It's bound to rain at some point.'

'I only hope it's worth it,' he said. 'We can see Tony and Ginger any time, and she's still got that awful Harman living with her, hasn't she?'

'Harman's not that bad when you get to know him, and he keeps her happy.' Connie sidestepped a puddle elaborately, pleased by the view of a narrow grey foot in pointed suede. 'And we *don't* see Ginger and Tony. Stop grousing, darling, it's fun to be going out and very kind of Lettice to ask us. Come off it, you're as pleased as I am to have a change of scene. And different food!'

'Humph,' he said. 'You're quite as good a cook as Lettice when you try.'

She accepted the compliment in silence as they were blown in to Lettice's hall.

'Frightful night!' Lettice was laughing, untouched by the weather, plump and sleek in her black silk trousers and silver shirt.

'I feel *guilty* dragging you all out! Only Roger and Sylvia had no way to come. Say nothing, *please*, I've already had enough from Ginger. What can we get you, to compensate?'

The room they entered, smoothing and shaking themselves free of raindrops, appeared crowded. Connie's glasses misted in the change of temperature and she had to clear the lower edges with a finger before she could recognise some and grin vaguely at other faces turned to watch her. How unimpressed should she be? She slunk after Lettice to join Harman at the table of bottles behind the feather-filled sofa. Everything Lettice owned was, like her, soft, voluptuous and shiny.

A thick white carpet dragged at her heels and the sofa, which now embraced a little woman in wool and a skeletal blonde, was covered in dark chintz with a metallic sheen. This same material, splashed with overblown roses, hung in festoons at the windows. The two comfortable chairs contained cats, one white Persian and a fluffy ginger tom, forcing the men in their dark suits to cluster near the sofa, bending towards the women like trees in a gale.

Harman presided over the bar like a comic magician, all cuff and cummerbund, patiently perspiring. He's good-natured, Connie thought, and that's all that matters. Just what a woman needs. No desire to prove himself or intrude or make people talk to him. A dumb waiter. Harman the barman. She liked him much better than Lettice's various husbands and assumed that Lettice found his dumbness relaxing.

'Hi Con!' he said. 'What's it to be?' A major speech. She felt welcomed.

'You know Ginger,' said Lettice, taking a glass from him and filling it with whisky. 'Take this, darling, for the moment and I'll introduce you.'

Ginger, the Master's wife, stood square before the fire with her chin raised high with what, if you didn't know about the chronically dislocated neck, appeared like arrogance. She wore her usual long hairy skirt and a shapeless jersey dressed up with swags of beads, and an unfortunate belt.

'Haven't seen you for yonks, Constance!' Ginger bellowed. 'Lovely fire – come and warm up.'

Connie levelled up beside her, struck as on every occasion they met by the handsome head, a profile like a Roman emperor, a splendid display of bones accentuated by its peculiar angle. 'It's been a very busy summer, somehow,' she murmured.

'What's that?' Ginger's shout seemed to draw all attention to them. Connie had forgotten the Bad Ear and shifted to her other side. 'Very busy,' she repeated.

'All those children, of course. Haven't seen them out yet this Season.'

'Oh no, they haven't hunted for some time.' There was no point in saying for how long, or why, or in feeling sad that Ginger had no interest in such trivia as adolescent children and the expense of livestock.

'Pity. The girl had a good seat. Your mother's well?' That, too. Ginger's perception of Connie was as a scion of the Bryant tree. Her husband Tony had served in the Brigadier's regiment; Ginger and Edith spoke the same language.

Lettice had brought the other women to their feet and shuffled the pack, drawing Mr Gibson and Roger across the carpet to the fire.

'Richard Gibson is my absolutely favourite banker!' she introduced him while the little grey man shifted his feet and looked too hot in a plum-coloured waistcoat and starched cuffs which grazed his knuckles. 'And you really know Roger already, don't you? It's absurd that you two have been eyeing each other for months and haven't done anything about introducing yourselves!'

Mr Gibson had raised a moist hand and grasped Connie's saying, 'How do you do?' She passed her hand on to Roger who caught it as if by mistake and unsure what to do with it. He held it for a moment, looking faintly surprised, and then dropped it. His head was level with hers and he seemed to gaze up at her, a forelock of dappled hair almost obscuring lustrous eyes with the enquiring look of an intelligent hound. So near he seemed a stranger and not at all like the man of her dreams, hound-faced with a long nose, narrow cheeks, and a wide mouth to balance the forehead, very pale; a starved animal beside the plump plum bank manager.

Connie blinked to cut Roger's inspection and said, 'Oh yes – I mean, not really. We've been very much on duty and rather preoccupied with, um, people. You know.' She could feel those eyes watching, observing, still, and turned to Ginger with relief. 'We both guide, you know. I mean,' with a silly laugh which sickened her, 'take guided walks, on Tuesdays.'

'On Tuesdays,' he confirmed. The voice was as low and melodious as she had imagined. When she glanced at him he was laughing. 'You make us sound like guide dogs.'

'That's what I was thinking!' And she laughed, too.

'One of these days I must go on one of these tours,' said Mr Gibson, rocking now like a weighted doll. 'Fascinating, I bet. All those things one doesn't know about Bath. It's one of your specialities, too, isn't it Lettice? How you all find the time!'

Lettice refilled glasses while Ginger talked of hounds and puppies, discovering for the room that the Gibsons had a cat and Roger's wife disliked dogs. Connie sheltered behind her whisky and a mask of enthusiasm, knowing that Ginger would entertain them and leave her in peace. Within her spectrum stood Roger's feet in dusty shoes, long grey flannels, a blazer unbuttoned to reveal a strip of cornflower-blue shirt. She would not raise her eyes higher than the knot of a dark tie and his only reality was the voice saying 'Sylvia doesn't like dogs' and the tapered, surprisingly tanned fingers moving the stem of the glass occasionally out of the picture towards his mouth. Lettice's hand removed the glass and his plunged to safety in a trouser pocket; the filled glass returned and the hand leaped back to receive it. As Ginger paused, Roger began to spin the stem between his fingers and thumb as though impatient at the delay, but once she was off again his grip tightened, the glass came to rest and he said: 'I wondered if we would meet.'

'So did I!' That sounded too eager. How spineless of him simply to wonder, if he had really wanted to meet her. 'Doing the same thing in the same place all the time, I suppose we could have introduced ourselves.' That was casual enough. 'Do you actually enjoy it?' She wanted to know that, and a direct question gave her the opportunity to look up at his face.

He seemed surprised, or perhaps that was the effect of eyebrows which, she noticed now, were thick and long and dark above the grey eyes. 'Enjoy the hectoring?' he asked.

'The whole act of making an impression, getting them on your side, getting them involved.' She had been so sure he felt as inadequate as she did, must know what she meant.

'Now you two,' Lettice's pink hand clasped Connie's wrist. 'You mustn't give away state secrets! And darling, you must come over and meet the other girls.'

Hugh was impressing the other girls with some hunting yarn, vying with Tony no doubt, directing the anecdote at Roger's wife. Lettice squeezed herself and Connie in between the men and cut straight through with the introductions. Mrs Gibson seemed relieved, quite grateful to be addressed. Sylvia Benefield checked Connie over from the hair combs to the high heels and back via her sapphire engagement ring. When their eyes met, Sylvia invited Connie to do likewise with an unwavering stare, and adjusted her hand around her gin and tonic to show the size of her diamonds and the length of her scarlet nails.

'No, we've not met before,' she said, with a swing of her pale gold bob, as if expecting disagreement.

'Stunning' Lettice had called her. Connie was stunned enough to be unable to focus on Mrs Gibson. In an effort not to be impressed she analysed the effect as: (item) one pair of amazed doe-eyes which seemed to occupy the whole head, a cross between Audrey Hepburn and a bush baby, and (item) an anorexic slimness giving the impression of bone-china fragility and expense. Apart from that, Connie forced herself to notice, the small mouth was already edged by deep, petulant lines and the little black dress accentuated matchstick limbs of more interest to a medical student. Can you ever be too rich or too thin? She looked both.

'You're Hugh's wife.' No more than a statement, but she produced it with a full headlamp blaze at Hugh.

'And you're Roger's,' Connie had taken enough whisky to answer.

'And Joyce is Richard's,' Lettice laughed. 'Thank God we've got that sorted out! Joyce has been advising me about Anastasia's raw chin – did you notice, darling? Apparently their cat's had it too and the vet said *acne*! Can you imagine? At her age! Menopausal acne – the imagination boggles!'

'Ah, but, Lettice dear.' Mrs Gibson patted at her hostess's arm and her cheeks grew pink. 'It's hormones, I gather. Both in adolescence and the Change, don't you know. I believe it's quite common.'

'Anastasia doesn't look common!' Sylvia made an oblique smile to include all but Mrs Gibson. 'Surely the beautiful Anastasia wouldn't have a common-cat complaint?'

'Oh but, Mrs Benefield,' Mrs Gibson hastened to explain, 'I didn't mean she was a common cat! No, not at all. I only meant—'

Sylvia swung the 400-watt gaze from face to face and murmured, 'Of course not, dear. I'm not fond of cats, myself. They say they're very female – and personally I prefer men.' The men purred. 'The way they ingratiate themselves, I can't stand that.'

'Is your cat cured now?' Connie asked Mrs Gibson, remembering she was there expressly to control Sylvia.

At dinner, in a room lined with dark blue felt and lit only by silver candles, Connie was seated diagonally opposite Roger and could appreciate him battling against Ginger's Bad Ear. Twice he caught her watching and allowed her to see, without moving a feature, that they shared a joke. The slightest frown, an imperceptible droop of the eyelids and a quiver at the end of that long mouth. No need to speak. Connie felt fortunate to have him at that distance rather than invisible beside her. She could attribute to him later any words she wished; for now all she wanted to remember was his face and its fleeting changes of expression.

Poor Harman plodded. Mrs Gibson, stranded between him and Hugh (who was preoccupied with Sylvia Benefield) was doing her best to interest him. Her ploy was to feed him questions. Each time he thought she had finished, and inserted the waiting fork into his mouth, she asked another. Connie could feel his convulsions against her sleeve as he swallowed yet another sprout and cube of steak without his customary twenty-one bites. Harman's mother, she could tell, had insisted; Harman sounded near death.

Lettice gathered the plates and dishes and replaced them with a cheese board, and Harman poured more wine. In a pause when all conversation was suspended, Lettice took charge and threw her remark at no one in particular. 'So what do you think about Cameron's latest, then? Is one supposed to applaud? With apologies to dear Richard, of course the rich bankers will get the money for flood defences instead of the poor farmers. Those posh boys who are running the country didn't stand up to the bankers when they were taking us all to the cleaners ages ago either, did they?'

'It's not just the bankers!' Roger surprised Connie by sounding quite passionate. She had not thought of him as being political: politics she associated with Hugh and Tony, and Hugh's instructions on how she should vote. She had learned to keep her own views quiet; they were cause for derision amongst the Tories. 'All his policies are undemocratic and elitist, isn't that blatantly obvious? No one in their right minds should support him for yet another period of feudal practices.'

'The Government,' Tony assumed his position as Chairman of the local Conservative Association, 'knows exactly what it's doing. You are obviously ignoring the state of our economy – handed down, may I say, from Blair and Co, and still being messed about by you Liberals. We should be allowed to get on with it without your interference.'

'The weak to the wall!' Roger sliced into the brie. 'Send the money to African despots and forget about family values at home!'

'That's utter nonsense, I'm afraid.' Hugh smiled apologetically towards Sylvia. 'We need a few more years of austerity to get the country on its feet, you must allow that. And where would we all be if we ignored the mayhem abroad, I ask? You see us as a blinkered little island with no role to play in the world.'

'Why not?' Roger pushed the cheese board towards Connie. 'Surely we should care more for our own people and leave the more aggressive countries to do the fighting? Where's the point in harping on about our long-distant role of owning an Empire? We don't even have a useful role in Europe.'

'Don't you *believe*,' said Mr Gibson, 'that we still have an important role to play? Look at the Common Market. If we opt out, Europe will be run by the Germans again and then –'

Both Tony and Hugh leapt to add their weight and Roger withdrew with a withering smile, only saying, 'I'm more concerned about how this country is managed, and getting some fairness into the politics here and now. It's absurd –'

Hugh received his bowl of Pavlova and covered it with cream from a silver jug. 'What a typical woolly-headed remark, if I may say so. You have no idea what we are doing and what we've accomplished despite your interference. If your lot would just lay off and let us get on with it –'

From Sylvia came an enormous yawn. 'I believe,' her voice was icy with disdain, 'that this is the most unutterably banal discussion. Isn't there some kind of law against terminal boredom? Lettice, really – can't you bang their heads together?'

Before they left the table Ginger tried to hit back at Roger's wife. Capable of cutting short any conversation quite as brusquely as Sylvia, she was not prepared to have her husband interrupted. And she couldn't stand a thin woman who smirked at them all enjoying lashings of Pavlova while murmuring that she never even tasted puddings.

'Money,' Ginger flung across the table, 'isn't everything!'

They all assimilated the fact. Sylvia, at whom the remark was evidently aimed, contemplated the rings on her left hand without agreeing.

'Not by a long chalk it isn't,' Ginger prompted.

Sylvia shrugged a beautifully draped shoulder pad. 'I don't know, it suits me quite well. If I hadn't been left a packet by my last husband I wouldn't be able to afford the present one, not however hard I worked. You haven't tried living on the proceeds of a little Latin coaching or you wouldn't make such an idiotic statement.

Money is the only thing we can't do without.'

'Some would dispute that,' said Ginger. 'I imagine your husband for one!'

'My husband certainly would not.' Sylvia's voice hissed over the sibilants like silk being drawn through a ring. 'He appreciates my good fortune quite as warmly as I do. Don't you, my dearest? How else could he indulge his little whims?'

Roger and his wife stared at each other without expression while the others pondered on that. Lettice, who professed to know him, was intrigued, but could imagine no suitably expensive whim; Connie felt only disgust that a wife could trot her husband out as a poor relation, a liability, even if she had an enormous legacy and a brilliant career. How dared she! Latin coaching to her sounded noble, erudite.

'Whims?' Tony voiced the question they felt too polite to ask, and then smothered it. 'You're right, we've all got 'em and it's a pleasant change to hear they're not being indulged by the welfare state. What some people are getting away with would make your hair stand on end! Have you heard this one?'

Sylvia dimmed her searchlights but kept Roger in her beam. Roger maintained an ambiguous expression, but Connie could see his wife's eyes glitter with contempt. What harm could he possibly have done her that she despised him so?

'I don't understand,' said Hugh as they drove home along a black satin road cross-hatched with lines of rain, 'why she married that man. Something fishy about him. He's not even a proper teacher, hasn't even got a decent job. Obviously a delinquent, not settled to anything. Not the type to make something of the tourist business either, and goodness knows that's exploitable! Funny that a woman like that settles for a chap without ambition. Don't you think?'

'Yes,' Connie said.

Chapter 6

Hallatrow Hall was in darkness. It was by now one o'clock in the morning and the kitchen was undisturbed. Hugh snapped on the lights as if hoping to catch an errant cockroach, waking Sheba who blinked, yawned, stretched and thumped her tail sleepily. Hugh then made his way to the drawing room to do the same light-flashing and returned.

'She's not in.'

'She might be in bed.'

'I'd take a bet on that.' He stood in the doorway rattling the money in his pocket. 'The first time she's on trust and look what happens! I should have known better. She's utterly unreliable. I should have known better than to trust her.'

'She's not –' Connie began. 'It's not –'

'Not to be trusted.' The pupils of his eyes darted. The money clinked. 'Treats us with complete contempt. Does exactly what she likes when she likes. She thinks nothing matters but her squalid little life out on the tiles with that layabout. She had no intention – no, listen to me – no intention of honouring our agreement. And you've put her up to this! You with your Yes darling, of course darling, do as you like darling. You have undermined my authority all along, all along the way. And look what you've got to show for it... Nothing! Well, it's too late now. It's too late. I wash my hands of her, I give up, there's nothing I can do now. She's no daughter of mine. No child of mine would openly defy me like this.'

'Darling, it's only just one o'clock and Jupiter's doesn't close till two.'

'That's got nothing to do with it.'

'She may be upstairs.' Connie pushed past him, switched on all the lights upstairs, glanced into Sally's room without hope and came slowly down again.

'I knew it.' He had time to consider. 'Well this time it will be a different story. I warned her. This time she won't find me so simple. I've tried – I really tried to be understanding, to allow her to prove she could behave responsibly. She knew she was on trust. We agreed. Yes Daddy, she said, I do understand, I know how you feel. Worthless! Her word is worthless!'

Sheba groaned, stretched her toes, heaved herself up and padded to her bowl.

'Worthless!'

Sheba slurped water, shook herself and gazed up at him.

'Go to bed!' he said to them both. 'I'll deal with her.'

Sheba slunk to her corner, flopped onto her blanket and lowered her nose to her paws. Connie could think of nothing helpful to say. Possibilities like: But this is not the first time, or, She has been out much later, or, At least we know she's with Tim, were not guaranteed to appease an irate father. Nor, she knew, would the sight of her anxious face calm him.

'Coffee?' she asked. That was a bright idea.

'Go to bed!' he repeated.

Upstairs, as she crept round the bedroom avoiding the creaking floorboards, listening through the open door to his stride across the hall, the clicking of light switches, the clink of a bottle on a glass, she heard a motorcycle purr, stutter and stop somewhere down the drive. She pulled a dressing gown over her nightdress and tiptoed to the top of the stairs. She thought she could hear Hugh pause and step back, footsteps on the gravel, urgent whispers, a key in the lock. The front door creaked, hesitated, creaked again.

'Aha!' cried Hugh like a pantomime villain. 'So it's you finally!'

'Crikey, Dad, you scared me! What on earth are you doing lurking in the hall? Have you just got in?'

'Who's that?' Hugh's voice rising.

'It's Tim, of course. He's just brought me home.'

The portico lamp blazed to illuminate the drive, and Connie could see through the staircase window the curve of the rose bed fading to the corner where Tim's motorcycle reflected little squares of brilliance. The rain had stopped. Steps again on the gravel, and a scattering noise like horses prancing, excited at a Meet.

'Dad, for Christ's sake! What are you doing?'

'Hey, hold still, Mr Bryant!'

Grunting, heavy breathing, a thwack of something hard hitting leather, incoherent human growls and then a wild excitement from Sheba.

Connie was stumbling down the stairs, hand over hand down the banister rail for support, bare feet hitting the cold stone of the hall, her dressing gown ballooning in the wind from the front door.

'Darling – for heaven's sake!' She darted out onto the gravel to drag her husband back with a strength she had no idea she possessed, but Sally clung to Tim and Hugh shrugged her off and charged out again.

Somehow in the tussle that ensued Tim managed to knock Hugh to the ground and stood over him looking more surprised than belligerent. With a cigarette tucked behind a ringed ear and a tangle of black curls escaping from the ribbon at the nape of his neck, he looked as if he were simply studying a cycle for faults. Connie and Sally each took a leather sleeve to restrain him as Hugh struggled to his feet. Connie then clasped Hugh's arm and pulled him indoors while he shouted, 'Get out of here before I kill you, do you hear me? And leave my daughter alone! Don't you ever —'

In the hall mirror he noticed that his lip was bleeding and he staggered close to examine it, seeming to grow in size as he registered the enormity of being struck by the younger man. For a moment he could find no words at all and then he rounded on his wife. 'Get that brawling whippersnapper off my land, do you hear? I'm calling the police.'

As Connie tightened her hold on his arm, Sally led Tim into the hall and for a moment they all clung and rocked together in a crazed mixture of comfort and aggression.

'Get him out of here!' Hugh yelled, dripping blood to the flagstones, dabbing at his lip with a cleanly folded handkerchief and managing to slap his daughter with his free hand.

'Christ, Daddy!' Sally screamed.

'I'll get you for that!' muttered Tim, gathering his powerful black-clad shoulders over bunched fists.

'No!' cried Connie. 'Stop it, stop it, stop it!'

Hugh was studying the blood on his handkerchief, back in his normal shape and size, almost thoughtful. In a voice nearly his own he said, 'Leave now, before I send for the police. You can both leave now. I want nothing more to do with either of you. You can go now, Sally, and not come back. I've finished with you. Do you hear me?'

'Fine,' said Sally. 'I'll go now. Come on, Tim.'

'Why not let's talk about it?' said Tim.

'Yes!' cried Connie.

'No.' Hugh pressed his lip and checked on the stain. 'If you go now, Sally,' his voice dangerously low, 'you won't come back. I'm making that absolutely clear. Do you understand me? If you walk out of that door, it's the end. You can choose. It's up to you. It will be your decision.'

Sally's fingers were locked with Tim's and she raised a face militant and undismayed.

'Sally,' said Connie, feeling the cold stone floor and the grit from the drive under her feet. 'Enough. This is absurd. Don't say anything else, any of you. Not a word more – please! Sally, take Sheba and then go to bed, now.'

Sally hesitated and then released Tim's fingers. 'I'll phone you,' she said, 'in the morning. Promise.' And she bent to lead Sheba to the kitchen. They watched in silence as she shut the kitchen door and then trailed upstairs.

'And Tim, home now. Sally will call you tomorrow.' Connie stood in the doorway as he crunched across the drive, turning up his jacket collar against renewed rain; then she closed the door and turned off the portico lamp.

For another hour Hugh stormed and grumbled about that pipsqueak, that lout, that layabout; that never in his life had he been so treated by anyone, led to brawling in his own driveway by a long-haired lout who wore earrings. He hadn't been able to control himself, opening the front door to be confronted by *that*! It had made his blood boil, Connie must understand that surely? All his rage channelled itself to Tim, Sally temporarily forgotten. Tim was never to darken their door again, never to be entertained, never mentioned. When he began to remember his daughter, Connie stopped the rush of edicts by wondering idly if Edith and her sister had heard the affray, or the Fosters? Sheba had made such a din! When he was calmer, almost chastened by the concern that outsiders might have overheard, she agreed that Tim would not be welcome in the house but at least Sally could meet him in town, or with Mark – they were all such friends.

They fell into bed arguing about non-essentials like Harman's supposed hold over Lettice and why she told everyone about her overdraft. Connie had neglected to switch on the electric blanket.

* * * * * * *

By lunchtime on Sunday, Hugh and Sally had made up their differences and last night's rain had washed the sky to a clear blue. Sally had apologised and explained why she had been later than agreed – circumstances beyond her control, she said, something about meeting friends of Mark just as they were leaving Jupiter's and it would have been so *rude* to dash off – and Hugh had explained his annoyance and sadness that she had broken her word. How would she have felt, if she had been him? Of course he had been furious, perhaps a little hasty, he couldn't think quite how it had all happened.

Hugh and Sally had collected rakes to begin the annual leaf-gathering, father and daughter in harmony. They had passed the Fosters in the yard and had received no strange looks or reference to being disturbed during the night. But Granny certainly did so at lunch.

'What exactly,' Edith asked, dusting an imaginary crumb from her table mat while Connie arranged the vegetables before her, 'was going on last night?'

'It sounded like sheer bloody murder to us,' said Aunt Fay receiving her plate with a happy smile. 'Thank you, dear.'

'And we're on the other side of the house, so goodness knows how it sounded on the road,' Edith added grimly.

Sally looked to her father, feeling by now that it was entirely his fault. The 'timing' agreement had been reinstated, for a probationary week, and she had even been allowed to telephone Tim. It was some kind of victory to have her father almost admit he had been in the wrong.

Hugh finished carving and sat down. 'An argument,' he said, dismissing it. 'Sally was late. And Sheba joined in. I only hope,' he was beginning to realise he had been too lenient, 'that she realises how much trouble she put us all to. I'm sorry if it woke you. It's up to Sally to see that it doesn't happen again.' He cut into his meat with an expression which left them all in no doubt as to whose fault it was.

'I sincerely hope it doesn't,' said Edith, refusing to eat until everyone was aware of her disapproval. 'In future, Sally, show a little more consideration for the rest of the world. Aunt Fay and I were most disturbed. We though at least the house was being ransacked. That is not amusing at our time of life.'

'I'm sorry, Granny.' Sally took a mouthful of red cabbage and continued, 'It was all a misunderstanding, but we've sorted it out now.'

Connie looked from her daughter to husband and wished she could kick them both, even kill them both. That they could swim through reconciliation after such a night and with such ease made her feel physically sick. She wished, as she had so often wished, that she had half their stamina, any degree of their ability to bounce back and forget so easily the pain they caused.

After lunch Sally and Hugh returned to their leaves and bonfires in the spinney and when Connie and Aunt Fay had cleared the kitchen they joined Edith in the drawing room with the Sunday papers.

'It's too beautiful a day to be cooped up indoors,' Edith complained, reaching a rheumatic hand for the magazine before her sister could get it. 'If I could move with *any* ease I'd be out there making a bonfire. I see that the Fosters are lending a hand at least.'

'Oh good,' said Connie brightly. 'That lets us off the hook then! We would only be in the way. Would you like the review section, Aunt Fay?'

'No dear, thank you. After last night's excitement I believe I'll take a little snooze, if you don't mind. We can't pretend we're getting any younger, can we?'

Edith snorted and rustled the magazine to show that she could, but gradually settled lower amongst the cushions in her chair and her lips slipped open even before Aunt Fay's regular breathing dominated the room.

Connie found herself reading words without meaning under the headline 'Is Ibsen Even More Relevant Today?' and flattened the paper on her lap. Aids, perhaps? Morality? Frustration? Despair? Then why didn't they say so? The article was close-packed with a sub-plot on symbolism, too complicated to follow when your eyes are tired. Hectoring.

The mirror reflected a thin aqua sky behind the windows, which mellowed the folds on the curtains and painted fingers of light and shade on the ceiling. Hectoring. Had Roger thought she meant he bullied, domineered yesterday evening? She could see his face quite plainly. Why hadn't she explained, or said something more interesting, more intelligent?

'Don't you think Ibsen is somehow even more relevant today?'

In the mirror those sleepy dark eyes widen a little, the broad mouth quirks. 'What an interesting concept. I must give that some thought. Tell me, dear Polly, for I can see that you are wise and have studied the subject. Tell me all you know so that I can explore your mind as I desire to know every part of you.'

Very easily she could dress Sir Roger in an intricately tied stock, high shirt points and a long-tailed coat of celestial blue.

He would call on her of a late afternoon when the Duchess of Hallatrow reclined on a chaise longue in the drawing room – dare one mention those ruby lips were snoring? – and her paid companion nodded in a corner. He would sit opposite Polly with a grave expression while she told him all her hopes and fears, his smile a caress, his eyes showing all the feeling he was forbidden to express in words.

But the daylight was still too strong for a romantic invitation to take a turn outside on the terrace and there was little more they could accomplish with their sleeping chaperones in the room. And besides, Miss Fay was awakening. Regretfully, Connie returned to the paper.

Chapter 7

In neither century could the warmth and gaiety of family life be maintained. By the end of November, Sally's agreement with her father had mutated to an arrangement with both parents that pleased no one in particular and made Edith very sour indeed.

Hugh remained inflexible about Sally's 'timing' and, having brought her to heel on that, had rashly conceded to Connie's suggestion that she could entertain at home in the old playroom.

The playroom, at the chilly end of the house, had been the scene of childhood parties, reasonably sound-and-child-proof with its linoleum floor and its gas fire caged in chicken wire. It now contained a television set and a square of maroon carpet which looked as if it came with Aunt Fay, and the nursery furniture from the Coach House. And gradually it filled with Sally's possessions from her bedroom, Mark's record player, an electric kettle and an assortment of mugs and glasses. Here Sally could bring her friends through a convenient side door from the yard, and as long as they disturbed no one with cars or motorcycles or loud music no questions were to be asked. In return for Sally sticking to a written list of rules, no one mentioned Tim, and Hugh promised to leave the playroom alone. For weeks Hugh had battled to perfect and enforce his Rules and had checked, the following morning, that the room was left tidy. For weeks Connie had followed him in case it was necessary to cajole or make excuses. But empty bottles were never found, cigarette ends had been scrupulously collected into envelopes and buried in the dustbin, the windows were always open, and the playroom looked merely draughty and in need of a spring clean. The battered sofa sagged a little more, but in the cold light of day seemed more familiar than ill-used.

* * * * * * *

By the end of November, Hugh was taking walks quite often without Sheba, spending more time at the Reference Library, and sometimes saying he would get himself a bite to eat at a pub, so don't wait lunch. His mother thought this unnecessary and wondered, often aloud, what Mrs Foster did all day now that little Emily was at school. But Hugh was in a much better temper as they approached Christmas and made none of his usual remarks about the prospect of having the house full of Connie's parents, who always joined them for the festivities. He relaxed his hold, too, on the playroom and listened less for departing guests. He seemed to have come to terms with his retirement and wrote fewer letters of application. The whole household settled to a new and quieter routine, less involved with each other, less openly critical.

* * * * * * *

By the end of November, Connie had organised a life of little rituals. She had her Tuesdays and Thursdays, of course. She met Lettice for lunch quite often to hear the latest gossip and fetched Sally from school when she had the car. Automatically she checked the dustbin after each of Sally's parties, fearful that one day there might be a fire, and she prepared food and vaguely cleaned the house with Aunt Fay's assistance as usual. But whenever she could she escaped with a book in the high-backed leather chair in the drawing room. She read more slowly now, sometimes not at all. The bookmark in *Letters from Bath (1766–1767)* by the Rev. John

Penrose had scarcely moved in a week. Often she stood at the mirror, unseeing, all-seeing, lost in the grey-green reflection of another world.

Hugh had caught her there and had noticed her preoccupation. 'You're getting as bad as Sally,' he remarked. 'Must be your second childhood! It doesn't help, you know – not with either of you – all this titivating in front of mirrors. A total waste of time, if you ask me.'

Edith had made her deprecatory sniff. 'Well I don't know, I'm sure, how you find the time for so much reading. At your age I'd have felt positively guilty sitting down with a book during the day time. It's funny how old habits die hard, don't you find? Couldn't even do it now. Even now, when there's precious little else I'm capable of, as the Lord knows, I still feel I should be doing something constructive. And oh, how I wish I could! What I'd give to be your age! Not a moment to be wasted, I've always said. Even Fay knits.'

Aunt Fay had worried that the meals were repetitive and ill-planned.

* * * * * * *

By the end of November, in the world beyond the mirror Polly's family had changed dramatically. Connie had soon tired of Hugo's anodyne charm and wanted more than a refurbished husband to dream of. She wanted, too, more distance from her children. And so she had woven for herself a broader tapestry, based now on Richardson and Fielding, lacking the delicacy of Georgette Heyer.

The Duchess of Hallatrow, it now turned out, was no duchess at all and Connie was discovering that Hallatrow Hall was being run as a house of ill repute. Polly's household had established itself in a new pattern, one of love and vice and intrigue and Connie found that she could step in and out of their lives with barely a backward glance. She felt at home with them in every room. She even caught glimpses of the Duchess and her friends in the stable yard when she was washing up in the kitchen.

The guillotine had been robbed several times of its intended victims; prisoners had been spirited away from under the executioners' noses. In their place there was usually to be found some small memento of an Englishman who called himself 'the Scarlet Pimpernel'. This elusive gentleman, identified only by his wife and Citizen Chauvelin, also lived in the Royal Crescent, Bath, as every tourist guide knows. What no one knew was the tragic background of young Polly, who arrived in England at a tender age and was placed by Sir Percy Blakeney in the household of the Duchess of Hallatrow.

Young Polly is a paragon indeed. Nature has adorned her with every charm in abundance, bedecked her with beauty, youth, sprightliness, innocence, modesty and much besides, and bestowed on her the sweetest temper and the tenderest heart. Her complexion owes more to the lily than the rose, her breast is of a whiteness that no lily, ivory or alabaster can match. Add to these qualities a dimple which the least smile discovers and a pair of sparkling eyes, and there she stands a nascent flower to inflame the passions of any saint, a vessel into which any man would willingly pour his soul. She also speaks fluent English – her mother having been the toast of London before her marriage to M. le Comte de Muide and setting up home with him in Paris – and she has been educated in every refinement. Now cruelly orphaned and reduced to working for her living, pretty Polly is in a privileged position at Hallatrow Hall as the Duchess' personal maid. No caller would dare trifle with her: all are in awe of the Duchess and her son Hugo who watches the girl as a farmer nurtures a ripening peach.

Polly enjoys her work. She paints the Duchess' face as if it were an expensively framed canvas, dresses her hair and sees that her clothes are in perfect order. Her province is the master bedroom above the drawing room and she only descends the staircase to join the other servants for meals or when required to help admit the gentlemen for one of the Duchess' salons or soirees. She is never involved in the riotous gatherings behind the drawing-room door, never follows a couple to one of the other rooms. Although many of the gentlemen eye her lasciviously, she maintains a downcast gaze, curtsies prettily and retires.

The Hall's situation so near to Bath makes it possible to attract many of the influential visitors to that city, as much as the local gentry. In the Season one might meet Britain's statesmen and heroes lounging in through the front door, and conversation will turn on the war and taxes. When Society has moved on to London, the Duchess lowers her sights to any man who can afford the dues. But always there is a throng of luscious females and the air vibrates to giggles and worldly chat, singing, laughing, ogling, and all that.

The women who come and go, overpainted, overdressed, selected for their physical charms, flaunting flesh and jewels, are insanely jealous of the beautiful, unsullied maid and the regret with which the gentlemen pass from her to join them through the drawing-room door. One Mistress Annie – a gorgeous bit of muslin with red hair, a lady of the night if ever there was one – is the favourite of Hugo, but bestows her favours on any visitor whatever his deportment. She particularly resents young Polly and keeps a cautious, captious eye on her. A red mane and voluptuous creamy breasts she knows are no match for such youth, such delicacy, such lively good humour, the faint but seductive French accent. Annie is already marked by her age and trade. Accustomed to attracting all eyes she is the first to sense a rival, and she will never forgive Polly for discovering her one day in the hayloft above the coach house. Polly will never forget that, either.

Exploring soon after her arrival at the Hall, Polly has ventured across the yard to the stables. Here the warmth and smell of the horses, the patient chomping and stamping and tail-swishing overwhelm her with memories of earlier, happier days when she would play in her father's mews behind the great house in Paris. She has so far shut Paris from her mind, has refused to think back to the horrors of lying entombed in an attic trunk while the Communards dragged her father and mother away to their certain deaths. But on this day, pressing her face against a chestnut flank not unlike that of her father's favourite mare, she gives way to all the grief she has been unable to express, and with her tears washes away her tragic Past and brings herself to contemplate her Future. She is kindly treated at the Hall, but there must be some freedom from the communal life, some secret, private place to which she can escape. The hatch to the hayloft stands open, the ladder invites, insists. She mounts the rungs two at a time, climbs up and up and up.

Only her pretty head appears above the beams and into the cathedral of rafters, the light filtered by swags of cobwebs and random heaps of hay clear enough for her to see, and to be seen. One glance is enough and she descends, hand grappling below hand, toes slipping and tripping, slithering all the way down until she hits the cobblestones of the coach house floor – and rushes, blind, back across the yard. One glance is enough. An unforgettable impression remains with her of layers of cream-coloured flesh surrounded by a spume of white linen and the hay, a wanton leg raised, black-stockinged to the thigh, the twin spheres of male buttocks superimposed and pumping – and slightly to one side, the mass of Annie's red-gold hair and those green-gold eyes.

In this hothouse of social and sexual intrigue emotions surge and swell, thrust, bloom, fester. The gentlemen come here to be titillated, diverted, the women for money or revenge. Over this altar of love, forever escorted by her lapdog, presides the Duchess with her arthritic fingers drumming on the head of her cane and her sharp but hooded eyes aware of every human desire, prepared to sell any soul. Polly has learned that she is not safe for long and dreads the day when wealth or birth enough will enter the Hall and persuade the mistress to part with the maid. Until that day arrives, however, she lives quite happily in this exotic paradise, content to wait and watch, learning art and artifice and, above all, learning to trust no one.

The inferior priestess, at her altar's side,
Trembling begins the sacred rites of pride.
Unnumbered treasures open at once, and here
The various offerings of the world appear;
From each she nicely culls with curious toil,
And decks the Goddess with the glittering spoil.

Much decking is required before the Duchess is equipped to appear in company. She sits before her mirror in the bay of her bedroom windows. Both she and the reflective glass are draped in muslin as protection against powder, but as the Duchess cannot see the image with much clarity the mirror is superfluous. The lovely Polly hovers, culling and toiling – the full-scale toilette is under way.

The Duchess has not adopted the simple new fashions from France. Younger women now cut and curl their hair close to the head and wear a velvet ribbon around the neck, unlike the

Duchess' ruffle; some sport a blood-red neck ribbon to ape the effect of the guillotine. The Duchess continues the practice of a complete 'head', a hairstyle set with lard, dusted with flour and caged at night in a net of silver to keep mice from nesting in it.

She also relies on beauty from pots and boxes, flasks and bottles, where the style of the day now runs to purity and nature. The Duchess insists on the old-fashioned white arsenic face with brilliant circles of rouge on the cheeks. Her dressing table supports an array of jars of pomade and rouge, pots of face- and hair-powder, crystal scent bottles, home-made ointments, Parisian paints with Spanish wool for their application, enamelled patch boxes, ring stands and clay hair-curlers, and a vial of Cagliostro's Water of Life – a guarantee to preserve youth and beauty forever. Polly has been quick to learn the English tricks, never practised by her avant-garde mother, and toils with pride in what she can achieve for the old woman.

Already Polly has dressed her mistress in her boned corset with its front and back lacing, her petticoats and chemise gown. Already she has applied the white lead and egg-white paste to prime the neck and face. She is mixing more lead powder with carmine from a porcelain pot to paint the cheeks and lips when Hugo enters the bedroom, and she has to hold the Duchess still while they talk.

'Sir Roger,' Hugo is saying, as he prowls the room, straightening a print of *Marriage à la Mode*, sniffing at a potpourri, 'is quite impossible to please. You would think he would be content with Charlotte, or would be mad for Laetitia. As a neighbour one would wish him satisfied. However –'

'However,' says the Duchess, irritably shrugging away from Polly and reaching an ivory stick to scratch at a movement on her scalp. 'We need not concern ourselves over Sir Roger. He enjoys our soirees and is happy whether winning or losing at the tables, and that is quite enough. Poor man, I fear he has a Secret Sorrow and it is enough that we can entertain him. Alone in that big house (and I hear he has other estates in Hampshire), such a waste for a single gentleman! If I had but a daughter… Such a wit, such a waste! If I were ten years younger –' she pauses to remove the ivory prong from her hair and employ it to pick at her false teeth, 'Well, maybe twenty. Such a fine figure of a man.' Her voice trails off as she allows memory and conjecture to mingle.

'But tonight –' Hugo returns to business.

'Mistress Annie will entertain him,' the Duchess muses, her attention still trapped by thoughts of herself and Sir Roger. 'Haven't you noticed her interest in him? She sees herself as the future Lady Beauchamp! Well, let her try. We can rely on Annie.'

'We shall not –' Hugo begins, but he knows they will. His control over Annie is limited at present to the act of copulation. Sir Roger adds tone to a party in December when much of Society has returned to London.

'Tonight,' he continues, unbuttoning his cut-away coat and swinging the tails aside as he takes a chair near his mother, 'we have the pleasure of a visit from an Assize Judge, and no effort must be spared in his entertainment. Word travels,' he adds. 'Make sure that the food is perfection and the women all look their best.'

The Duchess picks again at her teeth and then removes the lot. 'Polly!' she calls, and gestures dismissively at the array on the dressing table. Youth and beauty are a mere illusion after the age of twenty or so and the old woman's teeth were pulled decades ago. This false set, of which she is justly proud, has been assembled from extractions from bodies dead in European wars, far superior to those of porcelain or animal bones.

Polly cleans the teeth and returns them together with the cork plumpers to swell the Duchess' cheeks. She takes the opportunity to offer a choice of mouse-skin eyebrows.

Laetitia and Charlotte are announced with M. Andre who will dress the hair, and Hugo lounges off with a reminder: 'See that they know the arrangements for tonight. A little whist or piquet, perhaps. No serious gambling, mind.'

'Duchess!' cries Laetitia, a heavy rustle in taffeta. 'I have this moment heard—' 'Sit!' snaps the Duchess. 'Allow me a brief respite.' She sighs and sinks into her muslin powder-gown. 'I shall wear the wig, M. Andre. I have not the time or the strength for a head today.'

M. Andre the perruquier, another refugee from Paris, coveted by most of the wives of Bath, is here for his monthly visit. The Duchess without the use of her wig is a peculiar challenge – most women of her age have given in to a shaven head – and he is prepared with his false hair pieces and Macassar oil to mould an edifice to his fancy and to impress his other clients. He shrugs and bows, both to the Duchess in the mirror and to the assembled ladies, and proceeds to remove the packing and most of the lice from last month's arrangement. He pirouettes and pats while he cleanses the sparse hair with bran, and he controls his normal chatter because the Duchess' attention is elsewhere.

'What news?' she sighs. 'Polly!'

The maid is at the window again, against the light where she cannot be sure what the girl is doing. She should be sewing perfumed sachets into the linings of tonight's gown; she should not be staring into the garden.

'I have heard,' Laetitia continues, pulling her chair closer, almost tripping M. Andre, 'that Mistress Annie has an assignation with Sir Roger!'

'When?' The Duchess jerks forward and bran sprays to the

floor. Although she relies on Annie to entertain her most exacting guests she does not trust Annie's behaviour in her own time. Hugo would be no bar to such extra-mural activity, and Annie has pretensions to a better life.

'Right now!' Laetitia is a favoured gossip and somehow knows the latest before it has happened.

At the window, nimbly cutting one mouse-skin eyebrow to match the other, Polly can recognize the elegant form of Sir Roger on the terrace meeting Annie, who is wearing one of the daring new flimsy high-waisted gowns, half covered by a pelisse of magenta velvet.

She is insinuating her little hand through his arm and guiding him towards the laurels. Sir Roger Beauchamp – whose land marches with that of the Bryants, rising beyond the spinney and visible from the Duchess' bedroom window – has been a frequent visitor at the Hall and is quite the most handsome of men Polly has ever seen. She has watched him with a lively interest for many a month and knows that he, too, has noticed her. Her feelings, as she witnesses the familiarity of Annie's grasping hand, excessively scarlet-gloved on his pale sleeve, build to a turbulence of jealousy and despair.

The Duchess sucks at her teeth and lisps, 'Annie is not to be trusted.' With a petulant shrug she turns to the mirror to peer at the miniature garden that M. Andre has created in her powdered wig. 'A Guinea pig!' her carmine lips pronounce. 'A Guinea a year Pitt's now taxing us – extortion! We will have to cease the powdering. Who can afford it?' She can smile benevolently at her young employees; only because of her patronage could they afford powder.

Sir Roger is seen to draw away from Annie's insistent hand and to lead her safely back to the terrace. And Polly returns, content, to her mistress to apply a black taffeta patch or two over the more obvious pock marks.

* * * * * * *

Connie sat with *Clarissa* on her lap, facing her mother-in-law and Aunt Fay on the sofa and her husband yawning over the *Times* crossword beside the fire. Sally was entertaining someone in the playroom. Tim? Mark, even?

She already knew that Mark had been to one of Sally's parties in the playroom. Sally had told her, but Mark had not. That silence lay between them on Thursdays now and she had not had the courage to mention it herself. This absurd furtive behaviour! This underhand skulking, meeting on the sly. She had started it. For some stupid reason, like not wanting to antagonise Hugh, she had arranged the Thursday meetings with Mark – a nonsense subterfuge because Hugh knew they took place. By doing so she had encouraged the children to subversion. That was all her own fault and now she reaped the reward of not knowing if her son was in her own house. The enormity of all this, the absurdity that the entire family was creeping about behaving dishonestly, burying the truth, and that she had not only started it but had allowed it to continue and to grow, suddenly overwhelmed her. It was all her own fault.

'I have never,' Edith was saying, 'understood people who do crossword puzzles! Your father never did. He had occupations, hobbies. It seems to me a complete waste of time. What, I ask myself, are you accomplishing?'

She was asking herself; no one answered. Aunt Fay looked up from her knitting with her usual patient smile. Hugh poised his pen over the crossword, pursed his lips and then shook his head.

If, Connie continued to herself, she had said 'No, I won't have that –' If she had said 'All right, live in your bender but come home each week, each Thursday –' If she had said 'You must –' or 'We shall –' and had insisted that the family met periodically. If only she had said at the beginning that she would not accept such a break and that Hugh and Mark must fight it out there and then, and then accept their differences and find some common ground... But she had not. She was a passive wife, a spineless, fearful, conciliating and ultimately selfish woman who had preferred to accept a situation which she knew to be wrong, simply because she hadn't the courage to stand and fight. And by indulging herself with the simplistic excuse that she was keeping her husband happy, she was destroying her family and teaching the children deceit. Well, yes. True. But.

Hugh was glaring at her over his reading glasses. 'Do you know who Sally's got in there?' he asked. 'I'm not entirely happy with this arrangement. They could be getting up to anything.'

'They won't be late,' said Connie quickly. 'She's got a lot of homework to do for tomorrow, I know. They're all right.'

'Just what I'd expect from you,' he grumbled. 'Everything's always all right. You don't think. You have no idea.' But he returned to his crossword.

Edith made a look which implied several paragraphs of disapproval and condemnation, and a few more about her own restraint.

Connie sank deeper into her chair, half closing her eyes until the room blurred to a haze like an old print hung too long in sunlight. Faded, distant, the Hall and its inmates took on benign shapes and colouring and could be overpainted with bright new emotions. She could feel herself emerge from the cowed and hopeless housewife, a loser, a worrier, prey to guilts and fears, to butterfly out of this drab chrysalis and to take wing as pretty Polly. Polly with her youth and sparkle can accomplish anything and will never be miserable or middle-aged. Polly will never waste her precious time worrying, nor will her experience lead her to uncertainty. Polly is blithe and simple and sees everything in primary colours. Because of that – and with the added advantage of dimples, ivory skin, lustrous eyes, etcetera – Polly is the lively, lovely animal who can bring any man to a froth of foolishness. She smites where Connie can only be smitten. Polly is a different species and will enjoy a very different life. Connie eased out and spread her butterfly wings in the firelight, the dark undersides flattened to the carpet exposing only a brilliant surface.

* * * * * * *

On one cold dark evening when the winds are heard to moan down the chimneys and the last of the autumn leaves scurry frozen round the Corinthian columns of the portico, the amiable Polly is again assigned to the door. She enjoys these duties when a footman falls sick or is dismissed – a frequent occurrence because the Duchess will employ the most exquisite of young men and they seldom have the stamina or the temperament required. Polly enjoys these duties particularly because they allow her to see the faces of the gentlemen visitors, not merely their fine coats and curled and powdered hair she might otherwise glimpse down the stairwell from above. Many she now knows by name from greetings with Hugo in the hall or announcements by the steward at the drawing-room door. Florid cheek follows sallow skin, an impossibly thin man minces and chatters after the rotund and rolling gait of a local squire. Some chuck her under the chin or, alert for Hugo, slap her comely bottom or pinch her upper arm. She is now a part of the household, as familiar as the furniture and treated, more or less, the same.

This evening Hugo is not to be seen. An Assize Judge has been introduced and all attention is focused on his entertainment. Dressed in her most becoming grey gown, demure but provocative with mob cap perched on her golden curls, Polly receives coats and hats from the visitors and escorts them across the hall. Fat little Mr Gibson has passed through with a lugubrious young man whose silk stockings hang upon meagre shanks. Squire Framley, a favourite of the Duchess, a short, ill-made old man with wet lips and a rheumy eye, checks the hall for Hugo and then slides a warm velvet arm around Polly's waist, brings his steamy breath close to her face.

'Tell me where's your room, Missy. Upstairs, eh? They won't be missing us for a while, I'll wager!'

The front door is opened and closed behind them while Polly plunges and struggles and tries to slither from his grasp. A young footman would not dare to intervene and the steward is out of sight. Panting with fear and with her arms clamped between her body and the heaving bulk of the Squire's embroidered waistcoat, Polly can only arch and twist herself away, feel a damp paw tearing at the bodice of her gown, and watch those livid lips and great goggling eyes close in on her face. As she is on the point of resigning herself to the awfulness of such a kiss, the mouth opens with a cross between a belch and a groan, the thick clammy hands fall away and Polly stumbles into the arms of celestial blue. Sir Roger, of course.

Supporting her, easily encircling her with one arm, Sir Roger fires a cold command at what remains of Squire Framley, who shambles off towards the drawing-room door. Then he half carries swooning Polly to the staircase, pauses there staring down at her and says, with ill-concealed emotion and without his usual charming manners, 'Go to your room now, child! I'm sure they can manage without you for tonight!'

Polly gazes, breathless, up into eyes of an exceptional brilliance made more intense by the darkness of their lashes and brows. In confusion she tries to adjust the fichu at the neck of her gown across her naked bosom, but she cannot move or speak. She is caught like a marionette, bemused, stiff-limbed in his arms, pink-cheeked, lips parted, her dress torn – a seductive picture indeed.

His eyes narrow and his face shows only harsh features as he controls his passion and prepares to force her away from him. The look of faint amusement, the languid grace are gone. 'Go, run, you little fool!' he whispers urgently. 'Fly, fly away, my little bird! Look, I open my hand and you are free. If you do not fly instantly we are both doomed!'

She stares up at him, bewitched by the intensity of his expression, her spirits in a visible flutter. His words tell her to go, his eyes insist she stay. She feels like a rabbit transfixed by a candle in the dark, a child dazzled by sunlight on cut glass.

'Doomed,' he groans, devouring her with his eyes. 'Already it is too late. I have seen you, heard your laughter, watched you for many a day. You are youth, joy, all that is beauteous and true and I must have you! There is such a frail line dividing despair from joy. You alone can bring me pleasure. I know you have the power to cleanse, to heal. I can already feel –'

She knows that he will kiss her; she knows that his passion is as impetuous as her own. If only he would stop explaining. She is content to be cradled in his arms with her back against the banister post, but she is less trusting of fate than he and fears an interruption before his mouth meets hers. Indeed, at the very moment his long dark eyelashes fall to veil his contemplation of her face and she anticipates the long-craved arrival of his finely chiselled lips, a commotion is heard in the hall.

'Aha!' Hugo's cry echoes with his footsteps across the flagstones.

Polly can see his one hand on Sir Roger's collar, feels the blow from the other sting her cheek and throw her from the comfort of Sir Roger's embrace. She falls back until she is half lying on the stairs, her slippers lost, her skirts in disarray. The two men are struggling, Hugo with his fingers grasping the lace ruffles at Sir Roger's throat. In a moment Sir Roger, with a seemingly casual shrug, has thrown Hugo from him to the ground and is standing over him looking faintly amused.

'Really, my dear fellow!' he murmurs, flicking a raven curl off his face.

Hugo scrambles to his feet blustering and gathering himself to return to the fray. Polly leaps to restrain him, grasps his arm, watching with fascination as blood drips down from a cut on his lip. Hugo raises a finger to his mouth, sees the blood and turns on Sir Roger in awful wrath. 'That, sir, is beyond all!' he splutters. 'I insist on satisfaction!'

'No!' cries poor Polly, stumbling barefoot to Sir Roger, clutching at his hands, imploring. 'No, I pray you, stop! I shall explain. Please, please, dear sir – thank you, but will you not now join the others? I shall explain to Mr Bryant.'

Sir Roger gently sets her aside and dusts at a speck on his sleeve. 'Mark well what she has to tell you, sir,' he warns Hugo. 'And see that it does not recur. It was a pleasure to be of service to you, Mademoiselle.' And he sweeps her a deep bow.

As Sir Roger strolls towards the drawing room, Hugo dabs at the blood on his lip and glares at Polly. 'So, Miss?' he demands. 'It should be a good explanation!'

At the drawing-room door Sir Roger turns to observe them,

waits until he sees Hugo's shoulders drop and the tendons slacken in his neck. He then smiles faintly, sadly, in farewell to the charming maid and moves on to the alternative delights conceived by the Duchess.

* * * * * * *

'Constance!' Edith's voice came like a cannon shot from far away. 'What's wrong with the girl? One feels as if one is talking to oneself. Really, Constance, wake up! All this drifting and dreaming – you've no excuse for dropping off like this. When you are my age, perhaps. Though goodness knows I wouldn't want to waste a precious moment.'

Chapter 8

'It would be so much nicer – and, as Daddy says, more practical – to make a real holiday of it and come for more than the few days of Christmas. All that driving and shutting everything up and getting Tiggy to the cattery. And I'm hoping Archie might stay on for the weekend too. We see you both so seldom, my darling, it would be such a treat.' Connie's mother had written in November.

'She makes it sound like mobilising an army!' Hugh had commented. 'As if she had to close down something on the lines of Longleat and get the lions into foster homes – not just one tiny cottage and an ancient tomcat. And 'all that driving' they've managed every year. Good God, it's less than two hundred miles to Cambridge. However.' He knew she knew how he felt.

'I suppose Archie might stay on for the weekend, 'said Connie, 'as he's between wives he can't have much to hurry back for.'

Hugh had snorted. 'Your brother has always got some woman up his sleeve. I only hope the next is more – shall we say, *comme il faut*. Poor Marion is the only one I ever liked – and how long did she last?'

'Marion was hopeless for him, we all said that. Far too ordinary.'

'There – you're as bad as your mother!' Hugh knew that would strike. 'Nothing's good enough for dear Archie. And look what a mess he's made of his life. What a family!'

Connie had ignored the jibe. There was nothing wrong with her family, and Archie at least was fun. Like her mother, Connie was proud that Archie had consulting rooms in Harley Street and enough funds to live in style in a nearby mews house; unlike her mother, Connie delighted in the idea of having a brother who specialised in venereal diseases. Mary Johnston could not admit to 'my son the venereologist'. 'A doctor' she would smile, forbiddingly, 'A Harley Street consultant'. If anyone enquired further she would become vague – as she could on so many counts, anything difficult or controversial or unseemly – and would agonise instead about what she knew of his incredible lifestyle: 'Parties or theatres *every* night, and a permanent seat at the Albert Hall, isn't that quite immoral when you think how many people are starving?' The money involved in such hedonism distressed her as much as she was impressed that he could afford it. His relationships and divorces she refused to discuss, her other obsession being the Church.

'They won't want to be here for the Meet,' Sally had said. 'That's against Granny J's creed!'

'Nor Ginger and Tony's party,' Hugh had warned. 'But that's your problem, Constance. I'll take Mother.'

Mary and Victor Johnston arrived on the day of the Hunt's cocktail party, the day before the Meet at Hallatrow Hall. Edith, as widow of the Brigadier, Tony's old C.O. and a former Hunt secretary, was to be honoured guest at Tony's party, escorted by her son.

'If you'd like to …' Connie had suggested to her parents as she settled them into the blue room. 'But we thought you'd be tired and would prefer a quiet evening.'

'Nothing,' said her mother, 'would possess me to go anywhere. But some tea would be lovely, darling. Shall we come down?'

Connie's father would have liked any party. Long retired from the prep school where he had taught Maths and Games, and occupied now only in writing his local Parish history, he welcomed any diversion and even after 'all that driving' was ready for a party. Well into his second childhood, as he was happy to admit, he needed entertainment, treats, people and things to play with. Mary was a stern nanny, always tidying away his toys; at home he would escape to the Half Moon.

After Connie had left them; 'A dram,' he said, 'a drop of the hard stuff would meet the bill! Don't you feel a sense of anti-climax after all the bustle of getting here?'

His wife, unpacking socks and thermal vests, straightened to look at him and fingered her lustreless pearls. 'No,' she said, forbearing to condemn his habitual attempts at escape from bustle or boredom.

'I could take it down to slip in the tea.'

She tried to ignore the hip flask emerging from his pocket, to make no expression which could be taken as a plea.

'Nicer that way, of course.' He was watching her, playing with her, hoping for a reaction. 'But perhaps just a tot now?'

He had her there. She must allow that, in order to avoid his making an exhibition of the flask downstairs. Mary had such a nice idea of right and wrong: wrong was any unwarranted behaviour in company. In private she would put up with anything, any abuse, but in public one Anglo-Saxon word or his being the tiniest bit tipsy and she became positively Victorian, all mortification and ruffled feathers. Half the time she asked for it with her Church manners and Sunday face, all drawn in and disapproving when he opened the bottle before the sun rose over the yard arm. (What's so Christian about six o'clock, for heaven's sake?) That, naturally, gave him every excuse, encouraged him to pour the next. And if, like today, she made a great show of not noticing, how could a man withstand the challenge to push a little further?

Mary was folding wool and tweed into drawers as if they were here for a month. 'We had better go down now – I'll finish this later. We should say hello to Edith before she goes off to the party.'

Edith was already dressed in her amethysts and a purple satin kaftan, sipping China tea.

'Why Mary and Victor!' she exclaimed as if unaware of their arrival or amazed that they had been invited. 'How nice! And quite unchanged, I see. Fay, we shall need hot water.'

'I see *you've* changed,' Victor joked. 'Into your party togs! Off on the razzle-dazzle, I hear. Don't do anything I wouldn't!'

Mary hurried to the sofa, took Edith's spare hand in both of hers and bent to peck her cheek.

'So good to see you again.' Sincerely said, as she would delivering Meals on Wheels. Edith was quite five years older than her and qualified for compassion. She ran a hand down the back of her heather mix skirt and sat with knees and toes and wrists together. 'Tell me, how's your poor arthritis? Are you still getting a lot of pain?'

'Oh, you don't know!' Edith shifted slightly sideways, slightly away, and peered at Mary's bog-coloured blouse and Shetland cardigan. No, she hadn't changed. Still the moorland look, still those anxious eyes blinking, almost overflowing with goodwill and good intentions. A thinner, better-preserved version of Aunt Fay.

Victor was prowling, picking things up, glancing at book spines and china marks, disassociating himself from the women and the tea. 'And here's our host!' he cried when Hugh arrived, and 'abandoning me to the hens!' ruefully as Hugh escorted Edith from the room.

By the time they returned Mary, Victor and Aunt Fay had changed into lighter weights and shades of wool and Sally was answering questions about next summer's exams.

'We have heard,' said Edith as they settled to honey-baked ham and red cabbage in the dining room, 'that your brother is playing some role in trying to sabotage the Hunt!' She glared over her spectacles at Sally as if it were her responsibility.

Sally looked suitably surprised but glanced at her mother. Hugh caught the look and challenged: 'Did you know about this, Constance?'

That, Connie did know. Mark had also admitted with pride that he was being considered for leadership of the local Sabs. 'Don't tell Sals yet; she thinks I'm just playing about. You know, we're in a super position here with at least three hunts in reach and lots of locals dead keen to get them. That's why we're going to run our own show – we don't need normal help from outside the area any more. We're setting up headquarters in someone's squat in town. It's going to be very organised, just like running a proper business – though I don't think Dad'll be too impressed! Or Granny. Or some of your friends.'

'Or some of yours! Darling, have you stopped to think? As far as I know, what the Antis do is not only illegal but often reprehensible. You can't right a wrong with another one. The behaviour of some of these Antis is absolutely vicious; you can't condone that!'

'That's quite beside the point.' Mark had run on into explanations and justifications, his eyes alight in his hairy face, shining with conviction and moral purpose. And Connie had sighed and smiled at him across their Thursday coffee mugs, smiled indulgently she feared; far too indulgent. But what more could she do than draw his attention to what they all knew was wrong?

'Yes, I knew he –' she replied to Hugh. It sounded like an excuse already.

'You knew!' Edith was genuinely shocked.

'He's only keeping up with the 'Baz's,' comforted Sally. 'He's living amongst them; he can't not.'

'I must say that I approve of the principles –' Mary began.

'You know nothing about the practices!' Edith relegated her to

Aunt Fay's position. No one should be allowed woolly opinions on such a serious matter. 'How can I look Ginger and Tony in the face after this?'

'I wonder if Mark'll show his face tomorrow?' Victor mused. 'At your very own Meet – a bit near the bone! But if he's honest about it all I suppose he should. Gamekeeper turned poacher, so to speak. Sounds as if he's grown up.'

Saturday dawned crystal clear and bitter cold and Connie hoped her glasses hid her amusement as she watched through the kitchen window Emily and Lewis Foster re-polishing Pickle. This was to be Emily's great day. The new Harris tweed jacket and jodhpur boots had been paraded weeks ago, the tack relentlessly cleaned, and Pickle had been stabled for two nights just in case he might roll in some mud. This morning there was much shifting of straw and stuffing of hay nets by little Emily while her father fiddled and blew on his fingers trying to plait the shaggy mane. Connie and Sally had both shown him how; today it was his task.

'Would anyone mind, do you think?' he had ventured. 'Emily would so love to come to a hunt.'

'To the Meet, why not?' Connie had said. 'But she's not ready to follow and you'll find Pickle will be quite different when hounds are around. By all means bring them to the Meet, but hang on to him.'

Glasses of sweet sherry stood ready in the hall. Edith and Aunt Fay were dressed to survive any weather, Edith with a scarlet felt gangster hat set atop her headscarf at a sharp angle. Hugh was striding with his father-in-law, preparing to welcome his guests. It was his day, too.

'Don't you wish you had something to ride?' Sally linked arms between them. 'At times like this I feel quite sick with envy. I'd give anything to be young again.'

'Can't help but agree with that sentiment, my girl!' Hugh smiled into the past. 'You were much less trouble then! But make way for the next generation, here comes Emily. My, don't we look handsome!'

Hearing the first few animals clatter down the drive, the Fosters had emerged from the stable yard, Lewis holding Pickle by the snaffle, Annie aflame with her red hair and a golden anorak and her green eyes a-glint.

'Mine host!' She made a curtsy, graceful even in her green wellies. 'This is the most feudal thing I've ever seen! It suits you Hugh – you look great against a stately home and with minions bearing drinks on trays!'

Connie felt reassured that her jacket looked well used and her boots showed vintage mud. If you can't compete, merge. Lewis Foster was too keen to dress his family to match the popular ideal of Gentry; she wondered that Annie – who was 'quite a little socialist' according to Hugh – put up with such pretension. She also wondered what Hugh and Annie could have in common to outweigh their political prejudices. Now that a general election seemed inevitable Hugh had become louder in support of Cameron and had already been invited to join Tony's committee. How could 'quite a little socialist' become so friendly (as Edith hinted) with such a positive Conservative? A *spy*? Infiltrating the enemy camp? Visions of Annie slinking about the Coach House in a mask and a fedora pleased her. Even Lettice hadn't come up with that idea!

The drive was now filling with horses and ponies swirling the gravel, parading and backing into each other.

'You can be the first to have a sherry,' Connie said, offering the tray to Annie. 'Perhaps Daddy will let you have a sip of his, Emily? Pickle looks very smart; you have done well.'

'I'll take the tray, Mother,' Sally offered. 'There are some characters I even recognise! Would it be all right for Emily to follow as far as the crossroads? I've heard they're going to draw Farr's Wood first, and it's a quiet lane. I could go with Mr. Foster.'

Tony and Ginger arrived with the hounds, and the horses began to swing and sidestep excitedly while riders raised their glasses and their voices and turned gracefully in their saddles. As ever it made a beautiful picture.

'Doesn't it all look just like a greetings card?' Aunt Fay was hugging her sheepskin and beaming under a yellow woolly cap.

'Timeless,' said Victor. 'We could be a century back. Have you seen anything of my grandson?'

'Oh no!' Aunt Fay peeped over her shoulder and then towards the gates. 'Oh, he wouldn't, surely? Not here?'

'Drink up!' Connie was collecting glasses and Aunt Fay hurried to fetch a tray. Tony and the Huntsman, Bill Jenkins, gathered hounds and set off amongst a froth of tails along the drive followed by the hunters bunched together, fighting for space or position, followed by a trail of smaller ponies and the healthier onlookers. Lewis and Sally escorted Emily. They turned left, away from the village, and left again into the lane to Farr's Wood, and the commotion began when the hunt was spread like a ribbon down Farr's Lane.

On principle Mary Johnston had refused to have anything to do with the Meet, but she had allowed herself to watch the scene from her bedroom window. When the hunt moved off – quite the prettiest sight, whatever your principles – she had followed to the bathroom window at the end of the house with its view across the barley field to Farr's Wood. Mary could see the whole cavalcade. And the van blocking the end of the lane. She also was the first to see the motorcycles rounding the corner, passing the drive gates, turning left.

Trapped by the van with space enough only for the hounds to leak through, and anticipating trouble, Bill Jenkins turned his bay mare while Tony rode off to investigate. Fifty yards back, a gate into the barley field would free them. He waved a hand to the Field Master to clear a path and sounded his horn. To lose his hounds to the Antis behind a barricade was more of a danger than starting a panic down the lane, but human folly and animals' sense of claustrophobia filled the road with heaving, turning bloodstock, and horses were being funnelled down from the other end by rebel yells and the revving of machines.

'Clear the way!' Jenkins yelled, urging his mare forward against the hedge, twisting in his saddle to see the path close behind him. 'Let hounds through, for Chrissake!'

The Field Master, conveniently near the gateway, had anticipated the need for an escape valve. He had unhooked the five-barred gate by the time Jenkins arrived and was fighting to hold back those who had no control over their mounts.

'Madam, *please*!'

'This lot first,' Jenkins called to him as he passed. 'Half the pack's stuck behind them!' But he saw brindled bodies forcing through the hawthorn and encouraged them with the horn.

The sound of a hunting horn also stirs any experienced hunter. The melee by the gate worsened until, like the uncorking of a bottle, horses popped and cascaded into the barley field.

The notes of the horn reached down the lane to Pickle who was shivering with excitement. Near the end of the line, he had been more harassed than most by the motorcycles and was sidling with his tail pressed tight between his flanks and his ears flat against his plaits. A biker roared behind him again; there was no way home except forward. Lewis clung tight to bit and bridle, Sally turned to shout caution and found herself looking into a helmet which could only be Tim's.

'I don't *believe* it!' she cried. 'What are you *doing*?' Where's Mark?'

Lewis and Pickle were swept on and through the gate into the field where Pickle shook his head, flared his nostrils, snatched the bit from Lewis' grasp and galloped straight towards home. Emily clung to the saddle like a monkey with her eyes screwed shut, opened them in amazement when she felt Pickle lift into the air over the fence to the vegetable garden, and only fell when he skidded on the cobbles of the yard. By the time Lewis caught up, Emily was wrapped in blankets, unconscious and bloodstained in the Coach House.

Chapter 9

Lunch was late that day. Connie had been occupied with the Fosters – Emily was now in hospital with suspected concussion – and Hugh and Sally returned separately long after the hunt had left the barley field.

'If I had only known what you intended, dear.' Aunt Fay clattered knives and spoons round the scrubbed kitchen table and wondered if seven might be rather cramped and what would Edith say. 'If I had thought just soup and cheese, of course I would have laid before. Though perhaps in the dining room?'

Connie stirred the soup, half hearing her mother and Edith colluding against the Antis over the dregs of the sherry. Could Mark have been involved? 'This is only lunch!' she snapped and felt immediately guilty. 'But thank you so much for washing up all the glasses. That was a great help.'

'Oh, nothing at all.' Aunt Fay blushed and beamed and pulled at her yellow sweater. 'So nice to find somewhere I *can* be useful. Shall I bring everyone in now?'

'We were just saying—' said Edith as they filed in. 'Gracious, what a squeeze!'

'I really think—' said Hugh. 'And the table's only half set!'

'Choose your places,' said Connie. 'And darling, would you cut the bread?' 'Darling' can be an offensive endearment when used without reflection. She reached to touch his arm as he passed, to draw him to her, to excuse the kitchen, herself, the saboteurs, to show she shared his concern, to mitigate his anger; but he shrugged away.

'Did you see Mark?' he asked when he had settled, still muttering disapproval, at one corner of the table. 'By the time I got to the end of the lane the van had gone, but I saw you talking to the motorbike brigade, Sally.'

'Don't tell me,' Aunt Fay had an awful thought, 'that your Timothy was involved? Mercy! I didn't think of that when I heard about the cycles.'

Sally slurped a spoonful of broth with her eyes fixed on the cheese board. 'I didn't see Mark, and he's not 'my' Timothy.' That should be enough to shut them up. She was fed up with all of them, particularly with Tim. How *could* he! Without even telling her! He and Mark had both betrayed her. She was quite alone. Nobody understood. If they went on at her, as she knew they would, she'd be in tears.

'So Tim was there?' Mother being a pain.

'Obviously.'

'Did you talk to him?'

'Obviously.' With a withering look. Mother should understand.

'There's nothing obvious about it!' her father joined in. 'Watch your manners! Did that lout mention Mark or anything?'

Sally said nothing.

'I'm asking you!'

'And I'm not answering. What is this, a third degree or something?'

Hugh rose and banged on the table. 'Go to your room! Immediately! I won't have this insolence. How dare you speak to me like that!' His nose and forehead had mottled and his eyes were jumping.

'Righty-o!' Sally swung round the table and brushed past him to the door.

'That child,' said Edith as the door closed, 'should have her bottom spanked. As I've said before ...'

Granny Johnston folded her lips and closed her eyes as if in prayer. Far be it for her to comment, but Constance would never have spoken like that. Victor rolled his eyes in search of someone to share a joke, and Aunt Fay seized the opportunity to cut into the Stilton.

'I've had enough of this!' said Hugh. 'I'm not putting up with either of them any more. It's gone too far.' He glared at his wife. 'You can fetch Mark back, I want to talk to him.'

'I don't think—' Connie began.

'I'm not interested in what you think.' Hugh reached for the cheese. 'If you don't get him, I will. I want him back in this house by tomorrow. And Sally stays in her room.'

Self-pity, Connie said to herself as she drove to the river, will get you nowhere. Perhaps Hugh's right and feelings don't count. Sally must learn self-control. And it would be lovely to have Mark home for Christmas.

No one was at the encampment by the river. Connie ran the gauntlet of the railway line and like a thief crept into Mark's bender. All was warm and tidy, though the stove needed stoking. She broke some twigs and poked them into the embers and inspected his room. Rags drying on a line she recognised as a vest and pants and socks; the sleeping bags were neatly rolled. Her heart ached at the order of it all. She sat on the mattress to write her note: 'Please darling, you must come home. It's Christmas. It's time we all talked. I'll collect you tomorrow morning.'

On Sunday most of the family prayed. Mary, Edith and Aunt Fay went to church; Hugh, Victor and Sheba for a walk; Sally was allowed out to fetch Mark; and Connie, once she had thrown the joint and potatoes into the oven, prowled the house revelling in its emptiness. Not a second of such peace should be wasted. Lovingly she wandered round the drawing room, plumping cushions, caressing the backs of chairs. She smiled through the windows to the deserted terrace, through the mirror into the empty room. The Duchess and Hugo must be at church, too.

Sir Roger naturally knows their movements and has chosen this moment to ride up on his steel-grey gelding. There he goes now, past the arc of windows! Polly's heart flutters. Why here on a Sunday morning when none of the Duchess' ladies, nor the family, are at home? He sees her. He dismounts at the window.

'I must talk with you!' His voice and eyes through the glass urge her to respond.

Flutter, flutter, flutter. What violence does Sir Roger intend?

A moment later he joins her in the drawing room. 'I could not bear another day to pass without seeing you!'

Flutter, flutter, flutter. Polly may be virginal but she is not naïve. She too has been reading *Clarissa*, and she has seen her Adonis parading on the terrace with Annie. All men are rakes at heart. No maid should believe a word she is told. And yet …

Sir Roger crosses the room with a long and careless stride, the coat-tails of celestial blue floating behind him. 'No, wait till you have heard what I have to say.' The gravity of his expression disarms her and her heart melts in tenderness. She sinks into her mistress's chair and allows his pretty speech, his professions of love. She leans her golden curls against the high wing of polished leather and veils her eyes.

Although this view of her fires his desire to take her there and then, he stands aloof and paces the floor. He is deeply concerned, says he, that she is employed in such a house, exposed to the morals of such as Squire Framley, under the control of a libertine like Hugo. He has heard her history, has sought out Annie – the most willing of the Hallatrow ladies – in order only to discover more about her circumstances. The more he has heard, the more he fears for her. After finding her with Framley last night and seeing Hugo's disregard for her plight he is deeply concerned for her safety and anxious to offer her his protection. Here he pauses, gazing intensely down into her wide grey eyes. How could anyone place her in such a house? So innocent. So young.

'What protection could you give me, sir?' she asks, pert but breathless. 'As to innocence, I have been aware of the ways of the world since I was seven. Methinks your protection would be similar to Mr Bryant's, should he have his way, and less disinterested than the Duchess.'

Sir Roger's eyes smoulder. 'So that is what you think of me?'

For a moment he watches her with a brooding gaze and then reaching for her hand he pulls her up and into his embrace. 'You would be happier with me,' he drawls. 'Can you deny that? I would care for you; I would see that you were happy. If you stay here it will not be long before the Duchess puts you to other work downstairs.'

'And with you?' Polly asks faintly, fixing him with a limpid regard. 'How long before you tired of me and turned me loose like a spit dog which has run the wheel and served its purpose?'

He is intoxicated by her presence, clasps her body roughly against his, presses kisses to her hair, her cheek, her throat, his breath hot and harsh on her skin. 'If you were to marry me …'

'So there you are!' The Duchess is at the drawing-room door.

Polly jumps away, aflame with guilt, peering short-sightedly towards her. She sees a scarlet felt gangster hat perched on the Duchess' wig and, behind her, the apple cheeks and grizzled hair of Aunt Fay.

'We were wondering where you'd got to, dear.' Aunt Fay inched in round her sister, striding right through Sir Roger. 'The whole place seemed deserted. But you'll be pleased to hear, I know, that little Em'ly is home. We met the Fosters coming in from the hospital. It was very *mild* concussion apparently, and they said she'd be better off in her own surroundings now. Isn't that a relief? I knew you would be pleased, dear.'

'Oh, yes,' said Connie.

Chapter 10

By Christmas Eve, Mark and his family had come to some sort of understanding. Pressed by his sister he had arrived for his interview with Hugh. All afternoon their voices – Hugh's voice – could be heard from the playroom. When Hugh came out ('I wash my hands of him') Connie had taken over. He stayed the night, though he refused to join them for dinner. All next day, while the women festooned tinsel and silver balls about the house and decorated the front door knocker, he listened to or argued with his father, (when Hugh stormed out, Connie or Sally cajoled or pleaded him back). He allowed Connie to throw all his clothes into the washing machine, and he took a bath. By Tuesday he had agreed to stay for Christmas, and Hugh escorted him to check the bender and fetch a few belongings. But he refused to shave.

'It's nice and warm in here,' he told his mother, the first hint of humour he had shown. 'No, honest! It'll be okay while I'm in this cushy place, but when I'm home again I'll catch my death.'

Connie had felt more unhappy about the bender being 'home' than about the beard. His father had taken a stand for appearances. 'If, for whatever length of time, he wants to consider himself part of this family,' Hugh announced, 'he will jolly well do what he's told! That beard's an insult, and he knows it.'

'It's not exactly his choice to be here,' said Connie. 'He's only staying because we've asked him. Darling, there are so many more important things to discuss.'

'Discuss? I'm not discussing! By the time I've finished with him—'

'But exactly, darling. There are so many points it's important to make, don't waste your advantage over such a small one.'

'It may seem small to you, but it's part and parcel of his whole attitude. You have no idea. Back we go to the same old excuses. He's got to be brought into line. What you don't understand – good God, have you learned nothing? – is that discipline starts with self-discipline. He's got to sharpen up before we can get anywhere. It's like the Army. You've no idea about what makes a man! Your problem is that you don't *think*! If we allowed new recruits to swan around with beards and earrings we'd never be able to lick them into shape! It's a state of mind, all that.'

'Manners maketh man,' quoted Connie. 'A tidy mind in a tidy body.'

'Exactly. These old sayings were always true.'

'But they usually had their opposites. Like 'absence makes the heart grow fonder' and 'out of sight, out of mind'.'

'Not on this front. You leave this to me. It's an insult, at least to those that know better. Mother would understand. So would yours, believe me.'

'If you make a concession on something like this—'

'Why should I make concessions? It's not my job to make concessions!'

'He won't, Mother,' Sally warned, Mark's advocate again after a furious row about the hunt sabotage. 'It's part of his *personality*, don't you see? It's like asking him to go barefoot or to wear a skirt! Besides, they all call him Foxy because of it – it's the way they identify him, it makes him feel important. You can't make him shave.'

'Then he won't join us for meals,' said Hugh.

By the time Uncle Archie swirled his white MG to a halt at the front door and the family massed to greet him, they had found a compromise: Mark's whole coiffure was shorter, neater, trimmed by his mother, and everyone's pride and was intact.

'Uncle Archie'll soften them up,' Sally had tried to cheer Mark as they sat wrapping presents in the playroom. 'You'll see. He's the only civilised member of the family. Granny J will be mooning around him as per usual and won't notice the rest of us; he'll flatter groany-Granny until she purrs; he'll stop Mother fussing, and he'll balance Dad's power complex. A bit of fresh air will get into the house – and do we need it!'

Mark had been squatting by the gas fire slowly, carefully, folding shiny green paper around Sally's gifts for the family while she wrote labels from them both. 'This sellotape's hopeless,' he complained. 'It only sticks to itself. And this room's freezing; it's much warmer in the bender.'

Sally finished a label and watched his efforts. 'You know, it's good for you to be home for a bit. You're getting thoroughly spoilt in that bender. You've lost all touch with reality.'

'You must be joking!' For a moment he showed his old spark instead of the bovine gaze. 'You should see yourself; you should see Them! Who's in touch with reality, I'd like to know? They see nothing, they're aware of nothing, they care about nothing except themselves. It's quite shocking suddenly coming into all this again. It makes me want to vomit half the time. Don't you see how materialistic they are? Everything comes down to possessions and money. It's all wrong. And then, the amount of money they waste on food and drink! That's disgusting. They do nothing to help anyone worse off – they don't even think about it. They don't even seem to care about each other. They've got no idea how half the world lives. I bet—'

'Come off it!' Sally grabbed a box of soap and measured a scrap of paper to fit. 'Just what do you think you're doing to help other people? You can't condemn other people's way of life unless you're doing better. Sitting about talking about it and Being Aware, Man, doesn't help anyone. You're just as selfish in your own way. Just look how worried Mum's been about you!'

Their father banged on the window. 'I want help with the tree,' he called. 'Now!'

'That's your job,' said Sally. 'I'll have to decorate it.'

Uncle Archie arrived at teatime when the tree had been erected in the bay of the drawing room and draped with tiny white lights. His mother had been listening for the car and heard it before Sheba. She let out an audible and visible sigh, much like Sheba stretching before the fire. Christmas had begun.

'How', she cried as she shivered under the portico light, 'did you manage to fit all this in? I've never *seen* so many presents come out of such a small space! Mark, *help* him!' She, like Edith, had tried to accept Mark's arrival naturally, when he was finally allowed to meet them. The grandmothers had, in fact, behaved so 'naturally' that Sally and Connie had been forced from the room to control their giggles.

'How nice to see you again, Mark.' Edith's smile could have cut paper. 'Are you home for long, now?'

'Mark, my dear, how lovely! Now we'll all be here for Christmas! Are beards in again this year? I never understand fashions, I'm so out of touch. It makes you look very … doesn't it, Edith?'

Edith was busy not noticing the dirt ingrained on Mark's hands, her mauve shadowed eyes flicking from hand to jeans, hand to holey sweater, hand to shirt collar. 'Black seem to be in fashion this year, too,' she commented.

'Would you like me to darn that jersey, dear?' asked Aunt Fay. 'I'm sure I have some black wool upstairs.' Her expression doubted that anyone would have enough.

'Oh, this one's fine.' Mark felt deserted, washed up on an island, thrown to the hounds. These were his best clothes, on his mother's insistence, all clean. His hands he could do nothing about.

'Greetings, greetings, my dears!' Archie had struggled from his car and bear-hugged all within reach. 'Christ, the country's cold! In with you, quick – the kids will help me unload. Steady with that, it's booze. Godammit Mother, in you go!'

A vast coat made from Siberian foxes he threw into the hall: 'See, I'm prepared for frozen country seats! Just keep young Sheba off it, if you please! Where's the heir apparent? This bag weighs a ton, practically broke the back axle.'

But Mark had disappeared.

'It's the fur coat,' Sally apologised, dragging at the bag. She had seen eyes glowing red in the dark near the lime trees and had anticipated Mark's friends. Once she had told him what she thought about Tim and Saturday's ambush, and had discovered that he had driven the van, any discussion about the Boxing Day Meet was out. But she still had to protect him from Them.

'He's not still doing his boy-scout act, is he?' Archie had unpacked his crate of bottles, Sally had arranged his presents beneath the tree and he stood, feet astride, in front of the fire cradling the dregs of a neat whisky. 'Christ, I needed that! What a trip – the whole world's on the M4!'

His mother closed her eyes at the expletive and his father nudged him, delighted. 'Good to have you here, my boy! Positively hag-ridden, we've been – eh, Hugh?'

'How can you? All these lovely ladies! Edith, you're amazing – not a day older – and that frock's a stunner! And Aunt Fay, still the Penelope of Hallatrow, I see! When are you going to knit one of those gorgeous things for me? Every year I try. I know, I know, you're daunted by the *volume*!' Archie dug his thumbs into his waistcoat pockets, glancing down at the spread of his watch chain. 'I had to come straight from patients or I'd have got out of my three-piece suit. D'you want me to change, Con?'

Mark, from the door, beckoned Sally. 'Tim wants you,' he hissed.

'Well, I don't want him.'

'You must see him, at least. Come on,' and he pulled her out of the room.

Connie read Sally's mule face. She had forgotten that there would be a Boxing Day Meet and now knew that Mark would be leaving before then. He joined her later in the kitchen, leaned against the sink with his hands behind him.

'Sal's finished with Tim.'

'Completely?' Connie adjusted the grill and sprinkled herbs on lamb chops. 'Oh dear!'

'So she says. An ideological difference of opinion. Idiotic.'

'Are you,' Connie busied herself prodding at the potatoes, 'leaving on Boxing Day?'

'Thought I'd better warn you to save all the hassle later. I can't take all this Christmas bit. It's gross, all greed and commercialism. Money, money, money and what's in here for me? Ho, ho, ho! Bring on the next present! I wouldn't mind pushing off now, but suppose it'd be neater tomorrow. I'd have to go tomorrow, anyway.' He dipped a finger into the brandy butter. 'Whenever you like, but while it's daylight. I don't mind. While they're at church would probably be best.'

Connie peered at the grill pan. 'Probably.' She turned to look at him. 'You can't stay for dinner? We'll miss you and I've made lots of veggie stuffings and things you'd like.' It sounded like pleading, but she could see no answering concern; Mark seemed indifferent to any pain he caused, walled up in his separate world, a stranger. This moment she was struck by Hugh's words 'He's no longer my son.' Had those words wrought the change or was Hugh acknowledging a fact? Did Mark really feel he was no longer a part of the family? That possibility, and how she would feel if it had happened to her, split her head with a hail of sharp imagined tears, lacerating, drawing blood, causing physical pain. In the dead days of childhood she would have reached for him, scooped him up, cuddled him, smoothed it all away with warmth and pressure and nonsense murmurs until he was renewed, recharged with love and security. But today he stood aloof, separate, and the space between them yawned. Boredom? He seemed so far from her that she couldn't tell. If he didn't care, did it matter why?

The frozen tears hung on her eyelids, weighing her down, bowing her head. She was torn between an overwhelming concern to reassure him of their love and understanding and unaccountable rage that her beloved son could be so callous and so easily removed from any feeling for her.

'Well,' she said, 'you can take some of the dinner with you. Are Baz and BJ there? I'll do some up for them, too.'

'Thanks Mum. I think it's best not to tell the others.'

Again the subterfuge, secrets, whispers in the dark. And he is right. The arguments would be terrible and Hugh would throw him out immediately. Everyone would be upset. She nodded. 'Fetch them in,' was all she could trust herself to say.

Coffee and croissants and presents round the tree, a debris of crumbs and torn paper, Sheba snoring by the fire, Sally wading through to refill their cups.

'We'll have to have a bonfire this afternoon.' Hugh was merry, playing Father Christmas. 'Here's another one for you, Mark – another black shirt? Oh – a pity Marks and Sparks don't sell black underwear, but I suppose you can dye it!'

'I don't think that would be a good idea, Hugh dear,' said Granny Johnston. 'It might run.'

'Wouldn't make much difference,' Sally laughed.

'That's what's meant by the black sheep of the family,' Archie murmured to his father.

'And for you, Archie,' Hugh adjusted his glasses, 'from Aunt Fay and Mother.'

Aunt Fay clasped her hands and leaned forward.

'I wonder!' Archie kneaded the parcel wrapped in last year's ironed paper, pretended to rattle it against his ear and then tore through to a heap of multicoloured wool. 'I don't believe it! It's my year! Oh, you wonderful woman!' He staggered up and across to plant a kiss on her furry cheek.

'It's from us both, dear.' Aunt Fay beamed and chuckled while he approached Edith. 'But I do hope it *fits*!'

Archie threw off his jacket, hoisted his grey flannels and struggled into the enormous pullover.

'Fair Isle!' Connie admired it. 'Aunt Fay, you are clever!'

'Edith provided a lot of the wool,' Aunt Fay smiled to include her sister.

'It's magnificent,' said Archie, swaggering, hand on hip, through the mounds of paper. 'Don't I look pretty? And warm! I'll live in it.'

'Those of us who are going to church really should leave,' said Mary anxiously. 'Aren't we through? It's incredible – every year there seems to be more and more.' She sighed.

They set off in two cars, leaving Connie and Mark behind to clear up. Mark started a bonfire to please his father while Connie hoovered. In the kitchen she had plastic boxes of chestnut and mushroom stuffings, bread, mince pies, a jar of brandy butter, a bottle of wine.

'But I can't drive you,' she said.

'No problem. I'd arranged for Tim to be here just after eleven. Don't fuss, OK? See you next Thursday?'

When he had gone she found his new clothes all neatly stacked in the drawers in his room.

* * * * * * *

'Absent friends!' said Hugh.

Archie had toasted the cook, Victor his hosts, Connie the whole family and Sheba the dog who had somehow got hold of a turkey bone and been sick in a corner. Archie's bottles of champagne had been drunk before dinner; Hugh had opened a fourth bottle of claret.

'Absent friends!' It could be as well be 'Marks & Spencer!' or 'Sieg heil!' Connie stared down the table at her husband.

After a mammoth rage over lunch, fuelled by the grandmothers ('One might have expected it, that child has no manners.' 'It would have been polite to say goodbye at least, don't you think?'), Hugh had stormed in and out of the dining room where Connie was arranging the table for dinner.

'Ingratitude!' He was almost inarticulate.

Connie wove a garland of gold tinsel and ivy leaves along a row of scarlet candles on the white cloth.

'All the effort we made!'

She placed seven gold doilies on green felt around the table and folded red napkins onto the side plates.

'We'd all accepted him. No one mentioned the hunt – did anyone say anything?'

She laid the knives and forks, hesitated over the glasses.

'And all those presents! He got an entire refit out of us! Ha! No difficulty in taking, I notice! Not slow to accept all he could get!'

Connie lettered gold place cards, set them beside each glass, rearranged them to the centre of each mat.

'The *cowardice* of it! Just going off like that. *You* knew, of course; he told you. And you let him off. 'Off you go, darling, you know best. No need to apologise or explain. I'll wrap you up a little care package. Would you like some wine? A bottle of brandy to keep out the cold?' He mimicked a silly falsetto and rummaged in the sideboard to check on the brandy.

She sorted the little parcels wrapped in red foil and put one behind each place card and finished by crossing crackers between each pair of candles.

He followed her to the kitchen. 'And you said nothing! I know you. *Nothing*! No wonder that boy is a mess. You didn't think to hand him over to me. I'd have shown him! I'd have knocked some manners into him. No son of mine would have got away with it. No son of mine would skulk off like that, *desert*! Now I really wash my hands of him. This is the last straw; this is final. He won't crawl back now; I won't have him back! He's disgraced us with the Hunt and now he's proved he's not man enough to stand his ground. He's *nothing*. You're nothing! You both make me sick.' He searched round the dining table, straightening each chair. 'And Sally, too, mooning about the place because of that layabout – don't think I don't know! I wish I didn't have to go on with this farce. If it weren't for our guests I'd leave you to get on with it. But I at least have a sense of responsibility.'

Chapter 11

'We asked them for you!' Connie was telling her brother about the next drinking session, 'And because Boxing Day's such a write-off.'

'Bilious Boxing Day! Dare one ever drink again?' Archie pushed his cup across for more coffee. 'I thought we'd be doing something hideously healthy like watching chaps rushing about on horses. Not that I'm complaining,' he added quickly. 'Why for me, you old Con-trick?'

'We thought,' Connie glanced at her husband, 'you should be exposed to local talent. The Fosters you met last year – she's the beautiful redhead, remember? And Lettice is my great friend, not so much your cup of tea, perhaps. And a couple we don't know very well but she's extremely glamorous.'

'And she's for *me*? Tell me more!'

'Well, we couldn't go to a party of theirs last week and so it seemed appropriate to ask them back, but anyway,' laughing at his disappointment, 'I think she's just your type.'

Emily arrived with her parents and was seated on the sofa like a princess. She had been cultivating the air of an invalid, smiled faintly and thanked everyone for their solicitude. Her father fetched her peanuts and Sally admired the wasp effect of her stripy tights and new sweatshirt. A Cindy doll, with hair brushed and tied high like its owner's, was changed into various outfits, unpacked from a black plastic suitcase, Sally helping with the breeches and boots of full hunting kit.

'How's Pickle?' she asked.

'He's OK.' Emily cast her a pale, oblique look. 'He's got a bump on his leg, but he's not lame I think.'

'That's good.' Sally struggled to force the doll's sharp fingers through the cuff of its scarlet jacket. 'At least he's proved he's a great jumper.'

'Yes.' Emily watched her efforts and Lewis watched them both. 'But I'm not sure I'm ready for him, actually.'

'Not ready for all that, maybe!' Sally laughed, feeling that her reaction to such an adult phrase mattered. She searched for her mother, but Connie was welcoming an unknown, rather scruffy man and a fashion-plate in suede trousers. 'No way could you hold him like that – but that was our fault for suggesting it. He's safe as houses for hacking; you know that.'

Emily pushed a jockey cap onto the doll's head and it popped off across the rug. 'It never stays on!' she whined. 'Daddy says he's too strong for me. Daddy says I might have been *kilt*.' Big eyes. 'Kilt dead like Gran'ma!'

'I doubt it,' said Sally, unweaving the metallic hair and ramming the cap onto the doll again. 'There you are! No one wears a riding cap over a ponytail.'

'I did.' Emily's sigh was heroic. 'I might take up ballet instead, though. I'd like to be a ballet dancer and wear a fluffy skirt. Did you do ballet?'

'No,' said Sally. 'I was too busy mastering my pony. You know, you're a weed if you give up because of one fall. We'll help. You'll get your nerve back as soon as you're on him again, honest.'

Lewis had been not-attending to Edith's reminiscences and now, suggesting she might like to sit, brought her to the sofa. 'You don't think he's started a terrible habit?' he said to Sally. 'I've been so worried. And of course your mother's so busy at the moment, so extra busy, I couldn't bother her.'

Edith sniffed, and took Sally's place.

'*Pickle* won't have changed,' said Sally. 'Remember, we did say he'd be much peppier with hounds—'

'And those dreadful motor bicycles,' Edith added meanly.

'Yes, well.' Sally looked straight into Mr Foster's anxious face and saw no blame. He couldn't have connected Mark or Tim. 'I think it'd be awful for Emily to funk it now. He's a really nice little pony. No vices.'

'Who's got no vices?' Victor joined them. 'Sounds a dull chap!'

Archie had agreed with his sister immediately Sylvia Benefield entered the room, and Sylvia evidently knew and liked Archie's 'type'. He was lounging against the bookshelves, complimenting and questioning her, and her Walt Disney doe-eyes were widening and slowly blinking at him, excluding the rest of the party. Lettice, with Harman as if attached to her by a lead, held Connie and her mother with a story about an argumentative tourist. Hugh and Roger were being entertained by Annie.

Tourists of any kind bored Connie today. She peered towards Annie, vibrant in green and blues, actually wearing a skirt for a change. The central light, which Hugh considered necessary on such a dull day, lit sparks of red and gold in her hair and Connie felt that neither man would need encouragement to slink off with her into the laurels and undo all the buttons down the back of her blouse. But as hostess she could intervene.

'Emily's looking fine. No after-effects, I hope? What a terrible time you must have had.' As a mother she saw Annie quite differently; identified with her, sympathised.

'Oh, she's all right now. The doctor just said keep her quiet. Lewis is the one who's panicking, thinks she should take up something safer like dancing – I ask you! Do please go and calm him down.'

A plea for help? Dismissal? Connie felt like Annie's shadow, a monotone streak away from the light, a scavenger, a grey cat skulking at the fringe of the ginger kitten's playground. Obey or compete. She tried on a big smile and gave Annie to Roger. If he too could fall for such obvious charms he wasn't worth her interest.

'Have you heard about their daughter's adventure last Saturday?' she asked him. 'By all accounts she coped very bravely. Annie will tell you while I make my peace with Lewis – I feel most responsible for encouraging it.'

Against the fireplace with Lewis she enthused and encouraged and offered Sally to ride Pickle round the paddock to show that he had not gone mad. Lewis shone with gratitude.

'You know what one hears about ponies getting vicious, Mrs Bryant, getting vicious habits, getting the bit between their teeth? I was so worried that it might happen again. Nightmares, you know about her being killed. When I saw her there, like dead, in the yard –'

While Lewis stumbled on, Connie looked past his face into the mirror to see Annie lead Roger to the window. She was pointing – pointing out the direction of the Coach House, the shrubbery of laurels? Annie gave her peculiar laugh, half gurgle, half song, and leaned close against him to point further round the corner, her shoulder behind his shoulder, her hand on his collar, her cheek within a fraction of his. Hugh interrupted them with a glass jug of Bloody Mary.

* * * * * * *

The amiable Polly has been sent to the drawing room with a message for Sir Roger. She pushes her way through a merry throng just in time to catch Annie's lips enticingly close to Sir Roger's ear, to see her fingers clawing up the blue velvet sleeve, to hear her wicked laughter.

'Sir, a gentleman from your household –' Polly mumbles into her curtsy.

'What, child? Come, Polly, speak up!' He has turned from Annie and all his attention inclines to the charming young maid.

'A gentleman with a letter –' she clutches the letter in the folds of her skirt, unwilling to part with it and return him to Annie.

'Then I must follow you.' With a nod to Annie, he weaves his way after her to the quiet of the hall. 'You have the letter?'

Sir Roger reads its contents and smiles. 'Good!' he says. 'Encouraging news! But you, my sweetheart, you should not be in that room. Allow me to escort you to a safer part of the house. I want no one interfering with you again.'

'Except you, sir?'

'Except me, naturally.' His smile mocks himself as much as her. 'We understand each other, my pretty Polly. We understand each other perfectly!'

Pocketing the letter with one hand he employs the other to trace the curve of her shoulder and the line of her throat until he can tilt the head to an angle approaching his. The smile changes, fades, is replaced by a yearning passion. His fingers explore the contours of her breast while his lips …

* * * * * * *

'Connie!' Lettice's pink fingers were pinching her arm. 'Are you in there somewhere? What do we have to do to get through to you? You're getting as bad as my aunt's deaf Dalmatian! Come on, you're supposed to be entertaining us!'

Before the party ended, Roger sought out Connie in the kitchen where she was showing Lettice Aunt Fay's embroidered oven gloves. With guilty laughter they both jumped round. 'I thought – oh dear, I thought you were Aunt Fay!' Connie gasped.

'Never!'

He joined them. 'If she's the large woman in purple—'

'No that's my mother-in-law. Aunt Fay's her sister, she's the—'

'That's even less likely!'

All three of them laughed without control. 'Roger, really!' Lettice caught his arm for support. 'Why *less* likely? You flatter yourself! Oh, aren't we wicked?'

'I think – I think –' Connie couldn't continue, but she copied Lettice and allowed her hand to reach for his shoulder.

He smiled beautifully into both their faces and then hugged them together. With his head bowed between theirs, he murmured, 'You don't make me *feel* like either of those old ladies.'

'You certainly don't!' choked Lettice.

But Connie had forgotten what the joke was about and only noticed the tightening of his arm and his fingers reaching up her ribs. For a moment she turned her cheek against his and, almost by mistake, let her lips brush his ear. Opening her eyes she saw the purple shape of Edith at the kitchen door.

* * * * * * *

Victor was the only one who insisted on forty winks after lunch. Mary wanted to begin *A Life of Thomas Aquinas* given her for Christmas, on request, by her husband, but could not escape Edith on the sofa. Aunt Fay was content to knit. Sally, as promised, went off to school Pickle, and Hugh forced Archie and Sheba to take a walk. Sheltered by *Clarissa*, Connie sat back in the wing chair still shocked by her behaviour that morning. Demon drink! But he couldn't have noticed. After all, Lettice was there. Lettice started it, for heaven's sake! But Lettice could get away with it; Lettice was a familiar, touching kind of person, like Archie. And she, Connie, was not. But Roger didn't know that. Nor did Edith.

Sally, she knew, would go to the benders as soon as she had checked Pickle's leg. The schooling was an excuse to avoid a walk with her father. Would they be back from the Boxing Day Meet yet? What pranks today? One day someone would be killed.

I don't want to think about Mark and I won't think about Sally. I won't think. Come on, Polly! That slattern Dorcas has taken to her bed and the fire's smoking again. No parties tonight, it's Christmas. The visitors have left Bath for their Town houses or their country seats; even the local gentry are tied to their families at home. Only a few old friends remain at the Hall. On the sofa sits the Duchess with her wicked eye, guessing all about Sir Roger, chin-deep in delicious gossip with another old hag. Their powdered curls are nodding with the excitement of it. Annie, no doubt, in her gown of blues and greens is visiting Sir Roger, bent on seduction. Has she no shame?

Ribbons and silk taffeta and nodding curls above the over-painted faces. 'Do you know what I think? Do you know what I saw? That wicked girl and her wicked ways!' The Duchess nods and whispers; the other old lady sits with knees and wrists and ankles locked but her ears are wide open and she gasps at the story.

'My dear old Con!' A hoarse whisper that made her leap to clutch her book. 'Are you asleep, too? Look at them all! But why not, eh? You deserve it – all that cooking and planning, not a hitch. You deserve a gold star!'

She put on her glasses and looked around. Edith's chin had sunk onto the amethysts, her curls, cheeks and mouth drooping, reflecting purple from her dress. Mary had propped herself against a corner of the sofa, hands clasped round the book in her lap, her head tilted in an interested position. Aunt Fay on the uncomfortable buttoned chair had let her needles slip and her head fall back against the rust velvet, loudly snoring. Cautiously Connie followed her brother out of the room to prepare tea.

'Tell me about Sylvia.' Archie tried to cut a sliver of Christmas cake and rolled the crumbs into a ball. 'She's quite something. What a life! I get the impression she's a wee bit fed up with Roger the Lodger. Too pretty by half, I'd have thought.'

'Who? Which? They're both – I know nothing about them!'

'Oh really? If I were down here longer, I'd certainly give her a test drive. You were right, you know. She's available. Why are you being so prissy? You know, Hugh has really flattened you. You're becoming quite like Mama, and a bit before your time. Loosen up, girl, before it's too late!'

'Don't be so silly!' The kettle shrieked and Connie made the tea. 'I'm not you and I'm certainly not Mother! There is a middle line, you know.'

'Middle everything, that's you. You're making a thing of it. Dead boring, if you ask me. Snap out of it! I like Hugh. I admire him and the way he copes with you all. But he's getting fed up. There is a limit. Now that he's finding his feet again with this election business, he's ready to stray. You mark my words. There are lots of pretty girls around and that Foster wife has got her eye on him, I can tell you.'

'Has she?' Connie counted cups and saucers onto the tray and wondered how he knew. 'She's very married, and politically they don't match.'

'That,' said Archie, 'is codswallop! You obviously don't understand men! Or women either. I have never asked a girl her political creed before taking her to bed – or after, come to think of it! Don't be so naïve.'

'But Hugh's different. He certainly doesn't think like you.' He certainly did not, of that at least she was sure.

Archie rolled his eyes. 'God give me strength!' He popped the cake ball into his mouth and mumbled through it, 'You've been reading too much high falutin' stuff, just like Mama – there's too much 'delicacy' in those biographies. The well-brought-up husband has no carnal urges, no sensuality. He's supposed to sublimate or masturbate and be thankful if the little lady wife feels like uncrossing her legs once in a while. Marion was like that.' He swallowed thoughtfully. 'You can tell by the mouth.'

'Really?' Connie peered into the steel side of the oven and saw only a dark face and the shine on her nose.

'Not like that, you fool,' Archie choked on a crumb. 'You have to catch 'em unawares and then you see the droop, the down-pulled lines, that dreary discontent. I've seen it all. You just look at yourself in repose. All right, well look at the rest of them!'

'And Sylvia's doesn't?' Connie picked up the tray, smiling all her lines upwards.

'I haven't,' Archie's grin reached his ears, 'had the opportunity of seeing her in repose. But if I were pursuing her I'd certainly check!'

Chapter 12

'As we move inexorably towards the next General Election our thoughts should be geared to our Country's future … it is the Conservative Party which stands as the bulwark of our freedom … commitment to individual liberty … determination to defend the British way of life.'

Connie read the draft over Hugh's shoulder. 'Stirring stuff!' she said. 'Is that going out from you or from Lewis? I can't work out which of you is in charge of what.'

'You don't want to know – and don't get it in the butter!' Hugh added an 'and' in red felt-tip and deleted a full stop. 'It's no use you sitting on the fence; that gets us nowhere. You could at least try to help. If They get in we might as well leave the country. This election's crucial.'

'All elections are crucial. If that's Lewis's draft, do you think it's kind to use red ink? Isn't it rather schoolmaster-y?'

'This is for fund raising,' he said. 'As Treasurer, I'm going to sign it. Lewis is only Secretary of the Social Committee. At tonight's meeting we have to come up with some ideas. Have you got any?'

'I don't think God's on your side.' Connie was looking out of the window at a heavy sky. 'It's going to snow.'

'God seems to have left with your parents,' he said. 'But I think we'll manage. Why don't you come along, make your peace with Tony? I think he suspects you're in league with the Antis. Everyone knows about Mark now; it's most embarrassing. It would help if we could show a united front for a change.'

'Does Annie?'

'Funnily enough she does! She's what I would call a good wife.'

'Really?'

'Yes, really. She supports her husband; she believes in him.'

'That must be tricky if she's 'quite a little socialist' as you said. Some kind of sacrifice must be necessary?'

'Annie,' Hugh considered his own wife sadly, 'cares enough to do that. She's enthusiastic. Things matter to her. She would fight for what she believes in. There's nothing wrong in her supporting her husband and feeling strongly about politics in general.'

Connie laughed. 'I love the euphemism! Would you want me to vote for 'politics in general'?'

'You know what's expected of you. A vote for the other lot is worse than no vote at all in this area, and you're only being difficult when you talk like that. You have no idea about the issues involved. Don't be so silly. Can I at least say you'll address some envelopes?'

'Is Annie addressing envelopes?'

'I have no idea, though I should think she's too busy – she's started an Open University course, you know. My goodness, what a girl! You're the one with the spare time now. You've said you haven't got enough to do – well?'

'Addressing Party envelopes wasn't exactly what I was thinking of.'

'You haven't shown much interest in anything else. Come on, you need something to take you out of yourself. You can't sit around moping all day, it's unhealthy. You're getting very –' He gathered up his papers, at a loss for the word.

'Middle-aged? Boring? I know that, but do you think the envelopes will help?'

'Well, it's a beginning,' he said. 'Something you could do quite well. And it would be useful.'

'Yes,' said Connie.

The snow and the envelopes arrived together. Beautiful deep snow lightening the landscape, smoothing out the spinney, blocking out anything ugly and man-made. Sheba scampered like a puppy on the lawn, forking up the surface into frosted icing on a cake. Small birds and beasts made delicate tracks, the lime trees reached blue shadows across a sparkling white drive. Nothing moved on the road to the village. Hallatrow Hall was effectively snowed in.

Sally shut herself into the playroom with dismal or evocative music to help her much-postponed revision, emerging red-eyed to quarrel with her father at mealtimes. All she would tell Connie was that Tim despised her because she had no ideals. Tim was talking about moving in to the commune by the river, but was having a lot of stick from his family.

'Why don't you walk down to see if he's all right?' Connie asked. Meaning Mark.

'It's miles!' cried Sally. 'And back again.'

'If you cared—'

'Not *that* much! And anyway he's probably not there yet. I'll go when it thaws. Besides,' she added, 'I haven't decided.'

'Decided what?' Possibilities bombarded Connie's eyes in a shower of snapshots – Mark's bender gradually filling with her family; Sally riding a motorbike up against the hunt; Sally and Tim sleeping on the filthy floor of a squat, Sally and Tim strolling off into a bleak landscape without a wave or a backwards glance. 'Decided what?' She could hear her voice pitched high.

'Honestly, Mum! No need to be hysterical. It's my problem, OK?' And Sally added another pile of rubble to her barricade. On the other side, almost out of shouting range, her mother prowled up and down hoping for a signal, excluded even from sight of the problem.

Locked in, locked out, the family passed in corridors looking busy, idled in their own rooms or met in the kitchen to complain about the weather. Hugh cleared a path to the Coach House where he and Lewis revised canvassing lists; Connie helped Emily drag hay to the paddock to feed Pickle and spread envelopes all over the dining-room table.

'What's Annie doing?' she asked.

'Cooking a delicious-smelling stew – lentils and onions and garlic and things! Really sets the saliva flowing, as I told her! What's for lunch?'

'Soup and cheese,' said Connie. 'You can't expect two square meals a day. And envelopes too,' she added.

* * * * * * *

With the arrival of snow the Duchess' entertainments cease and the women of the Hall parade and yawn only for each other. Polly receives snaps and slaps upstairs from her bored mistress who has exhausted the subject of finding her maid tête a tête with Sir Roger. The Duchess, as much intrigued as incensed, has tried every approach to discover just one salacious detail and, disappointed, throws her now to Hugo.

'Yes, sir!' says Polly, pert, secure in her innocence.

Hugo's face mottles, his lips recede till they look like string and he juts forward a curdled chin.

'Enough! More than enough, Miss!' The pupils of his eyes dart from side to side in their glaucous pits. 'You have enjoyed the shelter of this house. You have been given privileges far above your station. And you have abused the kindness and the confidence of my mother. You have overstepped even that, you hussy! This now will end. I will allow no more. As you seem so set on philandering with our visitors, from today we offer you a new role. Dorcas will take over your duties with my mother and we shall see how you manage in the drawing room and beyond. Absolute obedience, mind, or you will be turned out. Perhaps,' the face relaxes and the lips lengthen into a leer, 'you will be more suited to earn your keep on your back?'

'I think – I believe –' Polly ducks behind the sofa, trying at the same time to appear brave, 'that Sir Percy Blakeney delivered me here with express instructions—'

'Sir Percy knew our business,' Hugo says curtly. 'The Duchess engaged to employ you, no more.'

'As her maid!'

'As whatever she wished. And it is you who have shown an inclination for the other.'

'I have not! I will not!'

'Mistress Annie will take you in hand now and teach you how to dress and how to behave. By the time the snows have cleared you will be ready.' Hugo turns and leaves her, strides away yelling, 'Annie!', and poor Polly takes a last glimpse of herself in the drawing-room mirror dressed as a simple maid.

When the snows clear Sir Roger will rescue her. When the snows clear she will escape and find honest work in Bath (though that is historically unlikely in that period and at that time of year). When the snows clear ...

* * * * * * *

Snow ploughs and gritters on the roads destroyed the unearthly peace and beauty of the countryside but freed Sally to take a bus into town.

'So nice for her,' said Aunt Fay, gazing forlornly out. 'A good walk is what we all need. Being cooped up like this makes one liverish. But I fear it's still too deep around here for that.' She huddled into her yellow jersey like a broody hen.

'Speak for yourself!' Edith delighted in her sister's frustration; nothing had changed for her. 'Though I think it would do Hugh good to venture a little further than the Coach House.'

At teatime when Connie lit the lamps and drew the curtains across a blue-grey twilight she became concerned that there was no sign of Sally; by the time it was truly dark she was worried.

'Thoughtless child!' said Edith, later, sipping her sherry. 'But I imagine you know what she was doing?' Meaning, I'm sure you have no idea. 'I doubt if the buses are running now.'

Hugh returned from the Coach House when supper was laid on the kitchen table, an official-looking file under his arm to explain his absence.

'Sally not back?' His need to apologise swung to accusation. 'Give me that layabout's number!'

Tim's father, on the demand for Sally, equally abruptly replied that he had seen neither of them for days.

'That lout's as bad as his son! No control over him, doesn't even care. Just like you – you'd make a great pair! If I hadn't come in – if I hadn't been around ...' He glanced with contempt at the food on the table. 'I'll get the police.'

Edith looked approving, Aunt Fay impressed.

'Don't you think we should—' Connie began.

'Oh, you eat – don't let me hold up your little pleasures! Don't worry about me.'

They sat obediently, listening to his voice in the hall. 'But that's not good enough! Let me speak to your superior. Then give me someone in charge. I can't believe that! You mean a girl has to be raped before you will do anything? Well, how do I know? You must have some procedure. For a start you could try that hippy lot down by the river. Well, I'm stuck in the country behind a wall of snow, aren't I? How do you expect me to get a car out?'

He stormed back into the kitchen muttering about the fool police, the rates, the country, dogs, the Labour council. His mother watched with an equally grim expression while he scooped a forkful of lentils into his mouth, followed swiftly by another.

'Digestion,' she said. 'Don't gobble. It won't do you any good, you know.'

'No, and lentils can be a wee bit indigestible,' agreed Aunt Fay, passing her plate to Connie. 'Just a *tea*spoonful, if you can spare it, dear – it's so good. And it makes a nice change. You haven't done this before, dear, have you?'

Hugh was not attending. 'You can phone her school friends,' he said. 'She could be with that girl – what's her name?'

'Debbie.' Connie sat listless, cut off from Hugh's drama. She had been through all of this before, all the fears and thoughts of rape, abduction, car accidents, crashed motorbikes. Sally should know better by now. There are telephones all over Bath. Why hadn't she phoned?

'Well, go on then!'

She phoned Debbie's mum just to pass the time and to save argument.

'Are the police going to the benders?' she asked.

'I doubt it. It would serve Mark right if they did. They said if she's over sixteen and only left this morning there could be lots of explanations, and to call again tomorrow. She's probably with a friend, he said. Really patronising, as if I couldn't have thought of that myself! But the fact remains, she should have rung. There's no excuse for that. When she comes in I'll crucify her.'

'Inexcusable,' Edith agreed, helping herself to a baked apple.

'A wee bit thoughtless,' said Aunt Fay pouring cream down the bottomless core cavity. 'Oh, my! Just look what I've done!'

Connie smiled at the plate of cream and loved Aunt Fay.

'She'd better have a damned good excuse.' Hugh's eyes and mouth were narrowing. 'If I find she's spent the night with that no-good –'

By the next day the trees and eaves were dripping and bare patches had begun to show on the drive. Sally phoned.

'Mum? Are you alone? Look, I'm sorry I didn't ring – it was all a bit chaotic and by the time I could it was too late and I didn't want to wake you up. Okay? Daddy would have been mad. Everything's fine now, all right? It's all sorted out. I found Tim. He's moved in with a super chap called Charles and he says I can stay too.'

'Stay?' Connie heard her voice squeak. 'Where? What for?'

'Stay with *them*. Don't panic – it's quite all right, Charles doesn't mind. We've worked it all out and Dad needn't get all uptight because there are lots of us. I'll tell you all about it when I see you. I've got to come back for some clothes – it's school tomorrow. Just smooth him down, right?'

Bees in the head. Connie walked around the table three times, patting each chair, counting, and then leaned against the sink staring out into the yard. Bees in the head, one thought buzzing at or after another. Bees in the head, messing up the picture, confusing the signals like atmospherics on the radio, crowding out the space where thoughts gather and sensations are received, buzzing and massing to obliterate the simple path of her perception. Thinking about bees, seeing bees, hearing bees. Half-thoughts, each with no form or conclusion, signifying nothing. Why? What? How? And a whole swarm of unfinished questions and answers. No, Sally could do her own explaining.

Which Sally, unlike Mark, was quite prepared to do.

'Listen Dad, it makes a lot of sense. No, really – okay, I've said I'm sorry – it saves all the trips into school. It saves – look, come and see the flat. Meet Charles. Honest, you'll like him. He's a businessman. An entrepreneur. He owns the Bull's Eye Restaurant *and* Jupiter's. He's rich! You'd approve, Dad. And the flat is amazing, it's just – amazing! All modern – fantastic! You see, you've got the wrong idea. There's nothing mucky about it. It's not a squat or anything. It's not like that at all. There are other girls. It'll be just like a family.'

'I can see absolutely no reason for it at all.' Sally was the only one who could divert Hugh. 'It's absolute nonsense – you live here! You've got a family here. What do you need a flat for?' He was genuinely confused.

'I'm seventeen now, Dad. It's time I tried a bit of independence. Most of my friends have moved on and out. I'm not talking about not taking 'A's or anything – that'll be easier living in town. Don't worry, I've got it all sussed.'

'You have, have you? And who do you think is going to pay for it, this independence? Ha!' He had found his stride. 'Don't expect any help from me.'

Sally looked sad and, to Connie, crafty. 'It's not like that. Charles doesn't want rent – he's rich, I told you. If I had my pocket money and the amount you'd save on feeding me I could manage. Otherwise I could stop school – which everyone else has done – and go on the dole. No problem. Perhaps that might be best, it's not getting me anywhere, just a waste of time.' She had passed him on the inside.

But Hugh was now running true to form. 'Well, that's fine, that's just fine! You know it all, of course. But I don't, funnily enough, accept that. What you do once you are sufficiently educated and able to make a career for yourself, you can choose. But certainly not now. You will stay here until then and do what you're told. If you move out, then that's your affair but you can expect nothing from me. Nothing! I'll stop your allowance, you'll get nothing from me. More than that—'

'Dad, listen!'

'I'm listening.' His lips and eyes had receded, signifying danger, a point at which Connie would withdraw.

But Sally had made her decision and was equal to her father. Quietly she said, 'I'm going, Dad, anyway. I've arranged it all; I can't back out now. Come on, let's be friends. Please? Come and meet Charles, you'll like him, honest! You'll see. You can meet the others and—'

'I shall certainly see this Charles – don't worry about that! And by the time I've finished with him you will wish I hadn't, I can assure you. I'll skin him alive. I'll crucify him. I'll—'

Sally packed what she could in plastic bags, leaving a bin liner of shirts and sweaters for her mother to bring later. (Hugh had refused the loan of a suitcase, or transport.)

'I shall visit this Charles if and when I wish,' he said before clipping Sheba onto a lead and slamming the front door. 'And rest assured, if you leave this house, if you dare to defy me, you will not come back. I hope this is clearly understood. I'll have none of this Mark nonsense with you, my girl. That will be final. Be under no illusions about it. Think *very* seriously.'

Sally looked at her mother with a strange new smile. 'Don't please say a thing, Mum! I'm going, right. I've decided. It isn't only Dad – this place is really getting me down. We'll be in touch – perhaps I'll see you with Mark on Thursdays.' And she gathered up her bags and splashed away down the drive, whistling.

Wham, bang, just-like-that, through the door and away. Away, off, gone. Silence. The extreme silence which follows extreme noise. After the volleys from the guns, no birds sing. Connie stood at the door peering after her daughter until she disappeared, a blur haloed by a watery sun, into a distance too far to be distinguished from all the other smudges of trees and bushes and puddles; until her vision dissolved into one great blur. She stood there for a while, blind and drained of anything but tears. Sally's departure had emptied the house. Nothing now remained.

* * * * * * *

Mistress Annie has the keys to a basement room beside the wine cellar (a dank dark room that survives in the twentieth century as air raid shelter and as store for apples and garden furniture). Holding a candle high above her flaming hair, Annie unlocks and heaves the door open and steps inside with no need to pretend a shudder of distaste. Something darts across the flagstones and disappears; threads from the low ceiling stroke and cling to Polly's face.

'Why are we looking in here?' Polly has no apprehension, only scoops up her grey skirts to protect the hem from the puddles that gleam in the candlelight and ducks to avoid the curtains of spider web. 'Why, there's nothing in here! And it's cold as a grave. Let's go back.'

'There is straw somewhere,' says Annie. 'I shall leave you the candle and you can find it for yourself. You have a choice, you see. This room has been used before by girls like you; some, it is said, have died here. You can choose this room or do as you are bid. Shall I leave you here to reflect and decide?'

Annie's kitten-face Polly now perceives as rat-face, the neat features pinched and pointed, the green eyes no longer languorous but needle-sharp, green ice. Polly darts to the entrance, clutches at the door post.

'No, no!' she cries. 'That was not Mr Bryant's intention. You are to teach me, to dress me. There is no choice!'

'Mr Bryant,' the rat-face snarls, triumphant, instantly superior, for she can claim to call him Hugo, 'Mr Bryant wishes you to know that there is a choice. Naturally you have a choice. We are all free to choose. Even a good wife is free to choose how deeply she supports her husband. We all have our duty and, for instance, as Hugo's wife I would know what support was due him and would behave accordingly. We have only to choose and then to obey.'

'There seems little difference,' says poor Polly.

'The difference lies in your willingness. Only you can make it easy for yourself. That is all that is asked of you.'

'Prostitution?' cries Polly.

'Isn't it all?' Annie sounds weary and follows her through the door. 'A woman's lot. There is only one alternative.'

As they mount the stairs, Polly hurries on. 'I cannot believe that! Not for me!' But curiosity overtakes fear. 'Are you truly to marry Mr Bryant?'

Annie turns, rat to kitten again. 'Why not?'

* * * * * * *

'We will see this man today.' Hugh swallowed his All-Bran and glared at his wife over his spectacles. 'You will come with me as witness. I want you to see and learn how to deal with such a worm, such a toad, such a – predator. It sounds to me as if Sally has been taken over, led astray by this charlatan. I'm reserving my judgement on her. No – I have a feeling, a strong feeling, that this Charles is something evil, like the Moonies, seducing young girls from their families. She says there are several of them there. Well?

We'll catch him in his lair. Now. The early bird catches the worm. Are you ready?'

Most of the night he had paced the bedroom, sometimes shouting, sometimes quiet, always returning to check that she was awake and could register his outrage and the various new fates planned for his children and their associates. By dawn he had rationalised Sally's behaviour and felt much better.

Charles's flat was on the corner of Kingsmead Square at the top of Avon Street, overlooking an expanse of cobbles and dappled sunlight under plane trees. No visitor could feel oppressed by these town houses, some decorated in the exuberant style of the early eighteenth century. Although the square had none of the scale and harmony of John Wood's creations, tourists would exclaim over its prettiness. Probably influenced by the trees. Probably only in summer sunshine. All Connie could see was peeling bark and dirty snow melting like the water ices her mother had sometimes made during the War. The whole square smelled of decay, as if beneath its dissolving blanket all was rotten.

She stood with Hugh under the naked branches of the biggest tree while he rang various doorbells – Sally had not given Charles's surname. Gazing at a dustcart collecting refuse from the back of the Co-op store that now took up most of the side street, Connie recalled that the nymphs of Avon Street had been notorious in the eighteenth and nineteenth centuries. Thank heaven Hugh had no interest in local history! He would have been quickest to draw parallels between the area's disreputable past and his daughter's questionable arrival there. A window above them screeched and a pale face peered down.

'Charles?' shouted Hugh. He would infinitely have preferred to shout 'Smith?' The familiarity jarred in the cold sunlight.

Wearing a royal-blue dressing gown which accentuated his

pallor and lank blond hair, Charles arrived at the door.

'Come in, come in! Christ, it's freezing!' He was clutching the blue velvet in folds across his chest and as he pattered up the stairs Connie tried not to notice the material pulled tight over his buttocks above long hairy legs. They followed him into a vast white room of breath-stopping heat.

'Christ!' he repeated. 'What's the time?' He looked at them now, blinking himself awake. 'Have we met? Look – settle yourselves down while I—'

But Hugh would not allow him to escape. 'My name's Bryant,' he announced, occupying the pale Casa Pupo rug.

'Oh, yes?' It meant nothing to Charles, who withdrew politely to the fringe, adjusting the cord of his dressing gown.

'Sally's father.'

'Oh, Sally?' He visibly sifted through the Sallys of his acquaintance.

'Sally Bryant.' Hugh rattled the change in his pocket.

'Oh, *Sally* – Tim's girl?' Charles looked relieved and moved behind the large white sofa towards a corner of white kitchen units. 'I need coffee – do you mind Instant?' And he filled the kettle.

'Now, look here –' Hugh needed some reaction and was not appeased by hearing his daughter so linked with Tim. 'We did not come here for coffee—'

'But do have some, all the same.' Charles was searching for cups. 'These kids!' He sighed. 'My one request – the *only* thing I insist on – is that they keep this place tidy. I can't abide a mess. They just don't think. Look at this now, I ask you!'

Connie from her station just inside the door had been looking, taking in the sleek modern furniture, the music centre, the slimline television, the one vast yellow canvas on the white wall. From the corner opposite the kitchen area a staircase spiralled up to the floor above and disappeared presumably to the floor below.

'They can do what they *like*,' Charles continued, rattling a spoon in thin china mugs, 'in the pit downstairs – I won't even *venture* down there! But here ....' He sighed again. 'Milk and sugar?'

Connie hurried across the Amtico tiles to receive the mugs and pass one to her husband.

'Now, *do* sit. Sally, you say? Very pretty girl, loads of personality. I've got my eye on her.'

Hugh, who had been about to settle on a white leather pouffe, straightened and almost spilled his coffee.

'I have suggested,' Charles sank into a corner of the sofa and crossed shiny knees with a graceful tweak at his dressing gown, 'that she might try waitressing at the Bull's Eye. I gather there's a money problem.' He did not look particularly concerned.

Connie sat carefully at the other end of the sofa and unbuttoned her coat.

'Money,' said Hugh, 'is not her only problem. What I want to know is what the hell she's doing here in the first place.'

Charles raised almost invisible eyebrows so that his face looked like a crumpled glove. 'You tell me,' he said. 'They come and they go. They're a nice bunch and I don't ask too many questions. If I like them and they behave themselves they're free to treat the place like home. I like to see it as a sort of moveable family. Most of them work for me, it gives me a sort of control.' He smiled wearily at Connie. 'You know what it's like at that age.'

'How many have you got?' Connie asked conversationally, pushing her coat off her shoulders while Hugh glared at her.

'I've no idea. As I said, they come and they go. It's up to them downstairs. Zoe sorts them out. She's my amanuensis. She runs the Bull's Eye – I leave that entirely up to her – and she recruits for Jupiter's when necessary. I don't know what I'd do without her.

She's housemother, the lot, but she's got a dicky heart and a lot more besides.' He sighed again and glanced at his watch. 'Oh, three or four girls are down there now. Your Sally is welcome to stay, as long as she gets on with the others and Zoe approves. Tim's proving quite a success at Jupiter's and I'm not complaining.'

'Do you realise that Sally is barely seventeen, is working for her A' levels and has a perfectly good home with us?' Hugh had been rehearsing and now spread out his cards. 'There is absolutely no reason for her to be here and I demand to know what the hell you're doing harbouring a minor.'

Charles contemplated him beneath lowered lids. 'Not exactly a minor,' he said, swinging off to make more coffee. 'That's between you and her, and you can leave me out of it. She seems happy enough with Tim and I'm not getting involved. She's your daughter.'

'Precisely!' barked Hugh.

'So it's up to you to sort out.' He stirred his coffee but did not return to the sofa. 'Look,' he said, 'this is not my problem. I've explained the set-up. I'm not seducing your daughter. I'm offering her work if she wants it, that's all. You talk to her, okay?'

Hugh paused with a visible effort to choke back his wrath. 'If she stays here,' the words slid out between his teeth, 'If she stays here with you and that –' no word suited his image of Tim, 'then she's no longer my daughter. She need never come back. You tell her that! Tell her I said so.' He dumped his coffee mug on the floor and flexing his fists, strode to the door. 'I'll have the police look into this. Be under no illusion about that! If she's not back tonight I'll have you hounded out of Bath. I know your game. I know what you're up to. I can deal with the likes of you!'

He held the door open for his wife and, without turning, slammed it behind them.

Chapter 13

'I don't trust that man one inch,' said Hugh as they picked their way through the slush towards Victoria Park. 'It won't be difficult to get something on him, you can rest assured. Too big for his boots, that one. And just look at that flat! He's not getting his cash from a restaurant and one seedy nightclub, I can tell you. I'll get something on him, don't you worry about that! I have my theories.'

'I'd have liked to meet Zoe,' said Connie. 'And to have seen more of the place. Didn't you think he looked like Christ? That long sad face and the drooping hair?' She made a double step to keep up with her husband as they turned into the wind of Queen Square. Habit with tour groups almost made her stop to consider the northern façade, Wood's Italian palace, but Hugh's head was down against the wind and he was checking his watch.

'More like Christ then you would care to imagine, once I've finished with him!' he threatened, pausing outside the Reference Library. 'I'm dropping in here now – you can take the car. I'll get a lift back with Annie when she collects Emily from school. If you're shopping, see you don't get a ticket.'

Connie continued into the Park through a fine drizzle of rain and aimlessly along the cobbles of the Royal Crescent. The pride of Bath's architecture, completed in 1775: almost twenty years before Polly leaves Hallatrow Hall. Connie felt detached enough from this scene to give Polly her place in history. Polly required more than personality, clothes and a potential lover before Connie could merge with her happily and she wanted to understand her situation. She must have arrived in England in 1793 when Louis was executed and the Terror was in full flood. And when she escapes to Bath in '95 – yes, she has to leave Hugo – that would be amongst bread riots and bankruptcy, poor harvests and one of the severest winters ever known. From this crescent the beautiful Elizabeth Linley had spurned her rich old suitor and eloped with Sheridan, one of the classic love affairs of the century. Here lived Sir Percy Blakeney – Orczy couldn't have placed him better than bang in the centre of the most beautiful terrace in the world. But, Connie feared, Sir Percy will be in London in January. Poor Polly.

Connie wandered back to town past the car parked in the Circus, past the Assembly Rooms and down the tourist beat to the Abbey, weary now but not inclined to go home. Anything was better than being forced to face Sally's departure. 'It isn't only Dad – this place is really getting me down.' Yes. For that I am entirely to blame and any changes I make now would be useless and too late. What, oh *what* can I do? I'll go to M & S and buy something silly and extravagant, something summery and jolly! That will surprise everyone. Something pink. Come on, Polly, coquelicot ribbons!

In Marks and Spencer she bought bread and frozen fish and leaned on the handrail of the escalator. Winter blouses were all On Sale and women hurried past with winter eyes. She took the next escalator down again and wandered amongst men's shirts. Boxer shorts made of pink and green stripes caught her eye, identical to those the children had given Hugh for Christmas, marked down. She stood there fingering the cotton, unable now to see the stripes, a small soft lump gagging her throat, a heavy weight slung somewhere around her pelvis. She could see Sally choosing, deciding, and later proudly showing them to Mark and giggling about turning Hugh into a trendy Dad. A hundred years ago. Blindly she turned and struggled against a tide towards the doors.

Mrs Bryant?'

She shook her head and ploughed on. If only she could get her arms above her ears and protect her face from prying eyes. If only she could melt and stream away, mere liquid instead of a pillar of flesh behind glass, the glasses as usual trapping drowning pools of tears.

A grip on her shoulder, restraint on the sleeve of her coat. She pulled against it and stumbled out through glass doors, from hot to cold, into a cross-stream of shoppers. The weight on her shoulder remained and forced her to make yet another turn.

'Now then!'

The side street was mercifully quiet and nothing bumped or harried her. She hooked her basket over her arm, removed her glasses and rubbed at the lenses and her cheeks with a mitten. Nothing would make her turn around. She could see the road and the pavement and the travel agency opposite, and she moved forward again.

The pressure on her shoulder was lighter now but a bulk of some person remained at her side. She walked on. It followed close. She turned under St Michael's arch into Abbey Green and could now see as far as the Abbey. With every step she felt stronger. She was walking to the Park, to the car, to drive home. Idiot to cry! In M & S of all places! What would anyone have thought? The bulk of her shadow remained and now felt like a part of her. At the other side of Abbey Churchyard the pressure became insistent.

'Please stop.'

She stopped. After what seemed a long time of silence she turned and looked at the edges of an old anorak on either side of the edges of a tweed jacket open over a checked shirt.

'You must be freezing!' she said and the sound of her normal voice surprised her.

She saw her children out on the hillside tobogganing or snow fighting, pink faces, purple hands, unzipped, unbuttoned, laughing, crying, labouring up to her open arms. 'Darlings, *you're* all wet!' She would swing them and cuddle them and zip them up and allow one more swoosh into the valley and then she would clutch two icy hands and drag them up the hill through the laurel bushes and home to peel off their wet clothes, and toast crumpets against the playroom fire.

'You're all wet!' she said.

'You're all wet,' said Roger. 'You're wetter! Come in here and warm up and we'll have a drink.' And he led her by the sleeve of her coat into a crowded pub.

In a corner, miraculously clear enough for two people to stand and steam like two horses in one stall, he brought her whisky and ginger and protected her from the crush by bracing an arm across her against the wall. 'Knock it back,' he said. 'Good girl! Shall we have another or escape this mass?'

'Escape,' she said.

He carried her basket. 'Do you mind walking, getting wetter? Everywhere will be packed out soon for the lunch hour and I can't abide so much humanity in the raw – all damp and giving off strange odours. Have you noticed the smell of fur coats and velour hats drying in a cheap restaurant? It's the aura of Bath somehow. A whiff of gentility, mothballs and lavender seeping out amongst the coffee and Bath buns. The rain seems to bring that out quite as much as the scent of good earth after a summer shower. Have you noticed how the rain –'

They passed the car in the Circus and Connie noticed a ticket plastered to the windscreen. The two-hour limit had seemed long enough; the warden ought to have been controlling excesses downtown. He must have been waiting with a stopwatch.

They cut down through the Park to the Botanical Gardens.

'Are you tired?' he asked. 'You must say.'

She shook her head, dazed not tired, not quite touching the ground, not quite aware of what she was doing or what she ought to do. He exclaimed about drifts of early snowdrops, despised the bourgeois crocus, drew her to touch the tendrils of witch hazel. Then she noticed they were back in the Crescent.

'Sylvia will be at Bridge,' he said. 'You are tired. We'll go in and dry off and I'll make toast.'

She had forgotten their address was the Royal Crescent.

'You sit,' he said, leading her into a lofty golden room overlooking the garden.

She sat while he kindled the dead fire and watched him toast bread on the tip of a fencing foil.

'There should be dripping – toast and dripping on a cold wet day, memories of childhood. But they don't come like that any more. Is there such a thing as dripping any more?'

He spread butter and what might be blackberry jam or caviar and handed her a plate, watching for an answer.

'It must be the beef itself,' she said carefully, as if at an audition. 'But it can't be the size of the joint, not quantity. Perhaps we're just too sophisticated now and our memories are faulty? Nostalgia can make the most awful things seem pleasant.' They were both pleased with her effort.

'Hygiene has ruined the taste of a lot of good old-fashioned food,' he added. 'Vim and Fairy Liquid don't improve the gravy. Better now? Warmer? You must have been hungry. I should have given you lunch.'

'Oh no. Really. This is –' She crunched the sweet toast and was surprised to find a sort of awareness returning like blood creeping into frozen limbs. Roger Benefield's flat! Well, now – fancy that!

And Roger sitting cross-legged on an opulent Turkish rug, watching her from under those heavy dark eyebrows. Sylvia at Bridge, didn't he say? Well! She noted the patina on good Regency furniture, the sheen of designer-draped curtains, the clever dull-gold walls and ceiling to show up the detail of white modillioned cornice and richly moulded architrave. How perfect, just like Sylvia! She felt like a spy, disloyal. Poor Sylvia at Bridge, not knowing that alien eyes were photographing her plaster mouldings and her carpet, captivating her husband perhaps. Connie felt positively normal again, better than normal. 'I am better!' She could smile again. 'Thank you. I'm sorry about—'

'Don't be.' He looked as pleased as if he had wrought a miracle, and offered coffee: 'Very black, I can't abide Instant.'

A shadow crossed her. Charles. 'Yes, very black.'

In the kitchen – built, he told her, from old church furniture – he set a filter with Brazilian coffee and laid Meissen teacups on a lacquer tray.

'Are you going to tell me what you were doing in Bath this morning? I thought Tuesday was your day? Somehow,' he was chatting on so that she was not compelled to answer, 'I felt that you lived in a blameless rural life way above the urban masses and only deigned to visit us for the Tuesday tourists. I see you as Lady Bountiful riding in ...'

She drew a breath and held it. She owed him some explanation, if only in thanks for his kindness, but could think of nothing to say. What had she been doing – weeping over the boxer shorts? There was no explaining the loss of her children, the loneliness, the despair, and no simple excuse like a cut finger or a broken leg. Physical pain is acceptable, easy to understand: she could tell him someone had stepped on her toes.

'No,' he said, quite suddenly, without turning from the coffee machine. 'Don't tell me! I don't want to know that you have finally murdered your mother-in-law – and I won't tell you about my compulsion to batter my students. Let's make a pact. No personal details, no drilling or dredging. We'll keep our illusions; we'll have a relationship built solely on fantasy. How about that? A bargain?'

Her smile spread as much from amusement as relief. Knowing nothing about each other they were unlikely to begin any kind of relationship, and she had her own fantasy about him anyway. 'Fine,' she said. 'Why not?'

'I can't stand analysis.' He said it with such force that she immediately wondered why. 'There will be no seeking of moral or motive, right?'

'Right!' she replied, almost laughing.

'It will cut a lot of unnecessary preamble. Come on, let's drink to it.' He carried the tray to the golden room, balanced it on a pile of magazines and sat beside her on the sofa. 'I feel I know you, as if I've always known you. It's very strange, but – well –' He busied himself pouring the coffee and then scowled and tossed the hair back from his forehead. 'I don't think we should share fantasies either. Does that leave us anything to talk about?'

'I'm sure we'll think of something,' she smiled. 'As long as you don't raise any more embargoes. We've managed so far.'

'Ah, but,' he said, 'we'll meet often now. Don't you think? Wouldn't you like to? Will you?' He sounded childishly earnest. 'It'll be a unique relationship – no possessiveness, no prying. Soon we'll have spring ...'

As he trailed into silence Connie wondered if spring was to be vetoed too and was about to laugh, but saw that it was no joke to him. 'Yes,' she agreed. 'Of course we can meet. And oh, what bliss spring will be after all this!'

They studied each other, each flaunting unmentionable desires and details. Did she want to murder her mother-in-law? Was he compelled to batter his students? Connie began to laugh until she couldn't stop, but managed to choke out, 'This is absurd!'

'Yes,' he said, but gravely. 'And absurdity is what we both need.'

On her way home she was still laughing. Had he invented this game to divert her, or was his need for such escape as great as hers? He had insisted they meet tomorrow after their separate Walks; that would be the test. She felt better. What Roger wanted she had no idea, but he had balanced the day and given her something new to think about.

The parking ticket she hid. The whole afternoon was her own responsibility. She felt equal to Hugh, who also returned in a happier frame of mind and made no mention of Sally.

But the lack of Sally hung over the house and the quietness of the four separate adults weighted the atmosphere and oppressed Connie again with Sally's remark 'this place is really getting me down'. Sally would be happier in Charles's white flat with Zoe as housemother. She wished she had met Zoe, imagined her as cosy and capable, much more cosy and capable than herself. Perhaps it was for the best. No one actually *likes* anyone else here, she realised as they settled in the drawing room to follow their separate interests – Connie with Lord Chesterfield's *Letters to His Son*, Hugh with the *Times* crossword, Aunt Fay her knitting, Edith yawning over her Patience cards.

* * * * * * *

'It is time,' sighs Polly, peering at her reflection in the Duchess' dressing-table mirror, 'to move on. I can rely on the Duchess no longer and Mr Bryant's plans for my future are probably worse than I can imagine.'

Annie's enthusiasm to dress her in white muslin like a nightdress with only one fine petticoat and a waist so high that it meets the plunge of the neckline is also suspicious. Is it to be bride or bed, or both? Pascal lamb. Mutton cloth. But common sense and the ever present threat of the cellar force Polly to agree and to suppress all her questions. Annie is not to be trusted. No one at Hallatrow Hall is to be trusted.

Tonight Annie arrives in spun gold, her hair unpowdered and nodding with scarlet plumes and ribands. All remark Hugo's interest in this firebird and whisper behind their fans about possible nuptials. Even the Duchess holds Annie with a special regard tonight, a calculating benevolence. Draped in imperial purple, the Duchess is seated beside a card table, her fingers twisting and twitching at a pack, her hooded eyes watching for any gentleman of fortune to join them. No one could venture to Hallatrow during the snows; now that the roads are considered passable will boredom bring in the prey? She doubts that anyone will care to make the journey from Bath: local squires offer lean pickings.

Framley is there already, and little Mr Gibson; both treated like household dogs by the Duchess. Neither is possessed of fame or fortune, neither will play for high stakes. Nor will they pay for a woman. A stranger enters with old Sir Andrew from the city, and the whole company turns to consider him.

'Mr Doo-clow,' the footman announces with his Somerset accent.

A cold, harsh face with eyes like ice pools, a skeletal frame with snow-white hands in sharp silhouette against a severe frock coat: Monsieur Duclos picks his way across to the fireplace.

Hugo greets him with a strange lack of enthusiasm, almost as if he were expected but unwelcome.

'*Enchanté!*' A formal bow and a glance to encompass the room, lingering more on furnishings than on personalities, a glance like a serpent's tongue to lick each face and pass on.

An unlikely candidate for the Waters, reflects the Duchess, turning a card. Not the dropsical, gouty type Sir Andrew usually accompanies. Nor does he look at home amongst the colour and frivolity in the drawing room. A spy from France? Surely too circumspect for an émigré? 'Fetch Polly,' she tells Annie. It is time for the child to prove her worth.

Polly is led into the room, trailed before M. Duclos, introduced by Hugo and abandoned. The Frenchman flicks a chill eye from toe to breast to face, receives two glasses of wine offered on a silver salver. Forcing one into her reluctant grasp he raises the other: '*A votre santé*, Mademoiselle!'

He seems to glance to Hugo for approval.

The evening passes in a series of these rituals. Ice-cold snow-white hands pressing another and another fragile glass stem between her fingers, the snake- like gaze darting from her to Hugo to the flirtations before the mirror, to the card table, and returning, always returning, to check the level of her wine.

'*A la patrie*, Mademoiselle!'

She is shocked more by the venom of his hiss than by the revolutionary turn of his words. By now the wine has dulled some senses, heightened others. She is aware of him as an evil force, but their conversation, such as it is, has become meaningless. She senses a connection, a collusion, with Hugo, some plot, but her only concern is that Hugo has promised her to the Frenchman. What, she wonders, can he want with her? He has shown her less interest than Squire Framley and seems unimpressed by the virginal nightdress.

Sir Roger arrives and Polly perceives him mistily as her saviour, turns with relief and welcomes him with notable warmth. The Duchess, too, greets him with pleasure and beckons him to join her in a hand of piquet. Hugo sneers but his face smooths into a thoughtful expression as he watches Sir Roger's elegant leg to his mother and the casual grace with which he takes Polly's hand. Hugo draws M. Duclos aside and, after a few words in the window bay, conducts him over to the Duchess. Polly's trap is sprung, for no reason that she can fathom, and she gazes shyly up into Sir Roger's demanding eyes.

'You see!' His voice is urgent and the eyes glitter. 'I knew they would bring you here! You are in grave danger. Please allow me to help you. Trust me and do just as I say.'

Sir Roger will not play cards tonight. Clasping Polly's white-gloved hand under his arm he leads her to exchange a few words with their host and then suggests they leave the party. Polly's blushes betray the flutter of her heart and the excitement charging her veins at the prospect of what is to follow. Sir Roger must as surely feel her heartbeat through the thin muslin as she shares the pulsating of his blood at her fingertips. Their bodies are already joined by the vibration between them and she aches for him to turn and enfold her in his arms.

Annie's jealousy has been assuaged by Hugo's attentions and she can smile her kitten smile as she leads her rival and Sir Roger to the blue room on the first floor. She can even wish them 'Goodnight' as if she means it while leaving her candle beside the curtained bed, and adds, for Polly's ears alone, 'Beware! He has a wife already!'

As the door closes behind Annie, Polly darts to the curtained window, peers towards the curtained bed, apprehensive, excited, fearful. The fumes of wine are blowing away, leaving her mind crystal clear like a new-washed goblet. So, Sir Roger is married! The heat has evaporated, her blood is clogged with ice. Sir Roger is no saviour but a libertine like all the rest. Bliss in, or anticipating, the marriage bed will not be hers. But she needs his help to escape.

She will flee to Bath, to the Crescent, to Sir Percy, who will find her proper employment. Perhaps she might become Lady Blakeney's maid. Once with the Blakeneys she will be safe from these false men.

'I need your help,' she gasps as he approaches, concealing now any hint of emotion beneath a downcast eye.

'And I yours,' says he, taking a hand and casually unbuttoning the white glove. While his wanton fancy roves unbounded over all her beauties and his imagination paints the charming maid in various ravishing forms, his heart melts with tenderness. He will take her now if he can, but if she refuses tonight she will be his before the week is out. 'You must leave here and I can help you. I feel as if I have always known you. Do please allow me to take you home with me to Widbrook and make you my wife.'

Flutter, flutter. How can he mean that? What does he mean? No, she can no longer believe that enchantment. 'How long is always?' she murmurs, watching her glove slip to the floor. How she had anticipated her disrobing, button by button, bow by bow! 'How can you know me when all my childhood I have lived in France, and since then closeted at Hallatrow?'

'Such a dear, literal creature!' Sir Roger takes her in his arms, tossing the second glove to the bed. 'Sometimes – very rarely – two souls meet knowing all there is to know about each other. They meet and they understand that they are destined for each other. Cannot you feel that now? There is no need for you to explain anything to me about yourself – I know and love everything about you. Your Past, your Future ...'

That experience, Polly considers, is one-sided (love and knowledge not appearing synonymous to her) and although her soul yields happily to his embrace it has no desire to become housewife at Widbrook until it knows more about his twinning with other souls, and whether she will be sharing the wifely duties with Another.

'My immediate Future,' she replies with a disarming smile, 'lies in Sir Percy's household in the Crescent where I shall be quite safe, I assure you. If you would be so kind as to escort me to Bath and if we can meet again in a less compromising situation, then I feel we shall understand each other very well indeed.'

He stands aside, regretful but with perfect grace, while she gathers up her gloves and adjusts the bed curtains. She will be his, of that he is quite certain. If not tonight, then he can still enjoy the pursuit. The light from Annie's candle glows through her virginal gown and onto his coat of celestial blue, and in the moment when their eyes meet their souls share a reluctance at parting.

'Then we shall know,' Polly encourages him. 'When we meet again we should understand each other better.'

Chapter 14

Spring blew in, as it does every year, unexpectedly. Winter had limped and dragged itself into gales of rain masking any bud or growth, trees had been stretched and torn, the river had swollen almost to the level of the meadows, and then one morning arrived like a child's paint box wrapped in a bright blue sky. And another. And another. Carpets of emerald grass unrolled splotched with daffodils, forsythia lit the depths of the spinney, the cherry trees blossomed in pink and white blobs like candyfloss along the edge of the paddock, and yesterday was forgotten.

It's like a miracle, Connie sighed at the bedroom window.

'It's like a miracle!' she cried as she strolled through the Park with Roger on Tuesday. 'And this avenue of double cherries is out of this world – no one could get away with a painting of this, it's far too theatrical!'

'Like sunset on the Alps!'

'Like the Taj Mahal by moonlight!'

'Have you seen the Taj Mahal by moonlight?'

'No, but what about the Alps?'

'I have, actually.'

He dropped her hand and hunched his shoulders, staring ahead, cut off behind a range of unshareable memories. With Sylvia? she wondered. No questions, no personal details. 'It's more honest that way,' he had said. 'No possibility for lies.'

Coming out of his gloom, returning briefly to her, he announced: 'Rilke said it's a pity nature is so *exaggerated* in Switzerland, how pretentious the lakes and mountains are. He put the blame on our grandparents and great-grandparents in their enthusiasm for collaborating with God to find the most mountainous mountains and the grandest reflections in the purest water, etcetera. Nice, don't you think? He also – Rilke, that is – remarked that it's odd that psychoanalysis (at least in Zurich) assumed its most intrusive forms there. Of course, that was before America took it up in such a big way.'

Isn't psychoanalysis taboo? Connie wondered. Too close to Sylvia?

'Nearly all these clean and angular young people are being analysed, he wrote. The result: a sterilised Swiss whose every corner is swept out and scrubbed. He wondered what kind of inner life there can be where the mind is as free of germs as an operating theatre and as glaringly illuminated. An interesting point. A *very* interesting point!' Roger had left her again, arguing with himself or gathering argument against someone else.

Connie dared not comment, and really had no comment to make. When he talked about poets and painters it was usually along some line she knew nothing about. She now knew all about his political interests, however, and the way he identified with nature, how he watched and felt and experienced everything and everyone he met (like D. H. Lawrence, he had told her). Most of the time she was with him she sensed a vibration of nerve ends, like a sea anemone wafting and sifting for new experience; then, for no obvious reason, he would plunge away from her into depths he refused to share, moody, melancholic. Their pact forbade questions, though both referred to details of home life where they helped describe or counterpoint something else.

Sylvia in reference to Bridge, for instance. Sylvia regarding trips to London, frequently. (Both London and Bridge – and perhaps Sylvia – ranking high on his list of least favourite things.) Connie had not been able to avoid mention of Mark and the benders (comparing pastoral scenes) or Sally and the white flat (interior decoration, with a nod towards Sylvia). She would have found an excuse to refer to her children anyway. Some of Roger's embargoes were convenient to them both but some, she realised, were imposed to inhibit, to frustrate. And only he, as he had made the rules, was allowed to break them.

Until they began their 'holidays', as they called their picnics in the country, they led each other on walks round the city exploring the waterways and alleys too distant or insignificant for tourists, and Connie found to her delight that Roger's interest in the eighteenth century was even more intense than her own.

At first they aped the Tourist Guide to each other, arguing about dates and comparing anecdotes: 'Imagine a day in Beau Nash's city –'

'Do you really say that *here*? Don't you find the traffic drowns you?'

'Jane Austen sat at this window writing to Cassandra –'

'Do you find time to tell them how she hated Bath? About her aunt being done for shoplifting? Have most of them even heard of her?'

'And the wind blew the Princess Victoria's skirts, exposing her frilly pantaloons, which is why she never returned to Bath and insisted on the blinds of her railway carriage—'

'That's only a theory! We're not allowed to say that!'

But when Roger instructed her on the difference between the Jacobins and the Girondins and displayed a lively knowledge of the French Revolution, Connie brought the game to the doorstep of her own fantasy.

'Let's pick a year,' she suggested. 'And return there. How about 1795?'

'Isn't that a bit late?' he objected. 'And you can't have much of Miss Austen. We'll miss all the building of importance, and Bath's already on the wane. That's a thoroughly nasty year for the poor in both countries. Bad weather, poor harvests, taxes and bread riots here, fears of invasion. And France was in a terrible mess, even the bread ration was curtailed and the poor were given rice they couldn't afford to cook. It's all very well for you – who were bound to be an aristo – but you might spare a thought for the less well off! It wasn't all minuets and Macaronis, by a long chalk.'

'But it was an exciting time to live.'

'An exciting time to die, more like.' He squinted at the Sainsbury's signs under the arc of Green Park Station. 'Starvation for the masses. Impossible prices for every necessity, the national debt doubled, mobs in the streets – even the Army forced to give up hair powder, my dear! The only real excitement I can see was in the grabbing of men to defend the country. You know, each parish had to raise a quota of recruits for the Army, and they used the prostitutes as decoys – rather like Sweeney Todd – 'Come on up, dearie,' wallop, thump, and on with the next. Twenty guineas a head.'

'I thought they used press gangs?' Connie saw that she could lead him on for ever and satisfy her need to know more about Polly's possible future in Bath. Roger would enjoy telling her. She wished he had not embargoed fantasies.

'The Fleet relied on press gangs. You couldn't exactly press for the Army, I imagine, too easy to desert. And the possibility of being invaded by the Frenchies did produce a patriotic fervour, particularly on the home front. Loyal Volunteers were also recruited – about eight hundred in Bath alone. We even had plans for a scorched earth policy if they got over here, shooting cattle and all that.'

'It was that real?'

'Oh, definitely. No one trusted the French. Apart from the chaos in Paris they were doing very well – and about to do better under Bonaparte.'

They had wandered up from Sainsbury's to Nelson Place and Nile Street, an area no tourist would wish to visit. 'Nelson hadn't really got off the ground by then, I suppose,' said Connie uncertainly. 'The battle of the Nile—'

'In the summer of '95,' he interrupted, 'an army formed in Hampshire under the Bourbon flag. Funded by the government. Arms and uniforms provided. The idea was to carry the war back into the enemy camp and forestall invasion. Four thousand or so set off from Southampton that summer and took over the fort at Quiberon, on the Brittany coast. But that fizzled out in local civil war. It's easy enough now to argue that Pitt was a bit of a twit not to be tougher with France – all those negotiations for peace when we had to fight them anyway, but then, the war was bankrupting us. We needed peace. Oh, the nonsense of war and the need to rattle sabres and appear equal! It's so easy to argue either way, for and against force. What's the difference now, eh? What has changed? What have we learned? When will we ever learn?'

Connie remembered Hugh's remarks at Lettice's dinner party and remained silent. She had no desire to argue either way.

At home Hugh had tacked a map to the kitchen wall and covered it with coloured squares and pins which corresponded to lists in a smart new ledger on his desk. As Treasurer and leader of the Finance & General Purposes Committee he was enjoying fitting names to squares, experienced canvassers and helpers in red, new volunteers in pencil. Lewis Foster (Chairman of the Social Committee) had none of Hugh's organisational experience, and part of Hugh's pleasure came from showing him and Annie the latest pattern. Although still too early to solicit electoral views and intentions (a euphemism for hard sell), Hugh and Tony had drawn up a military operation: salvoes of leaflets to be followed by regiments of doorstep callers, to be followed by reminders and the collecting of postal votes and, in some areas, offers of transport to the polling stations.

'We'll try moving Mrs Midgley from here to here,' he explained to Annie, taking a red pin from a blue square to a pink. 'She's very experienced and knows just how to handle the 'don't knows'. I'm sure she won't mind swapping her area, and we'll give her Judith to train up. Will you make a note of that for Lewis? It might affect who she invites to her Bring & Buy.'

Annie rested one tightly clad hip on the kitchen table and allowed her flaming curls to fall over her face while she made the note. Hugh watched her with more than conservative interest. 'And in that case we'll be able to move Sandra into Judith's place,' she suggested.

'Good girl! I'd forgotten about her.' He added a green pin to the blue square. 'You're a Godsend,' he told her. 'What would I do without you?'

She flashed freckles and green light and Aunt Fay came in to make the tea.

'Edith thought you'd be in here,' she giggled, coy, with a hint of a question. 'Don't mind me, please. A cuppa for you, too?'

Annie slid off the table and smoothed the jeans down her thighs as if she were performing a striptease. She too had learned to disregard Aunt Fay. 'No thanks, I've got to be off to fetch Emily. Come over later Hugh, if Connie's not back. We haven't arranged who's to phone the changes.' Without waiting for a reply she sauntered out, leaving Hugh grinning at his map on the wall.

'Connie's out to lunch again?' Edith joined them with an obvious glance through the window as Annie crossed the yard. 'I've been wanting to get you alone, Hugh, to find out what exactly is the position with Sally. These non-committal answers, don't you know. So secretive. I assume she *is* still attending school? This flat with the woman Zoe – it's all very unorthodox. If she were my daughter—'

The face Hugh turned to her showed no emotion. He was leaving Sally to his wife for the time being, letting them both get on with it. Then he would pounce. At present he was too busy. Roger Benefield looked a harmless type, a bit of a weed, rather effeminate. And he had checked up on Charles Swain and was secretly impressed by what he was making from his endeavours. The detail was to follow. Free enterprise Hugh respected, and for the present he had decided to ignore Tim and any implications from his living in Kingsmead Square with Sally. Without financial backing Sally would be forced to come home soon anyway, with her tail between her legs, and then he would deal with her. She would have to learn the hard way now.

'Connie's dealing with Sally,' he answered his mother. Connie could cope with the questions; that would serve her right. 'If you will excuse me, I must get my lists in order. There's an F & G P meeting tomorrow.'

'What I don't understand,' said Edith to Aunt Fay after he left, 'is how that Foster woman manages to reconcile her work for the Party with her conscience. I'd been led to believe she was quite a Pinko.'

'Can Lewis give you a lift to the meeting tomorrow?' Connie said at dinner that night. 'Sally's asked me to meet Zoe because on Mondays the restaurant's closed, and I'd need the car.'

'You haven't actually met her yet?' Edith registered her disapproval by dropping wrist and bracelet on the table, clunk, and widening her eyes at her son.

Hugh paused to weigh advantage with annoyance and surprised them all by agreeing. 'Though I don't like you driving at night. Mind you park sensibly, there's a lot of vandalism in that area.'

'Avon Street,' Connie had said to Roger, anxious, wanting it to be a joke. 'The nymphs of Avon Street. It's amazing how a long-dead reputation remains. Doesn't one think automatically of past centuries? Brothels and prostitution?'

Roger had hunched his shoulders and turned away. 'Why not?' he muttered. 'And the house is in Kingsmead Square.'

'Do you know Charles?' she had asked, surprised that he knew the address, aware of one of his moods and for once hoping to trap it. 'That would be a stroke of luck! I can't get anything sensible out of Sally except that he's 'amazing' and the whole set-up's 'brill'. It seems they all work for him in exchange for bed and board. What I really want to know is—'

'I believe I've met him.' Roger froze the conversation. 'Mutual friends.'

'There's someone called Max, Sally's been going on about,' Connie pressed on. 'It sounds as if he's always around but doesn't live there. I hear more about him than Tim. Does that name ring a bell?'

They had driven to Stourhead to look at the trees. Roger frowned across the lake and turned abruptly along a track towards the rhododendrons. 'I imagine that's Max Masterman, our SDP Chairman. He was Sylvia's analyst.' He was hurrying now and she had difficulty keeping up.

Oh! Embargoes, vetoes, closed doors. Connie hadn't the courage to continue. Sylvia's *analyst*! Two taboos for the price of one! She sensed that, despite the political interest, whatever she asked would receive no answer, and followed him in silence.

Chapter 15

Max Masterman was in the main room with Charles when Sally led Connie in. The heat was less oppressive than she remembered and Gregorian chant echoed from the four corners.

'This is my mother,' said Sally.

Both men rose to shake her hand; Charles in a warm grasp, Max with a flourish of cold fingertips.

'A pleasure, Mrs Bryant!' Beneath a forehead immensely domed, dark eyes gleamed like brackish water, something flickering, darting within. Although there was nothing of the skeleton about Max, Connie was reminded of M. Duclos: a similar mincing gait, the same exhibition of white hands, the reptilian glance. The eyes somehow held her attention, although they flashed onto Sally. She felt that he had seen right into and through her, and as if he, too, focused on some faint memory. '*Enchanté*, Mademoiselle!' But it was Charles who today wore white.

'I'm taking Mother to meet Zoe,' said Sally.

'Not in the hell hole!' Charles shuddered. 'Bring her up, dear.'

'Oh no, really I'd like to—' Connie was determined to look downstairs.

'Ah well, a pin to see the peep show! But do return immediately. We don't often have the opportunity to meet mothers.'

'Charles calls it Hell,' Sally said as Connie trod carefully down the spiral staircase, 'but I don't think he's ever been down here. We can get in through this door, you see, so we don't have to bother him coming and going.'

'Does he own the whole house?' Roger had said house, not flat.

Connie surveyed a litter of mattresses, duvets and sleeping bags. 'I'm not surprised he doesn't come down here, this room's a tip! Darling, really!' She noticed familiar garments in a heap near the window. 'Do you all sleep in here?'

Sally switched on the ceiling light and the jumble looked worse piled against violent yellow walls. 'No, Zoe's room's through here and Tim and Adrian sort of share this one.' A smaller, neater space, with a double bed, Connie noted. 'And the bathroom's here. It's only a bit chaotic in the morning, but luckily we don't all get up at the same time. The view's nice, isn't it?'

Connie was looking out onto Avon Street, trying to work out who used the double bed. 'How many of you?' she asked faintly.

'Only three of us girls. We're not very tidy, I'm afraid. Poor Zoe! They'll all be in soon and you can meet them; they've gone to the pub. Come and see Zoe, I've warned her you're coming.'

Zoe's room, overlooking the plane trees, glowed like a ruby under crimson flock wallpaper, crimson chiffon lampshades with golden tassels, a crimson velour counterpane. Connie felt as if she had entered a Victorian auditorium, a bordello. On every surface antique dolls sat, leaned, lolled; a hundred eyes turned to the door. Amongst them, just another pair of boot-button eyes, a tiny woman perched on an overstuffed chair, her doll's feet not quite reaching the carpet.

'Darlinks!' Zoe clapped grotesquely rheumatic hands and a wobbly scarlet smile split her face. 'Come in, come in! Mrs Bryant! Sally has told me all about you.'

Connie wondered what, and should she be flattered. 'And me about you!' She tried to look equally delighted, equally informed.

'A little drinkie?' Zoe slithered forward in her chair until her toes touched the floor and reached a shaky hand towards a tray of bottles.

'Oh no, really –'

'Charles said we were to go upstairs, Zoe. Max is here.'

'Good, good. Your mother will enjoy that more. Have you seen the way they insist on living, the dear children? I tell you I despair! But as long as they are happy.' Zoe writhed and wriggled and stood up, not much more than half Connie's height.

'You'll love Max, darlink. He's like one of my boys.'

Connie wondered about both points as they clattered slowly up the staircase.

'Zoe!' Max dug his hands into the sofa cushions to propel his body to its full height and then bent double to kiss each of her cheeks. 'I thought you'd gone to ground tonight! How's the shoulder? Did those fairy pills help?'

'So much better, darlink, thank you. As for always, you know just what Zoe needs. A little more of that and I'd be flying off! You have *such* good care for me, does he not, Charlie? But now, have you met Mrs Bryant? Isn't she just like Sally? Come on, come on darlink – sit by me and Charlie will fix us a lovely little drinkie. Don't you just love this apartment?'

Zoe's accent had swung from middle Europe to mid-Atlantic as her enthusiasm mounted. Her quivering hands plucked at Connie's sleeve and they sank together into the white cushions. Max was watching. As a psychiatrist, Connie supposed, that was his job. Perhaps he was Zoe's analyst, too.

'Opiates for the people,' he murmured. 'Just let me know when they run out.'

His voice contained deep brown tones like his eyes, unruffled, mesmeric, flecked with cynicism. Connie sensed a tension between him and her daughter and was beginning to wonder about his role in the household when bells rang and doors banged below.

'That,' sighed Charles as he handed out glasses of colourless liquid, 'sounds like the return of the Light Brigade. Perhaps we should disconnect their bell?'

'Disconnect parts of their anatomy!' Max suggested as yelps and scuffles filtered up the staircase. 'They were supposed to get all that out of their systems before they came home. Really Charles, you're a lax father figure!'

'My children!' Zoe's ill-sketched mouth trembled. 'They are happy.'

'More like half-cut,' said Max taking a swig from his glass.

Sally giggled and caught her mother's eye.

Trying to look amused, unconcerned, Connie copied Max and choked. The limpid liquid tasted like gas, lighted gas, and scorched her gums. 'Goodness!!' she cried, still smiling bravely.

'*Eau de vie*,' Charles explained.

'Oh dear what?' said Sally.

'*Quelle vie*?' said Zoe.

'*Quelle horreur*!' said Max as Zoe's 'children' bounded into the room.

Sally had described Amanda as an escaped Sloane and Sharon as a bit Punk. Amanda had been sent to Bath on a secretarial course, hated both the work and her flatmates and had drifted via Jupiter's to Charles's house; Sharon had left a local school and been thrown out by her parents 'because they don't like her hair'. The girls shrieked and chattered with Sally while Tim greeted Connie and vaguely referred to the other young man as Adrian.

'And how's Mr Bryant?' Tim enquired, as if speaking of an invalid.

'Oh, he's fine. Very well, thank you.' There seemed nothing she could add to encourage him.

'Seen Mark?' Tim lit a stub of cigarette from above his ear. 'He looks okay.'

'Yes. Oh, yes he does.' Not strictly true. It had been a harsh winter on the riverbank and she was still concerned about his health.

'Heard about the Peace Convoy?'

'You mean to Stonehenge?' Who had not? 'I thought it was banned this year?'

'Always is.' Tim sniffed. 'Mark's going.'

'Going? How can he go?' Connie felt the familiar rattle of fear in her gut and saw flashes of newsreel from past years, broken vans and lorryloads of hippies battling with police.

'They're all going. Baz's got hold of a bus.'

'A *bus*?'

'A sort of bus.' Tim shrugged. 'Which sort of works.'

Adrian sniggered. 'Wouldn't catch me!' he said. 'Asking for trouble.'

'All that energy.' Max had been listening. 'If only there was some way to channel it to some good cause.'

'Cause enough to get them somewhere to live,' said Tim.

'But Mark and Baz *have* somewhere to live.' Connie realised as she said it that she had missed the point. No one bothered to answer. She sipped her drink, gathering a mouthful of saliva to dilute each drop, and noticed with relief that Sally was sharing hers with Amanda and Sharon. Pushing herself up and out of the cushions, she joined them at the window.

'Are you all working every night at the Bull's Eye?' she asked, hoping she sounded more friendly than inquisitive. Would that allow Sally enough time for her homework?

'Uh-huh,' said Amanda, widening vague grey eyes and arching her neck so that a cascade of brown hair flopped over her shoulder to mingle with a collection of gold chains. 'But Charlie says we can have a go at Jupiter's some weekends, if the restaurant's not too busy. I'd prefer that. Waitressing can get a bit bor-ing.'

'What would you do at Jupiter's?' Visions of them accepting ten cents a dance wearing something even more revealing than Sharon's mini skirt and string vest.

'Oh, check-in, bar – that sort of thing.'

'Better money at Bull's Eye, though,' Sharon piped up, her shocking-pink cockscomb nodding. 'We get to keep our tips, y'see. Charles says that's fair. Don't get tips at the bar.'

'They buy you drinks, though,' said Amanda.

'*Some* do. But it's only the fat old farts.'

'So what?'

'So what are they after, then?' Sharon looked as if she knew and Sally tactfully led her mother away.

'They're nice, aren't they?' she said. 'Sharon's a bit wild sometimes but she's funny, and we're all getting at Amanda to stop her being twittish. They're a good laugh. Anyway, I like them.' She sounded defensive.

'So do I,' said Connie with a shade too much enthusiasm. 'Look darling, I really should go now.'

'Have another drink. You haven't talked to Max.'

'Why should I talk to Max? And darling, I hope you aren't drinking as much as everyone else seems to be. It's—'

'Oh, don't fuss! We can't afford to – and you'll be pleased to hear that Charles only sees that we're fed. Usually at the Bull's Eye, of course. He doesn't offer us this yukky stuff, it's kept for Zoe. She's the one for the little drinkies, but she needs it for her arthritis. Poor old thing, sometimes she can hardly move. But Max fixes that, he's got all sorts of divine pills. She goes quite bonkers on them sometimes.'

'You're not…?' Connie couldn't think quite how to express her fears. Max as the dispenser of purple hearts, or the modern equivalent, suddenly struck her as a possibility. 'What does Max exactly do here so much of the time? From the way you talk it sounds as if he practically lives here.' Perhaps she sounded anxious, critical. She thought she caught a furtive look in Sally's eyes, a flicker that at home preceded something devious.

'He doesn't exactly do anything, for heaven's sake!' Sally laughed. 'He's a friend of Charles and he's a shrink, and I think he's got shares in Jupiter's or something. He actually lives somewhere behind the Crescent, in St. James's Square I believe. He's known Zoe and Charles for years, and he brings rich clients into the Bull's Eye quite often – they're always good tippers, anyway.'

Connie saw that she would be told no more and felt the heat of Max's attention like a laser on the back of her neck. She didn't like the sound of Jupiter's, or the rich old men Max took to the Bull's Eye, or Sharon's knowing remark about what they were after. All her maternal instincts warned her against Max and increased her fears for Sally.

'We're off to get a pizza.' Tim appeared beside Sally, dropping an arm onto her shoulders and pulling her against his chest. Her lack of ideals must have been forgiven. 'Coming, Sals?'

'I really must be going,' said Connie.

No one tried to stop her. The young were scuffling by the spiral stair, Max and Charles lounged in opposite corners of the sofa with Zoe propped like a doll between them. Their six eyes were fixed on her, unblinking.

'We will take care of your Sally,' said Zoe, her smile quivering and jumping. 'She is happy with us – yes, darlink?'

'Oh yes,' Sally muttered, guarding her eyes from her mother.

Connie drove home with care, and with a sense of loss far deeper than before. Zoe and Charles playing at mothers and fathers seemed silly, peculiarly self-conscious, roles forced on them and manipulated by Max. She saw Max alone as the predator, the power through which she was losing her daughter.

* * * * * * *

The lovely Polly, when Sir Roger arrives as though to escort her for a drive round his estate, shines forth with more gaiety and sprightliness than usual. Hugo too appears in good humour, now that he sees she understands her new role. Her comportment last night must have pleased Sir Roger. Even M. Duclos has agreed that she can be employed to suit his ends, although Hugo is still apprehensive about using her as a spy. However, M. Duclos pays well for Hugo's information and what he expects from Polly will be added to the Hallatrow account.

Polly is now dressed in a more conventional robe of lemon sarcenet with a stylish green cloak borrowed from Annie. As she bids farewell to Hugo and allows Sir Roger to hand her into his phaeton, she sees only springtime and promise, the wisteria clouding the portico in a smoke haze, bluebells misting the bare earth under the limes. As they bowl down the drive she watches eagerly for each landmark until Hallatrow Hall lies behind unfamiliar trees and hedgerows and she is free, closing a chapter, heading a fresh new page.

With a great sigh, more of joy than sorrow, she turns to her companion to find him watching her sadly. Such dreams as he had still remain, but now he is pierced by dread that other hands might touch her first, that the innocence might be coarsened by Bath society, even that she might be forced into marriage with some moral bigot who would insist on his own conjugal rights, leaving no space for Sir Roger's own fulfilment.

'Shall I lose you now?' he asks, 'to the fleshpots of Bath? When you were caged at Hallatrow I knew I could pluck you out at any moment; with Lady Blakeney you could be travelling, you could be in their townhouse, you will have more liberty...' He dwells on her liberty with a sullen face. 'But you will not forget me? I shall call –'

'Oh yes, yes! Dear kind Sir! All will be splendid at Bath, I know it!'

Later, as the carriage passes through the South Gate of the city and rattles over cobbled streets, she becomes apprehensive. What if Sir Percy has forgotten her, if Lady Blakeney has no room for her, no friend in need of a maid? Nonsense! In the Queen of English watering places, the holiday resort of the fashionable world, there must be work and shelter for an enterprising young woman. She can become a milliner, a seamstress, a laundry maid, even. Such a city must require multitudes of women to serve its visitors.

The four horses trot smartly round the Circus and along Brock Street and swing into the dazzling ellipse of The Crescent, the whole intensity of the sun seemingly concentrated in this saucer of buildings. As Polly hovers on the broad pavement blinking at pillar and pediment, Sir Roger takes her hand to lead her to the door of number sixteen. 'John Wood says that this stone holds sunlight like a honeycomb holds honey,' he remarks, unable to bring himself to say goodbye. 'On such a day as this –'

She frees her hand, but with reluctance. 'I shall walk to the end and back,' she decides. 'I must savour this moment between my two different lives. Thank you very kindly, dear Sir, for all your help. I know we shall meet again.' She cannot admit to fear, nor to the impulse to accept his offer and return with him to Widbrook and whatever that life might hold. If he remains as witness her resolve could crumble. That graceful figure in top boots and a coat of forget-me-not blue is all she knows to trust, and yet she cannot believe him. She hurries away and he watches her to the end of the crescent with a grave expression, then climbs back into the phaeton and is gone.

The bell at number sixteen clangs and echoes in the basement. And again. A wind blows clouds over the sun and whips at Polly's cloak. Again she pulls the bell. No one answers, for Sir Percy and his wife are indeed in London and the housekeeper is asleep.

Much later she retraces the route taken by Sir Roger's carriage, down amongst the heavy rumble of carts and drays, the bawling of street vendors, the hustle of sedan chairs. Glancing at taverns they passed she is aware that she has no money and nowhere to stay. As it grows dark and the streets within the city walls narrower and more crowded, she gathers courage to enter the White Hart Inn, the terminal of the London–Bath coaching route outside the Pump Room, recently refurbished with stabling for three hundred horses and twelve four-horse coaches. Pushing forward through the throng she discovers an ostler and asks faintly for a room. He looks up and down and into her cloak, notes the lack even of a reticule or muff and tells her to take her custom elsewhere.

'I'll buy you a drink, dearie!'

She shrinks away and escapes through the stables. It seems that the streets are full of beggars and tramps, pickpockets and prostitutes, and as dangerous as the inn. She veers back to the warmth of the alehouse, deciding to try once more for a room for the night – tomorrow she can decide how to pay.

A girl younger than Polly clutches at her skirt. 'I seed you!' The pinched face gleams sickly white in the glare of a lantern. 'I seed you come and I seed you go. Don't you know nuffing? That don't work, being all hoity-toity, that don't. You want to ask the gen'leman for a drink. Act friendly. Know what I mean? Our Mam c'd tell you.'

Polly looks at her, weary, vague, confused by the tumult of voices and laughter and the rattle of dice, the heat and sweat, the volume of noise. A fat man jostles past her with tankards overbrimming, and a brown stain spreads down her sleeve.

'You got nowhere to go? I seed you! You come back with me? Our Mam needs another girl since Our Jenny fell in river. Come!' The small fingers pluck at Polly's cloak and she follows the waif out into the street, along past the Cross Bath and into darkened alleys to Avon Street.

Our Mam, crippled by disease, creeps about the house in Avon Street with the help of a broken chair. Unable to straighten her back and unsteady on her feet, she bows over her support and shuffles down the grim passage to find light. The girl Eliza is told to raise the candle at all angles while Our Mam cocks her head and leers sideways up at Polly. She is doll-sized and doll-shaped, an ancient rag doll with boot-button eyes.

'She'll do,' the old woman cackles. 'Been dismissed, 'ave you? Not with child, I 'ope? Seein' as you're a friend of Liza you c'n 'ave lodgings 'ere – in return for services, mind! Liza'll tell you. No tricks, mind! Our Jim'll tan your hide if there's any tricks.'

Eliza whisks Polly down treacherous stairs to the bowels of the house below street level before she can change her mind. 'You'll do!' she squeaks. 'You c'n stay! Not with child, are you? Our Jenny were – that's why she ended it in river. You can sleep here with me and Lydia. The bed upstairs is for the gen'lemen. You'll see tomorrow – and after Our Mam'll give you bread.'

They lie on sacks on the floor, Polly clutching Annie's cloak around her. She could never sleep here, the cold and damp and dark strike her like the cellar at Hallatrow Hall. Annie's talk of freedom to choose! She has chosen this.

Later, when Eliza is snuffling and snoring and scratching in her sleep, Lydia enters with a stub of candle casting weird light and shadow across her naked bosom and painted face. 'New one?' she asks without interest. 'Look-ee 'ere! A whole shilling from a gent I took in the stables – don't-ee tell or I'll kill 'ee! There's enough farmers in for market. A right boar I just had upstairs and your Mam's none too pleased coz he won't make a soldier!' She yawns and scratches, wraps her shilling in her pocket and a sack across her shoulders, settles beside the child and blows out the candle.

'Tomorrow,' Polly says to herself, 'I will escape and find honest work.'

Chapter 16

'Bath in the eighteenth century was, as I've already told you, devoted to self-indulgence and dissipation – described by one as 'a valley of pleasure but a sink of iniquity'. The bathing here at the beginning of the century was not only mixed sexes but also *nude*.' Connie paused for effect, wondering if her bunch of bored students was still listening.

Adults, particularly Americans, could survive two hours of detail with more stamina and enthusiasm than their guide, but school parties tended to flag as they left the city boundary and saved their interest for the promised later exploration of Bath's shops. Connie had learned to cut out dates and all but the main personalities, but if a harassed escort set a time she was forced to fill it. She saved the baths till last.

'This bathing was really a spectator sport as much as a healthy or social occupation. Fun for everyone! The bathers performed and the audience encouraged them. A bit like a present-day football match, if you see what I mean. They even threw things into the water. This was frowned on of course – there was a fine of 3/6d, for instance, for throwing a dead cat.' Pause for reaction. 'And although there was plenty of this hot water welling up from the springs, no one washed much in those days so it was pretty filthy too. Imagine!' A few 'ughs' and 'glugs' from those who were not swapping chocolate bars or gum. 'However, it all became much more civilised as the century went on. Women wore these big canvas shifts – dresses that wouldn't cling to the figure when wet – and bonnets or chip hats, and pushed little floating dishes in front of them holding a nosegay (against the smell) and a hanky, snuffbox, patches to stick on their spots – though they didn't stick very well in the sweaty steam of the baths. And the men wore canvas drawers and a canvas waistcoat, which must have been rather uncomfortable after the earlier freedom of sloshing about naked. But it was still rather rowdy and neither Fanny Burney nor Jane Austen allowed a character of theirs into the baths. Smollett, however –'

Yawn. Well, we can forget about him. Connie managed a peep at her watch. 'We'll walk along here now under the Colonnades – which were built to protect the bathers and promenaders from the rain on their way to the Pump Room. And then we'll be back where we started from.'

Enthusiasm, and a brisk return to duty by the escort. 'Wasn't that interesting, girls! I must say I was fascinated by –'

The girls had arrived early and Connie had had no chance to talk with Roger before the Walk. She hurried now across the Abbey churchyard to explain that she must see Mark today, and was flattered by his disappointment.

'Tomorrow, then? We shouldn't waste this lovely weather. We could leave earlier tomorrow, I could pick you up at the house?'

'That's a good idea.' Why feel guilt? She usually told them all at supper where she had been; Hugh didn't seem to mind; only Edith drooped her eyelids and pursed her lips as if sucking lemons.

At the railway bridge, listening for trains, Connie felt as hesitant as she would peering through someone's curtained window, uninvited, snooping. There should be a bell, some warning. The boys might be bathing, asleep, running about naked – anything. She hurried along the concrete blocks under the bridge, threw herself onto the fence, her heart pounding, and was greeted by a furious bark. A bundle of fur hurtled across the clearing snapping and snarling, hit the fence, fell back and then crouched down over its front paws, tail and bottom high, a-quiver. Dog and woman stared. The dog yuffed, rolled its eyes under shaggy eyebrows and wagged its body. Connie decided not to cross the fence. No one seemed to have heard; the camp appeared deserted, not even a wisp of smoke escaped from a fairy-tale chimney.

'Mark!' she called. 'Baz?'

The dog whooped and woofed, scampered in a circle and returned to its strange position. Connie noticed bluebells in the undergrowth and a patch of young shoots on newly-dug earth. The riverbank looked almost like a garden today, its ragged patches dressed pale green, and she was cheered that the boys were finally cultivating it. She could give Mark geranium cuttings, and lavatera seed that grow anywhere.

'Mark!' she shouted.

The dog charged around again and disappeared into Mark's bender. When eventually it reappeared three forms staggered out behind it like moles flushed from a tunnel, staggered and blinked and wandered without direction.

'Mark!' she shouted.

The dog romped up to her with a shoe in its mouth, dropped the shoe and barked again. The boys followed the noise as if blind. Half dressed in an assortment of frayed and filthy jeans and vests they swayed before her. Their appearance frightened her; she wished she hadn't come, wished she could hide, run away. They probably wouldn't notice. How could they be drunk, she thought, at this time of day?

'Mark,' she said. 'Is the dog safe?'

Mark grinned stupidly. ''Course she is. Come on in and meet her.' He reached to hold the fence down for his mother and missed. Sweat shone on his white skin and the beard looked matted like a bird's nest. 'Sorry we're not, um –' He dropped his chin to stare down his body, and pushed folds of vest into his belt. Connie climbed over the fence and the dog leaped to lick her hands and face.

'Down, Legs!' Mark growled. 'She's a bit, um – Come on in.' He wandered towards the bender, still digging at his vest. The other two watched and swayed with vacant smiles. Groping to raise the door flap, Mark turned. 'Sorry we're a bit, um – pissed.'

Baz giggled. 'St-stoned,' he corrected.

'Spaced out, man!' Connie had not been introduced to BJ but had heard from Sally that he was leader of the pack. He seemed to her to be older and in a better state than the other two.

They all crowded into the inner room where Mark and Baz fell onto the mattress. A sickly, unfamiliar smell filled the tent; the stove felt warm and through its little door Connie could see a glow in the embers.

'Why don't we all have some coffee?' she asked, hearing her voice dance and enthuse like a nursery-school teacher.

BJ agreed and set to work. The dog thrust its wet muzzle against her skirt and Mark muttered 'Down, Legs! Why don't you sit down too, Mum?'

She heaped Nescafe into mugs and decided to risk a corner of the carpet so that she could face them all. They drank the bitter coffee in silence, the boys in a row like three monkeys, sipping, sighing, staring ahead. Not until they had finished dared she speak.

'What kind of dog is Legs? Does he belong to anyone?'

'She's mine!' Mark's pride sounded positively paternal. 'Hannibal gave her to me. She's a lurcher, very intelligent.'

A lurcher. More likely very dangerous. The puppy rolled its eyes and yawned as they all considered it.

'Not a *pure*-bred lurcher, she's not,' said BJ, 'more of a cross.'

'She's not very *cross*,' said Mark. They all laughed. 'Hannibal's got the mother up at Bannerdown.'

Connie had read that hippies were gathering at Bannerdown and the police now had new powers to remove trespassers. 'Is that part of the Peace Convoy?' she asked, relieved to find such an easy lead to the purpose of her visit.

'A bit,' said Mark, playing with Legs as if that were no concern of his.

'A good bit,' BJ added. 'They can't turn us off there until they've found some permanent site for travellers. That's the whole point.'

What point, Connie felt she couldn't ask.

'They've got a statutory duty,' Baz explained, slipping on the long word. 'And anyway that's where the transport is now, that's where we go from.'

'Are you going?'

'Sure we're going.'

'But why, when you know there will be trouble and they won't let you anywhere near Stonehenge? Why don't you go off into Wales or somewhere peaceful if you want a change? I can't see the point in antagonising everyone.'

'That is the point, don't you see?' Mark set down his mug and Connie saw that his hand shook, that he was sick and should be going nowhere but home. 'We've tried everything else, no one will listen. The only way to make any impression is if we band together. At least they're aware of us then.'

'To what *end*?' Connie felt the sting of tears, the frustration of an old argument which always turned full circle upon itself, and took a gulp of the revolting coffee to steady herself. 'That's idiotic. That doesn't accomplish anything!'

'You'd write a letter to *The Times*, I suppose?' sneered BJ. 'What you don't realise is we're the dregs, we're unacceptable, we're guilty until proved innocent – just because we look like we do and live like we do. You won't understand that. You just follow Mark down the street some time and watch the reaction! I invite you to drive with me just a few hundred yards in our van – and I'll bet you we'll be stopped and questioned by the Pigs. And 'questioned' is a polite way of putting it. They just grab you and slap a conviction. It's like that, no joking! It's automatic that we're high or up to no good, whatever we say. You'd see.'

'But why cement that view? Why fuel it? Why not live quietly, peacefully?'

'You try to do that, Mam! All we want is somewhere to do just that. We know what we want, we're just like everyone else. We want to live like man is supposed to live, without all this technology, close to the earth. But that's considered deviant nowadays, that's not on, that's anti-social. We want to be self-sufficient, to be left alone, but society's not like that any more. It's all do this, do that; in particular, *don't* do that. We're not doing anybody any harm, but you wouldn't think it. They're out to get us – but we won't be got. No, Sir! The only way to fight them is together – solidarity, y'know.'

Hence the Convoy? She wanted to ask. But he would only agree and that would explain nothing more to her. How many of the Convoy were idealists? 'They're discussing setting up permanent sites,' she said. 'Why not wait and see?'

All three laughed and BJ rolled a cigarette, drew on it and passed it to Baz.

'Have you met Max Masterman?' she asked Mark, remembering last night and her other fears.

'Max? Uh-huh.' Mark tickled the dog.

She wished she had Mark alone. 'I'm rather worried about him and Sally. Do you know anything about him?'

'Max?' Mark's glazed eye looked furtive. 'Nothing particular.'

'Max?' Baz, Connie noticed, showed his first real interest.

Possibly, she thought, Max was connected in some way with the hippies; he had appeared very interested in the young. Possibly, it came to her in flashes like an ancient movie, drugs: Zoe's fairy pills, the boys' strange behaviour – not drink but drugs. Max was a drug pusher! Vague fears accelerated to horror. Of course!

'You don't have to worry about Max and *Sally*,' Baz laughed.

'No Mum, honest! She's fine. She's really happy in that place, she told me. And Max, he's okay, he won't do her any harm. Honest.'

You can't argue with such honesty. Connie returned to concern for her son. 'Why not come home with me now, if only for a few days, just for a change? If you are moving on –' She had to sound casual. They were all waiting for an unacceptable remark, she could feel it.

'Don't think Sheba'd like Legs, do you? Or Dad.' He had practised his excuse. 'But I'll see you on Thursday, right?'

All three watched to see how she took it and she passed the test with a smile which carried her through the bridge and back as far as the car.

* * * * * * *

All night poor Polly can neither sleep nor rest on the cold cellar floor. Nothing, she decided, will press her into Lydia's mould. To be parted from her virginity by a drunken farmer in town for the cattle market, or a coal haulier from Radstock, or a syphilitic soldier, is a far worse fate than the life of a sybarite at Hallatrow Hall. And if she were to be reduced to prostitution in town she would keep her own shillings, not become a slave in this dubious business enterprise. While Eliza and Lydia still snore and snuffle she creeps up the stairs and escapes into the dawn.

Drawn towards the heart of the city she watches the gentry arrive in their sedan chairs for the morning's bathing. Dropsical gentlemen of enormous girth, a child with scrofulous ulcers, elderly women swathed in towel and turban are helped from the chairs to limp and lope to the slips to the King's Bath where they wallow in their yellow linen and emerge later flushed and sweating to be carried home to their lodgings. Polly lingers and watches as the bathing becomes more riotous and the company gathers in the new Pump Room to observe the antics below and to drink the waters. She could discover the Superintendent of the Baths and offer her services as a guide, but the state of most of the bathers, their diseased bodies and sores and dirt, and the thought of escorting such a mass of discharge into the sulphurous steam fills her with repugnance. Why did she fly from Hallatrow? Hugo and Annie seem like angels in heaven compared with the heat and flavour of this hellish company.

By noon when the Abbey bells summon the faithful and the fashionable, Polly is faint with hunger and despair. Two coffee houses have turned her away; they have servants enough. Back in the churchyard she notices Eliza begging for pennies, and Eliza recognises her.

'You silly girl you – I seed you! Wa-cha want to go for? Our Mam were that put out. And Our Jim's 'ere on the lookout for yer so come on now—' Eliza glimpses crimson velvet emerging from the Abbey on the arm of a gouty gentleman. 'Hey, Will!' and she is off, followed by another urchin. While she flatters the crimson lady and pleads for a coin, Will snakes a hand into the man's coat skirts and Polly slips away.

She has never walked so far, crossing and recrossing the same streets and alleys, oblivious to the dust of buildings and rebuilding, the rattle of carts and carriages, the mingling of beautiful people with the lame, the deformed and the vicious. No longer does she remark a pretty gown or a particularly grotesque figure, a pleasing smile or a leer. Nor does she notice M. Duclos crow-black in the shadows of the colonnade. Her head resounds to a murmuring like a hive of bees. She wanders on, incapable now of deciding where to apply for work and without the will to do so. In the courtyard of the White Hart she rests against the wall, thoughtless, unseeing.

Eliza is plucking at her sleeve. Before her towers what must be Our Jim, with a young Army captain.

'We've employment for you. No need to be squeamish, Miss.' The big man's eyes scan her like a horse dealer's. 'Good money if you enlist a man for Cap'n Gibbon here. Easy money. Wa-cha say?'

The mouth of the recruiting officer twists to show what he thinks of such transactions. He takes snuff and drawls, 'Payments e-only on the result, my man. E-only when signed and sealed, do you understand?'

'She'll bring 'em in.' Jim has sized up his cattle. 'Never fear. Come on, girl – is it to be with us or the river?'

With her back against the wall, poor Polly can shrink no farther. Wildly she turns her head, peering out into a throng that shows no interest in a girl in conversation with two men and a child.

'Mistress Polly?' Up steps M. Duclos, the curls of his wig obscuring much of his domed forehead, the dark eyes steady on her but alive with stratagems and spoils. He extends a white hand and makes play of shaking back his cuff and wafting her fingers to his lips. '*Quelle surprise*! I did not expect to find you here. And your friends?' He sweeps an ironic bow and just touches Eliza's head. 'Such pleasure! May I escort you, Mademoiselle?'

The voice is low and light and any menace is reserved in the eyes that flicker now from face to face as he offers her his arm and turns on a scarlet heel. No one speaks as he leads her away. His sleeve feels cold and slippery under her hand like the skin of a snake, but she is swooning with relief at her rescue and would have clutched naked steel or fire to escape her fate in Avon Street.

'You will take a chair to my lodgings,' M. Duclos tells her, his tone still smooth but now inviting no argument, 'where I will attend you on the instant.'

A chair is summoned and she sits erect with her eyes closed as it sways and lurches away uphill to the north of the city, behind the Crescent and into a new square. Propelled by some outside force she sounds the bell at the door where she is set down, and enters without a word when the door opens. The butler shows no surprise at seeing a young lady unattended but ushers her into the library where she sits obedient, without interest in her surroundings. When M. Duclos arrives she neither moves nor raises her head. Someone later pushes a tray of bread and a bowl of broth before her. When she has eaten she looks up to see the Frenchman draped across a chair observing her.

'I knew your father,' he remarks, pouring her wine from a very small decanter.

She blinks over adjustment from the horrors of the city, to this house, and then back across the years to Paris and memories she had always avoided. Most of all, of her father. M. Duclos can never have been a friend of her father!

'There are plots against us, against our country,' he says, the dark eyes boring into her skull through her eyeballs, forcing, drilling deeper and deeper through their sockets, penetrating her very mind. 'Plots against *la France*.'

His voice is deep dark velvet, soft, enfolding. She sinks little by little into its embrace, caressed, calmed, lulled by a susurrus of familiar words and phrases. And then: 'Beauchamp – Sir Roger Beauchamp,' he says.

Again she is forced to blink in order to understand. Sir Roger? What connection can this man have with Sir Roger, too?

'I believe,' the velvet tones slide now, the finest silk, 'that your friend Sir Roger knows of this plot; I believe he would tell you.'

'No, no,' she murmurs, aware only of a shadow.

'You care for your country – you are your father's daughter.' (Political factions young Polly knows nothing about; she only senses good and evil, which we know have no relevance in politics.) 'I will give you shelter. I will not inform M. Bryant where you abide. I will feed and protect you and will place you in the path of Sir Roger. In small return for my patronage all I ask of you is to discover this information to me. This will make no harm to Sir Roger, he need know nothing of our exchange. That goes, *bien entendue*?'

Polly's sense of evil has been dulled by the strange wine. She sees only sunlit images of Sir Roger's handsome head, his elegant form, hears again his offer of marriage, recognises that Sir Roger is her sole means of escape. '*Entendu,*' she agrees. 'But he may not tell me.'

'He will.' M. Duclos's expression is similar to Jim's. Each knows the bargaining power of a maidenhead. 'Tomorrow,' he says, 'Sir Roger will be at the Pump Room at ten o'clock. That I know. For now you will wish to repose yourself, I am sure. I shall have you conducted to your room.'

Chapter 17

'Shall I compare thee to a summer's day?'

Roger lay in the long grass beside a stream at Nettleton, delighted to ecstasy by the sunlight burning into his bare arms and filtering on to pools of fading bluebells across the water.

'You can't,' said Connie, stripping grass seed from a stem between her teeth. 'More like an autumn's day I fear! But I'm sure today measures up to Shakespeare's. What bliss to have this sunshine and such peace. Even the woodpigeons laid on to coo! You've arranged it all quite beautifully.'

He rolled on to his back to gaze at the sky. 'It's a beautiful sonnet,' he murmured. 'They all are. And they don't fit my theory. Have you noticed how most writing, modern writing, particularly letters or poems addressed to someone, are designed to draw attention to the author? It's all 'Look what I have to say, or what I've been clever enough to recognise, or how I interpret it!' It's all narcissism. All modern art is egocentric, subjective.'

'Oh, I don't know.' She could think of no examples either way. Roger would do this, make some strange statement and then ask her opinion to support it. It made her feel nervous and stupid and she was beginning to wonder if he did it on purpose. Would Sylvia instantly produce chapter and verse, argue, cut him down? She doubted that. Perhaps it was a product of Latin coaching. Perhaps it was his way to show superiority. 'I simply don't know. I don't understand modern poetry. You tell me.'

He loved that. Sylvia probably ignored him and polished her jewels and flipped through *House & Garden*. 'Nowadays it would be something like: Shall I compare thee to my bank balance – or my other clients – or my golf clubs – or that divine little bistro I discovered on Fulham Road! At best it would be 'my vegetable plot' or 'my roses'. All possessive and personal. And this work of art would go on to demonstrate the author's cunning or prowess. The only detachment is to be found in lists and *aides memoire*.'

'That's silly,' she said. 'You weren't talking about detachment.'

He sighed and said, 'How very perceptive. You know, there are cleverpusses who'd take that *really* seriously and turn their tiny brains inside out to get at the fundament, the nub, the reason behind the reason. Those bloody Freudians! They're out to kill all spontaneity and romance. Oh, *hell*!' He shouted that to the sky, startling Connie and the woodpigeons, and sat up to dig his heels into the grass and glare across at the bluebells.

'I'm *sorry*!' He twisted away from her so that she could only hear his anguish. 'I didn't mean to bring that up. I'd no intention – ha! Read what you will into that!'

She had never seen him behave so and could think of nothing safe to say. She reached a hand to touch his shoulder and he flinched.

'I can't bear it,' she said. 'Won't you tell me?' The embargoes flapped and waddled like carrion crows around them. 'It's absurd that we can't talk about anything that matters!'

'Absurdity,' he muttered. 'All is absurdity. Sisyphus and his bloody stone. Do you realise – ? No, don't! Stay just as you are. That's what I like about you. That's what I love –' He swung round to stare at her without any emotion that she could interpret as love. 'Just an endlessly repeated pattern, no meaning to it at all. We think we have knowledge and understanding, but that makes no difference. The same old urges, the same mistakes repeated, time after time, generation after generation. I ask you, where's the meaning in all that?'

With time to think, she felt sure she could come up with something. 'Surely we learn by our mistakes?'

'We *do*? You're joking! We repeat and repeat, in a blind search for fulfilment perhaps – we *have* to give it a reason, make it sound logical! Those psychiatric mandarins who sit in judgement over us, they're no better, but they tidy it all into boxes. So neat, so clever! If you've read Freud you'll see the absurdity of that. Jung and his myths. The human desire to find an answer, to explain the silly pattern. There *is* no explanation!'

Does it matter? she wondered. And why pick on me? Do you do this to Sylvia, and does she understand? Connie wanted, more than anything at that moment, to comfort him. All her maternal instincts gathered to soothe and protect. Hugh didn't need her; the children were making it quite apparent that they wanted no help or involvement from her. And here was Roger demanding reassurance like a child – and she could think of nothing to say.

'Look,' she said, 'it's a beautiful day, and this is quite the prettiest spot for a picnic. Let's enjoy it while we can. Isn't it time to open the wine?' She spread the cloth and arranged the sandwiches she had made. He took the bottle and uncorked it. They faced each other across the space she had created and slowly his torment changed to a sort of laughter.

'I love you,' he said as if he meant it. 'I really do. Come over here,' and he pulled her across to him. 'A loaf of bread beneath the bough, a flask of wine, a book of verse – and thou beside me singing in the wilderness – Oh wilderness were paradise enow!'

'It's ham sandwiches, I'm afraid,' she said after he had held her for some time but showed no inclination to kiss her. 'And there's a wasp drowning in your wine.'

They wandered along the edge of the stream picking cow parsley and sniffing the garlic flowers in the shade. Everything smelled green, succulent, the only sound an occasional splash and the tinkle of water over stones.

'You know Max Masterman, don't you?' Roger had broken the rules with the release of some kind of personal detail (if only she could work out what it was) and it was only fair for her to sound him out about Sylvia's analyst.

'I do,' Roger replied with his closing-down expression and a burst of speed up the bank and into the meadow. 'Why?' He turned at the top of the bank to challenge her, with no offer of a hand, suspicious.

'I'm worried about him and Sally.'

'Max and *Sally*?' His face cleared. He sounded like Baz but was watching her more closely and without Baz's cackle of laughter. 'Why?' he asked, more lightly.

'Well.' She tried to break a stem, twisted it, pulled, and discarded the frayed mess. 'I won't bore you with the details but I've a suspicion he deals in drugs. Do you think that's possible? I mean –' She didn't want to mention Sylvia and that he should have some knowledge of Max's practices.

He reached a hand down the bank for her now, all smiles. 'I think that's most unlikely,' he reassured her. 'I'd never imagine him as a drug pusher.' He smiled away downstream into the half-tones under oak trees. 'And I'm sure he won't harm Sally. Save your fears for something more tangible, dearie.'

They strolled on in harmony, Roger entertaining her with snatches of poetry or silly jokes about Friesian cows. By the time they thought of driving home, shadows reached long and low over the water meadows. 'Will you be gated for being late?' he asked. 'Will the Duchess be waiting at the window?'

Connie stopped dead. 'What did you say?'

'It's all right, dearie – I was only making a rather crude allusion to your mother-in-law and her somewhat duchessy way of dressing. No offence intended, I assure you!'

'You think she looks like a duchess? That's fascinating, so do I!'

'Very mildly fascinating, I suppose.' He dismissed it. 'You can blame me, if it will help. Do you think it will set tongues wagging?' He sounded as if he rather hoped it would.

Edith and Aunt Fay were nowhere to be seen. Nor was Hugh. Connie had the kitchen to herself.

****

Our lovely Polly awakes with renewed innocence and joy to a sparkling day. She has slept soundly and without fear in M. Duclos's house, and anticipation of seeing Sir Roger springs her out of bed and to the window. Yes, a jewel of a day, a day to be treasured! Today she will put off those Miss-ish airs – a habit which does not come naturally to her, nor becomes her – and will accept Sir Roger's proposal, whatever it may be. That decision taken, she floats about the room in her shift, peeping at herself in the mirror, smiling, teasing her hair into a halo of light. Her lemon-yellow dress and petticoats have been cleaned for her and the stains of ale and mud removed from Annie's green cloak. She dresses, makes a few more pirouettes before the glass and skips downstairs.

M. Duclos has been pacing the hall and invites her to join him for breakfast while he sends for a chair to carry her to the Pump Room. She had forgotten her mission for him but now renews her pledge to discover any plot against France.

'I shall wait,' he tells her. 'I shall be waiting. I shall be there.'

For a moment she is sobered by his ominous tone and then, '*D'accord*,' she says. Sir Roger can deal with him.

At the Pump Room she leaves her chair with the grace of a lady of fashion, enters the building with equal aplomb and is swallowed by a crowd so great that she can see or identify no one. Up and down she hurries, in and out and around chattering groups. No need to look at faces; all the gentlemen are either too fat or too thin to be her hero. The Tompion clock strikes the half-hour. She could weep with vexation but is saved that ignominy by a hint of blue over by the pump where the prescribed three pints of water are being drunk by those with the health to do so. Sir Roger is in conversation with the same recruiting officer who had been bribing Our Jim.

Polly waits and watches, anxious now not to be recognised, until the young captain bows out and Sir Roger turns his attention to the antics in the King's Bath. As she approaches he swings his quizzing glass to focus on her and exclaims: 'My dearest child! Why here? Is Lady Blakeney with you? I had not expected— !' Again her appearance has overwhelmed him, ruffled his complaisance to reveal what could be taken for a natural emotion.

'Lady Blakeney is not at home,' she replies and against all reason now bursts into tears.

Sir Roger leads her out – neither of them noticing M. Duclos sheltered near the door – and sends a boy for his carriage. He tilts her face to mop the tears and gazes deep into her eyes. 'You will come with me now?'

As they bowl through the countryside in his phaeton she tells him all, including her strange mission for the Frenchman, while he clasps her hands, observes every shadow cross her face, waits gravely for her to finish. 'I cannot understand,' she exclaims at the end, 'why M. Duclos should think that you, who I believe never leave this country, are involved in some plot against France. You are not a sailor; you are not in the Army – or have you been recruited by that military gentleman? No, I cannot believe that! Do you have any idea what it is he suspects?'

They have reached the hamlet of Nettleton and Sir Roger orders his coachman to stop the carriage and rest the horses. 'It is a perfect day,' he remarks. 'Shall we walk in the water meadows and, if you wish, I will tell you what your friend fears.'

'He is not my friend!'

'You owe him some explanation, though, and we must decide what that shall be. Fortunately,' Sir Roger leads her through the long grass and meadowsweet towards the stream, his gaze fixed on the mist of bluebells under the beech trees, 'I am as aware of M. Duclos as he is of me. He is a professional politician, a strong republican as perhaps you have noticed? A Jacobin, in short. And he has wind of plans to restore the monarchy in France. For some time now we have been raising an army near my estates in Hampshire to sail under the Bourbon flag. All is nearly prepared. Very soon an Armada of four thousand men funded by our government will cross the Channel to help the Royalists. What support we shall find there remains to be seen, but it should forestall any invasion attempts on these shores for a while.'

They pause beside the stream and Polly stoops to gather the lacy sprays of cow parsley. 'But why should M. Duclos be here rather than in Hampshire? Why was he at Hallatrow Hall? Surely he must have spies who can count the soldiers, watch their movements, where the army is gathering?'

Sir Roger is contemplating her with an expression which has little to do with spies and troop movements. 'The grass is quite dry,' he points out. 'Shall we sit and listen to the doves up there in the trees, and forget about the French? "Come live with me and be my love, and we will all the pleasures prove –" '

He shrugs off the coat of forget-me-not blue, takes her in a passionate embrace and they sink down together until the grasses meet above their heads. 'By shallow rivers –' he murmurs hot against her cheek, his hand rifling her petticoats.

* * * * * * *

'Mrs Bryant?'

Connie jumped, her eyes misted still with bluebells and blue sky, still gazing upwards through the fronds of grass. Automatically she smoothed her skirt, touched the golden curls which Sir Roger must have ruffled into disarray; guiltily she returned to the kitchen and her whisk in a bowl of eggs. 'I'm sorry,' she said for no good reason, playing for time.

Lewis Foster hesitated in the doorway from the yard, delighted to find Mrs B in, fearful of intruding. She looked a picture there by that antique pine table beating up something, the perfect wife with her sleeves rolled up, arms a healthy pink from the afternoon's sun. Probably been planting out tomatoes or weeding the borders; now getting on with supper. Not like some he could mention. 'I don't want to bother you.'

'Of course not! Do please come in.' That lovely smile she had, really welcoming, putting aside the beater.

'Don't let me interrupt. I can't stop for long, I've got Emily in a bath.'

'I'm sure she'll be all right. How about a drink?' To his amazement she got a bottle from under the sink and thick tumblers, sloshed in the whisky and filled them from the tap. Not her usual style; he felt one of the family, very honoured.

'Cheers!' he said. 'This is nice. But don't let me hold you up. I'll just sit here.'

'Is Annie back?' she asked, pushing up her sleeves and sitting opposite him as if she had all the time in the world.

'Oh, that's what I came to say – no, she's not. Weren't they going to some meeting or something? I'd have thought they'd be back by now.'

'I think it was Mrs Midgley's Tea, wasn't it? You know, a Bring & Buy for Party funds. Surely you should know that? Perhaps they stopped off for a drink on their way home.'

Mrs B didn't seem fussed, but then it wasn't in her to be suspicious. Seven-thirty was not the time to come in (or not come in!) from a tea party. That he also knew. And no supper laid for Emily. He had been weighing it up for some time now and had decided Mrs B must be warned. Not to gossip, not to ask for sympathy, she would understand. For her own good.

'Do you think – er, there might be something going on between them? Between your husband and my Annie, I mean? I don't want to worry you, but they do seem to be seeing rather a lot of each other, don't you think? I mean, Annie's always going off for little walks – to cool her head from her studies is what she says. But I don't think there's much studying going on. She's doing an Open University degree, you know.' He was proud of that.

'Yes, I know. I mean, I know about the degree course.'

Mrs B looked flustered and he regretted breaking it to her like that. Perhaps he should have confronted Annie first, but she would only have laughed at him.

'Hugh's been going for walks, too,' she said rather vaguely, as if she didn't understand or didn't care. 'But what surprises me is that they use the Tory party as a cover. I thought Annie was Labour. That's the strange thing.'

'Annie went Lib Dem a bit back. They do that, you know, quite a lot of the Lefts are coming round to our way of thinking via the Alliance. I ask you, what's the point of voting for them?' He hadn't thought of Mrs B being anything other than Conservative – Mr B hadn't hinted – but now he had a nasty feeling, seeing her look like that. The last thing he wanted was to upset her. 'You know what I mean,' he added, to water it down. 'Although she says she doesn't like Cameron she's right behind us, I think – she must be.' He'd assumed she must be. All those little jibes and snide remarks were just Annie being difficult as she'd always been, trying to confuse him.

'It seems odd to me.' Mrs B finished her drink, too polite to argue.

'But that's not the point.' He drank up, too, feeling quite bold. It had been at least a triple-blip whisky by his reckoning. 'What do you think we should do about them?'

'Do?' She fetched the bottle and poured them both another without asking. 'I don't see what we can do. It can't be very serious – they don't really have the opportunity to go to bed together, do they?'

He was shocked. Fancy her being so matter-of-fact! She sounded almost like Annie. But of course she was still trying to work it all out. 'I was thinking of sounding Annie out, though I don't think it'll help much. I wondered if you'd talk to Mr Bryant? If they both know we know…'

'Oh I don't know about that.' She looked as if that would be interfering, as if she'd rather not know or appear to know. 'If they're not doing any harm.'

Here he felt he had to make a stand. She might be a woman, but that was too much. 'Harm?' he said, as gently as possible. 'They are harming our marriages, they are threatening the whole fabric of our families! If this is allowed to go on, heaven knows where it will end! It's got to be stopped before some really serious harm's done.'

The Bryant car spun down the drive and swirled into the yard. Lewis looked at Mrs B meaningfully. 'We really ought to talk to them,' he said, drinking his whisky too quickly and choking. 'For the sake of our marriages.'

****

His hand rifling her petticoats, his voice hot, muffled with desire. And the grasses fluttering, waving, against a sky of forget-me-not blue. No more words, no more French politics, until the rising and falling, soaring and dying is done and Polly lies abandoned and in some confusion to focus again on the blue above. No blood and guts, no screams of agony. Virginity lost but also regained. Sir Roger had swept her clean of all the fears and squalor of Avon Street and has rededicated by his kisses the battered temple of her soul. Now she can look on him as an equal.

'You have a wife already?' Now, also, she can raise Annie's warning.

Sir Roger falls on his back beside her, gazing up into the same sky. 'I have.' He sighs but makes no other movement away from her. 'And I will tell you about that, too.'

Their bodies rest against each other as in a twin coffin, shrouded in meadowsweet and the tall grasses, while he tells her about Sylvia: her terrible childbirth, their stillborn son and how, ever since, she has been demented, childlike, shut away on his estates in Hampshire in the care of his old nurse.

'And Widbrook?' she asks. 'How long will you remain at Widbrook?'

'If you were there,' he rolls over to contemplate the flutter of a pulse in her soft white neck, 'I would remain for eternity – hours, days, years, for ever. Widbrook was left to me when my maternal grandfather died and I am engaged in restoring the old house. When that is done – I had intended to return to Hampshire; I must return there briefly tomorrow. But after the Armadilla has sailed, if you were there I would make Widbrook my home. Nurse will care for Sylvia, there is nothing she wants from me. Although there is no possibility that I can make you my wife in name, in all else we will 'all the pleasures prove'. Come? You will?'

'And M. Duclos – what of him? What do I tell him?'

Sir Roger sits up to consider the uncertain darkness far down the stream. 'Aye, M. Duclos,' he mutters. 'Not only Duclos but also your guardian Hugo Bryant. They are in league, those two. Hugo wants no part in our support for the Comte d'Artois. He watches me, and Duclos waits on him. For now it would be dangerous for you to be seen at Widbrook, while I am seldom there.' He frowns out across the sea of wild flowers. 'I could return you to the Duchess – Duclos would anticipate that – on the understanding that I am making ready the house to receive you as its mistress. I could arrange that you return to the Hall as a daughter. The Duchess I am sure would protect you.'

'And M. Duclos?' Can she now trust her lover to see that she is safe from the debauchery at Hallatrow Hall? She quite enjoys the idea of parading this arrangement before Mistress Annie. She feels safe now with Sir Roger and gives herself willingly into his hands. No longer need she fear for her future. Sir Roger will take care of her and every detail until they are united forever at Widbrook.

'Duclos will no doubt follow you there and you can tell him – tell him that my interest now lies in Somerset, that I am no longer involved in recruiting. You can tell him that I am a libertine, that lust and lechery have got the better of me, that I am a lost cause, irretrievably lost to the rapture of your embrace! He will believe that. Anyone would believe that. I believe that!' And he falls on her again with a passion too impetuous for her to resist.

The grasses sing and Polly is overcome by inexpressible tenderness, all on a summer's day.

Chapter 18

No, said Mark. He'd changed his mind. BJ had gone to Stonehenge but he and Baz thought it was all too much hassle; besides, they had a job to do.

Connie's relief exploded across the café table and drew pale glances from the Thursday dole crowd. If she had prayed for it she would now be on her knees in thanksgiving; instead she knocked the tomato sauce bottle and embarrassed her son even more by not noticing. 'Darling, I'm so – I'm sure it was the right decision. Much more sensible! And a *job* you say?'

Sunshine belted through the window making a halo of Mark's bushy hair, dazzling her eyes with tears, shading his face so that she could not see his expression. Legs whined and pulled at her string while Mark scooped the sauce onto his plate with a paper napkin.

'Not really that kind of a job,' he said. 'We've got this room in the squat where we're monitoring *police* activity –'

'Police activity? I thought they were monitoring yours?'

'Two can play that game,' he growled. 'We're keeping records of their behaviour. It's going to be a sort of mammoth fact sheet. Time somebody did it. No point waffling when you get to court – you need hard facts, dates, places, how they carry on. We've got to be prepared. Can't do any Sabbing in the summer, while the hunts are laid off, and it all ties in. We're getting to be a sort of news centre – see what I mean? – it's all being sent in to us!' His voice sounded as if he were grinning. 'I told you I'd be running a proper business before long, remember?'

'Yes darling.' She remembered. 'Are you still living in the benders?' Perhaps he would come home, now that he had an 'office' to escape to.

'We don't want to give that up, particularly now. Anyway there's no room at the squat – we need the space for the paperwork.' He sounded efficient, though she wondered about the paperwork. He had never been tidy at home and she doubted if anyone could read his handwriting.

'We're doing it for Max,' he said.

'*Max*?'

'Well, *indirectly* for him. He's interested, you know, in police brutality – law and order, that sort of thing.'

She wanted to warn him, but of what? 'Why is Max so interested?'

'Oh, politics, you know. The behaviour of Cameron's pigs. Ammunition at the election. That sort of thing. He's some kind of news bloke for the Alliance. Well, we don't mind who gives us the paper, do we? Doesn't make any difference to us. It's a bit of a laugh really – he thinks we're sort of spying for him.'

* * * * * * *

The Bath Chronicle – June 18, 1795

Six thouſand uniform ſuits are making in London partly for the emigrant corps deſtined for the coaſt of Brittany, and partly for the recruits expected to be found there. The buttons bear in the centre an impression of the antient Crown of France ſurrounded by three *fleurs de lys*.

June 25, 1795

The nine regiments of French Emigrants in the pay of Great Britain, which continue on the Continent, have received orders to embark without the leaſt delay; they are deſtined to form the ſecond diviſion of the Royal army in Brittany.

July 23, 1795

Their mageſties and the Princeſſes have laudably determined to diſcontinue the uſe of hair-powder.

And a recipe on

How to boil Rice, to make it an excellent ſubſtitute for Bread.

Expedition to the Coaſt of France.
Quiberon Bay, July 23, at noon: The expedition is at length terminated. The whole Emigrant army is either killed, or wounded, or taken priſoners. On the 21st, at night, this disaſterous event happened.

* * * * * * *

Connie left the Reference Library lisping. She had stopped there to check the fines of 1646 for throwing things into the Baths – 3/4d for a dead cat, 6/8d for a clothed person (more, or less, for a naked person?) – and had been seduced by the newspaper files on microfiche. Just a quick look through 1795 proved irresistible. How little the local paper had changed. Jobs for honest domestics, horses for sale, houses for hire, garden produce – 'Brown Globe Artichoke Plants, at two pounds ten shillings per hundred'. Little hard news.

Sylvia was playing bridge and Roger had invited Connie to tea. He must be proving something because, since that first day, he had never again taken her into his house. She felt she understood him quite well now. Although they both enjoyed their picnics out in the countryside, perhaps the time had come. Perhaps he needed the privacy of walls, the protection of a known space, before he could say anything, do anything that mattered?

As she crossed the Park and followed the curve of the Crescent pavement she was wondering what she herself needed. Did she want him to jump on her, declare love or lust? Could she, after all those years of unquestioned fidelity, suddenly leap into bed with another man? Sir Roger could get away with anything; she had no qualms or conscience about anything she did with Roger's shadow. Now that she was getting to know the handsome gentleman with the saturnine smile, she was even reconciled to not living happily ever after as Lady Beauchamp – the delicious delightful moments alone with him (and she hoped for many more) were reward enough. No need with Sir Roger to worry about fidelity, treachery or the Future. Polly is a simple, unconcerned, adventurous young woman, the opposite in every respect to Connie. And Polly doesn't have to consider Hugo's feelings. Would she, Connie, fall blithely into Roger's bed? Unblithely, then? When it came to the crunch – it wouldn't be fair on Hugh, but yes, she probably would. The possibility excited her, quickened her step.

Roger welcomed her with his usual apologetic smile and holding a cucumber. 'I'd thought we'd have cucumber sandwiches – very appropriate for a formal invitation to tea – but I've made a hash of the bread and this isn't slicing well either. How people manage with something squidgy like a tomato, I can't imagine!' He looked endearingly helpless, slightly wicked with the forelock falling over his eyes, like a small boy caught attempting a good deed. His smile warmed her and she wanted to reach across that invisible barrier between them and hug him. She was touched by his efforts to make a really 'formal' tea. So sweet of him! What had she ever done, so obviously for him?

Tea was laid on a card table in the drawing room; an unnecessary number of crumbling crust-less sandwiches and, she noticed, three of everything.

'A real tea party,' she remarked, sadly. 'Is it a birthday?'

He laughed. 'Don't think I'd celebrate *that*! No, I've asked Max Masterman along – you know, you keep asking about him. And he's keen to meet you.'

Oh, *really*? 'But we've met already.' She tried not to sound ungrateful, disappointed. 'What a nice idea.'

'Come and look at my etchings before he arrives. I've been wanting to show you, I'm rather proud of them and you'll be interested.'

He led her into a room dominated by a four-poster bed. If Max hadn't been invited she would have been frightened by the indelicacy of cucumber, etchings, bedroom. It was as if he were deliberately leading her on, making some kind of statement. She felt embarrassed standing in Sylvia's bedroom on her lime-green carpet, staring at a slinky silk dressing gown and swansdown mules placed almost by design, everything just so as if expecting a camera crew from *Interiors*.

'Your eighteenth century aristocrats,' Roger was saying, 'had a mania for erotic pictures. These were all the rage in your favourite years. Not particularly erotic nowadays, perhaps. Hogarth's *Marriage à la Mode* of the 1740s, here, are more pretty than improper, and the Gillray is more of a record of what's on sale for sex, a pictorial satire if you like. Rowlandson produced these, here, for the Prince Regent.'

He had moved on, leaving her to wonder about the bed, far too neat and cunningly tucked and pleated for casual sex. On either side hung paintings of a very modern young man, naked and rather green, the brushwork concentrating on his genitalia. Connie turned quickly to a print of a fully clothed and be-wigged lady in a bath showing a little too much ankle. Sylvia's pictures – assuming the young man belonged to Sylvia – suited the colours of the room but, to Connie, jarred with everything else. Strange, for a well-known interior decorator.

'You were admiring Neville,' said Roger. 'Much argument has passed over hanging him here, I can tell you!'

'I'm not surprised.' But even interior decorators must be allowed lapses of taste in their own bedrooms. 'Still, you don't have to look at him – from bed, I mean.'

He laughed at that. She should not have mentioned the bed. The bedroom overlooked the garden and she caught a movement amongst the rosebushes. Putting on her glasses again, removed to study the prints, she saw a figure strolling towards the window. A moment later and the face was pressed against a pane, flattening the nose, but even with that distortion Connie recognised Max.

'Wait for me before you start!' he called, and disappeared.

Roger laughed again and saying 'Good old Max!' hurried past her to greet Sylvia's analyst at the kitchen door.

'It's not on, I know, to spy through bedroom windows!' Max had a forced, jokey air today, as if he were trying to make the right impression while not knowing what it should be. 'But I have a key, you see, to the garden gate so that I can take a short cut. It's ten minutes longer to walk round. I live just behind the Crescent, you see, and dear Roger took pity on my shoe leather.'

While he talked he was watching her, probably anticipating resentment, disbelief, aggression. Connie kept her face, she hoped, expressionless. She didn't like his easy familiarity. A psychiatrist should have more restraint.

'I was showing Connie my etchings,' said Roger with unwarranted pride. 'And I don't think she's too keen on Neville, are you dearie?'

She didn't care for that, either. He seemed almost to be laughing at her and his familiarity in front of Max seemed almost coarse. She ignored them both.

'Neville's not everybody's cup of tea,' said Max as they returned to the kitchen.

Did he admire Sylvia's taste in pictures? 'But you're honoured to be given the opportunity to decide.'

Connie sat tidily, formally, knees and ankles together, just like her mother, while Max sprawled his arms and legs to occupy most of the apricot-coloured sofa. Demonstrating he felt at ease, at home, she thought. Roger fussed with the tea, apologised about the sandwiches, courted them both, tried to relax Connie and amuse Max.

'For Christ's sake, Roger, sit down!' Max patted the sofa and withdrew a leg to make space. 'Doesn't he make you nervous?' he asked Connie.

'No, not really,' she replied, as coldly as possible without being rude.

'Connie's worried about Sally,' said Roger.

Connie felt the heat rise up her neck to flood her face. Max was the last person with whom she would discuss Sally. She was surprised at Roger.

'Ah Sally!' Max waved an arm in a vaguely expressive gesture. 'A super girl, Sally. You've no call to be worried about her, my dear. She knows just what she's doing.'

What a silly remark! Or perhaps it was deeply meaningful. Psychiatrists, Connie recalled, are supposed never to tell you anything but to lead you to make your own judgements. She wouldn't demean herself by asking what he meant. Nor, sadly, dared she mention Mark and Max's support for the police monitoring, though she would dearly have loved to show him that she knew. He must think she was very stupid and out of touch. By now she was feeling annoyed enough to forget about Roger, annoyed enough to refuse more tea and to flounce out and go home and vote Conservative. That would show him! Max, she had sensed all along, was a parcel of all that was evil – in either century – nasty, mean, devious, and smiling at her as if he knew exactly what she was thinking.

'I was introduced to your husband the other day,' Max said with a serpent's eye and flicker of the tongue so similar to Connie's image of M. Duclos that she showed the remark more surprise than it deserved. 'One of those political bun fights; a rallying of our troops before we even know when the battle will commence.' He paused, made a cathedral of his long white fingers to the bridge of his nose. 'You weren't there.'

'Why should I be?' Nothing would induce her at this moment to declare that she preferred his Party.

'I only wondered at his being there with a recognised Liberal. Perhaps you have met the lovely Mrs Foster?'

'We both know her well, she lives next door to us.' It would be nice to be able to add: 'and actually I was with her husband at the time'. The desire to hit him, hurt him, destroy him, was growing to suffocate her. 'She might be changing sides, you know.' That should concern him! If he were as keen as Hugh, he would rush straight round to Annie and reclaim her with honeyed policies.

'Perhaps,' he said, as if he could rely on her, and Connie wondered yet again if Annie was some kind of spy reporting back on Hugh's kitchen map and Mrs Midgley's Bring & Buy tea party.

'I think we can count on Connie,' said Roger with a sweetly

intimate smile that at any other time would have melted her heart. 'Connie thinks just as we do on all the main topics.'

But she couldn't swallow the link with Max and, making a show of checking her watch, cried, 'Goodness, if I don't leave now I'll be snarled up in the rush hour! No, please don't move. It was really interesting to meet you again.'

Roger escorted her out to the street where he held her hands and gave her one of his special smiles, apologetic, amused, rueful. 'He's not usually so bitchy,' Roger said. 'I don't understand it.'

Connie sat in the car waiting for the traffic to pass, filled, overspilling, overwhelmed by an emotion which could only be hatred. She hated Max. He was M. Duclos incarnate, loathsome, evil. She watched her hands trembling on the steering wheel as if they were not a part of her. Never before had she felt such hostility, such a strange conviction. Max was the agent of doom. Max would bring them all crashing down.

* * * * * * *

Sir Roger takes his leave of lovely Polly with much rapturous sighing and with promises to return early the next day before he sets off for Hampshire.

'If only I could keep you with me,' he groans. 'I cannot bear to be parted from you for one hour. But you are safer here and the Duchess has promised to care for you like a daughter. Remember we must keep up the pretence that I am very much occupied at Widbrook and have no intention of leaving Somerset County. Should you meet M. Duclos –'

'M. Duclos will hear no truth from me.'

'Good, brave Polly!' He sweeps her into an embrace of such passion that her senses reel, but this surge of delight must be stemmed and he rides away with many a turn of the head and many a wave.

Mistress Annie has observed all from a high window. She, like Hugo, is engaged in passing secrets of troop movements to M. Duclos in exchange for handsome reward. Both she and Hugo are delighted to have poor Polly back at the Hall. By watching and questioning her, they know they should hear all they need about Sir Roger. How endearing, how positively naïve of him to entrust his betrothed to the Duchess until Widbrook is prepared to his satisfaction to receive her! Annie, now promised to Hugo and so no longer interested in Sir Roger, had forgotten the rumours of his being married already.

She greets Polly warmly, leads her swiftly past the cellar stair, shows her to her own room where a cot has been set up for her 'sister'. Offering the choice of her dresses, she asks how Polly enjoyed her visit to Bath and listens with true amazement to her adventures.

'Will M. Duclos be here tonight?' asks Polly, anxious to disillusion that evil man about Sir Roger.

'He may be.' Annie would prefer to sell that information herself.

Later, M. Duclos hears the same story from them all, with the embellishment from Polly that Sir Roger is lost to the Cause because of his desire for her. She tells him this so prettily, with such modest confusion, that he has to believe her.

'So he will remain here?' M. Duclos presses. 'He will not leave Widbrook?'

'No, sir. He told me—'

'*Entendu*.'

Duclos and Hugo plot together that the very next night they will surprise Sir Roger in his home, take him prisoner and interrogate him. If he is no longer in charge of the Armadilla recruitment, he will know who is. He will also have a fair idea of when the expedition is due to embark. The time of watching and waiting is over.

* * * * * * *

Aunt Fay was watching for Connie's return.

'My dear, at last! Come quickly, please!' Her fingers were plucking at the ends of her pink cardigan, dragging it to more than usual dips and distortions. 'Sally's home and in such a state! Hugh can't cope with her and I must admit I cannot understand a word she says. She is quite distraught, poor lamb.'

Connie rushed past her and past Edith like a monolith in the hall, to the kitchen, where Sally crouched sobbing against the table. Hugh stopped mid-pace, shoulders hunched, hands rattling the change in his pockets, and turned an accusing eye on his wife.

'I can't get any sense out of her. Rushing in, quite hysterical. Where have you been, for heaven's sake? You deal with her!' But he looked vulnerable, helpless, and the accusation was tipped with relief at seeing her.

'Darling!' Connie dropped to the floor beside her daughter, pulling her from the table into her arms. 'Darling, what is it? What's the matter? Sweetie, *tell* me! What's happened?'

Sally choked and howled and clung tightly to her mother, rubbing wet hair and face against her neck, gusting great moans into her ear. 'I can't, I can't – horrible, horrible –'

'Come on, darling.' Connie pulled her up, groped for a chair and cradled her more effectively on her lap, scooping her close, murmuring, stroking, soothing. 'Come on, darling. Tell me. Don't cry. Come on, sweetie, please. Darling, please.'

Gradually the sobs became mixed with sighs, quietened to a whimper. 'H-horrible!' she repeated, scrubbing her hands over her face, knuckling her eyes. 'Mum, she's dead! Horribly sick and dead!'

'Who? Who's dead, sweetie?'

'Z-Zoe! Mandy and me f-found her. All spilt drink and sick and – ugh! C-completely dead. Ch-Charles said.'

'Charles was there?'

'He came down. He was awfully upset and he got the doctor. He couldn't get hold of Max. And then he drove me home. I said Mandy and Sharon could come, you wouldn't mind, but they said they'd stay. Someone has to do the Bull's Eye. Sh-Sharon was being very practical. But I c-couldn't bear to be there tonight. I know I'm a wimp, but it was all so –' Sally shuddered and hid her face.

'No, you're quite right, darling. It's all right now, darling. You're all right here. Come on now.' Connie fumbled for a handkerchief in her pocket, mopped Sally's face. 'Come on, blow! That's better!'

Just like her baby again. Poor little Sally, wickedly brave, galloping away leaving Daddy and Mummy terrified for her, and then the fall and the screams and the tears as she and Hugh panted down the lane to rescue her. The same heart-stopping sobs and wails, the same tear-strewn cuddles and relief. All Connie could feel now, as before, was relief that Sally was unhurt. And, as before, she then held out a hand to Hugh, to console, for consolation. And he was there to take it. She burst into tears.

It was a strange week. Sally had end-of-term exams; mock-mock, as she called them, and not that funny. Hugh restrained himself from asking about her future plans or her past activity, or from making any remarks about her being suddenly at home. He and Connie watched each other, noticed each other; any smile or gesture seemed significant; they kept meeting or passing on the stairs, stepping aside with a laugh. Laughing. Connie felt she hadn't laughed for years. Not since they moved from the Coach

House and the children grew up. Both she and Hugh fussed over Sally, asked about her mock-mock papers, read them through, tried to understand them, drove her to school, fetched her home, took mugs of coffee to her room. Mealtimes were enlivened by feeble jokes about Biology or History or French (following the exam of the day) and by parental attempts at wit or comprehension. Aunt Fay expanded, competed, became even more girlish and giggly in her pleasure at this change of spirit in the house. Granny made her remarks, which everyone found clever and amusing.

Connie found that she was too busy for Roger, just at the moment. Max had not only spoilt the tea party but somehow had wormed his way between them. She would have liked to discuss this with Roger, but sensed that Max slotted into most embargoes. For now, her family involved her and she returned to what seemed like a life of childhood, all dew and sunlight, bright colours, song.

The exams over, Sally said she must face the flat in Avon Street. She had phoned Charles, she had met Mandy one afternoon. An inquest was being held on Zoe's death. There were plans to refurbish Hell. Lots of plans.

'I think –' said Connie. 'Couldn't you work at the Bull's Eye from here during the summer holidays? I'm sure you'd be happier in the country. You could teach Emily to ride – Mr Foster said he wants her to have proper lessons.'

Hugh put on an expression disturbingly familiar to all and Sally began her mule face, but stopped. 'Look, I've got to go back, you must see that. Like remounting after a fall. I must go back and sort things out, sort out feelings and everything. I'll be back, I promise. Please don't be annoyed. It's not that I don't want to be here – you've both been super. Just give me time.'

When she had gone Hugh said, 'If she's gone back because of that vagabond, I'll—'

Edith said, 'And so she comes and goes as she pleases, just as she pleases, just as usual. Whatever changes?'

Aunt Fay looked mournfully from one to the other and took up her knitting with a sigh.

Chapter 19

But the first one home was Mark.

After a glorious June, July dismayed the local Conservative Association with storms. Cold drizzly days alternated with fearsome forecasts for their Garden Party at Hallatrow Hall.

'A fete worse than death!' Edith was reduced to remarking. Hundreds would come if the sun shone, with no particular interest that their fun-money would print blue leaflets to be scattered in the Fall. If it rained the harvest would be decimated, depressing the F & G P Committee as much as the farmers. The 21st July had been marked in diaries for months past.

'The day the Armadilla was wiped out at Quiberon Bay,' said Connie.

'Armadillos live in South America,' said Hugh. 'And they still exist, to my knowledge. You must get your facts straight, darling.' She had been much more sensible recently, much more human. She had been missing the children, of course – something that happened to most women at some point – though it was all her fault that they weren't at home now. He assumed she had come round to his way of thinking and as soon as Sally had sorted herself out things would get back to normal. Mark he was not so sure about. The boy seemed to have learned nothing and it was coming up to two years that he'd been dug into that igloo by the river. Mark's behaviour with the Hunt was unforgivable: it was only the Bryant good name that had saved them from being ostracised by anyone who mattered. Hugh looked on Mark as a rather nasty sore. If it were up to him he would leave it to heal in its own time, but Connie insisted on scratching at it, keeping it open, drawing attention to it. Mark was their failure, some kind of genetic throwback, something which perhaps recurred in her family, that he preferred to ignore.

'The Spanish Armada,' said Edith, 'may have taken place in July but that has absolutely nothing to do with our Fete! Just what are the contingency plans, Hugh? There are the stables, and, if you must, I suppose the playroom can be used, but I don't want the hoi polloi loose in the house.'

'Certainly not!' said Hugh. 'But I hadn't thought about the playroom. That's your job, Connie. You and Annie must work out alternatives for the most vulnerable stalls.'

'We have agreed that my White Elephant stall is to be under the cedar tree.' Aunt Fay's jumble rose in every conversation now. 'And I truly believe we'll be protected from anything God may send.'

'Let us pray God sends you someone who cares enough about wet elephants,' said Hugh. 'Get the joke? The pet show will have to be in the stables, I suppose. Where's Annie? If this weather goes on we really must sort something out.'

And along the drive trudged Mark with Legs tugging at her string. Sheba, frantic, led them to the kitchen door where they all stood, stunned to silence at the sight of the bedraggled pair.

'Darling!' cried Connie, pulling her son inside while Legs pranced and woofed and Sheba backed and snarled. 'Down Sheba! Darling, shut Sheba out for a minute, please.'

'I don't see—' Hugh began, but instant action became necessary and he pushed Sheba outside. 'What on earth is this?'

Legs fawned, shook droplets of mud over the tiles and rolled onto her back, waving her paws.

'What a sweet doggie!' said Aunt Fay. 'What breed is it, Mark?'

'She's an almost-pure-bred lurcher.' Mark's pride cheered his expression, straightened his back. 'She's very intelligent.'

'Humph!' said Hugh. 'If you're staying she'll have to go in the stables. She's filthy and it's not fair on Sheba.' Territorial rights. They glowered at each other.

'But she can stay here for now, can't she? Do take that string off, she'll strangle herself.' Connie was already thinking of compromises. The playroom didn't matter, and if Mark wanted to be with his dog they could make up a bed for him there. 'Darling, it's a lovely surprise to see you! Are you hungry?'

Mark looked his shambliest, like an old tramp, battered, tired, grey. Connie was aware of Edith and Hugh making judgements.

'We'll have tea now. Aunt Fay's made a cake! Why don't we all sit down?'

'To what,' said Hugh as they settled round the table, 'do we owe this privilege? Has the igloo blown down? Are you moving on to pastures new?'

Mark screeched his chair across the tiles, dumped his elbows on the table like heavy baggage and stared wearily at his father, his eyes blank, uninformative. Everything about him needed a good wash. The hair and the beard formed a protective helmet now, a greasy Balaclava; his hands, they all noticed before he shoved them up his sleeves, were black. He seemed unaware of his effect, but turned his eyes to his mother.

'We've been done,' he said. 'Busted. They came early this morning.'

'Who? What?' Warring tribes, pillage, reprisals; Connie was confused by her interpretation of Mark's primitive appearance, by thoughts of the Bourbon army.

'The Pigs of course,' Mark sighed. 'A dawn raid complete with dogs. You can imagine it.'

'Pigs? Dogs?' Hugh was startled from his pose of disgust against the Constituency map.

'The police. An Alsatian. Poor Legs went bananas. There we were, fast asleep—'

'What,' asked Hugh, 'did the police want? Not that I'm at all surprised. I've been expecting this for some time. You can't just take over someone's property like that. It's not only illegal but infuriating for the people who own it. How would you like it if I came and camped in your garden? And the lack of sanitation – it's disgusting!'

'They were after the grass,' Mark said with another sigh.

'The *grass*?' Aunt Fay giggled. 'You'd think –'

'Hash, pot – you know.'

'Cannabis? Did you have some there?' Connie should have known. Supplied by Max, no doubt.

''Course we did. You saw it growing, didn't you? We weren't hiding anything. Just for home consumption – wasn't doing any harm. Anyway, in they rush, maximum fuss, all over the place, take this, take that, and bundle us off in the van. Me and Baz and Legs and the 'evidence' – a few miserable little plants.' He stared at each of them in turn.

Aunt Fay hugged herself. 'How absolutely thrilling!' she cried. 'Just like a film!'

Edith was more down to earth. 'And what happened at the police station?'

'They locked us up, didn't they? Beat us up, too, for no reason at all – Baz's got a real shiner! Hours and bloody hours messing us about. And we've got to go back on Wednesday before the Magistrates. I ask you, for nothing! Just a few bloody plants.'

'That's enough!' Hugh had taken it all in now. 'If you swear once more you're out, my boy! This is disgraceful! And I suppose

I'm standing bail? You've given this as your address? Has Basil gone home to his parents? I can't believe it!' But he looked as if he well could. 'Eat your cake and then you can put that animal in the stable and go and have a bath. We'll go into the details later.' He left the kitchen.

'Well I never did!' said Aunt Fay. 'Well I – Here's a nice big bit of cake, dear. And shouldn't we give your doggie something? He looks awfully thin.'

'Do you think it was because of your monitoring?' Connie asked. 'Do they know?'

'Probably.' Mark crumbled his cake, picking out seeds with a black fingernail. 'I'd better check with someone before Wednesday. They didn't seem to be worse than their usual charming selves, but it's hard to tell.'

'The Bath police are awfully charming, aren't they?' said Aunt Fay, mixing Pal and Winalot and squatting beside Legs so that all could see the tops of her lisle stockings disappearing into her lock-knit knickers. 'Come on little doggie – there, that's better isn't it? There is one very nice young policeman I was talking to the other day. He was telling me all the trouble they're having with the flowers – vandalism, don't you know. People just uproot those lovely geraniums and petunias at dead of night and leave them scattered in the road! Isn't that *wicked*? Enough to make one lose one's faith in human nature. I told him—'

'I'm amazed you have even seen a policeman on the streets,' said Edith. 'By all accounts they're desperately understaffed. And those there are are fully stretched coping with types like Mark.'

Her eyes were fixed on Mark's fingernail and Connie anticipated one of her remarks. 'Darling, I think we'd better settle Legs in the stable while you go and have a bath. You've got lots of clean clothes upstairs.'

'Better phone Max first.'

'No,' she said, more firmly than any of them expected. 'Bath first. And take some shampoo with you.'

Max was out each time Mark called. Connie accompanied her son to the Magistrate's Court where he and Baz were each fined £50 with £21 costs, on the understanding that they kept away from the benders.

'One hundred pounds!' Hugh exclaimed. 'I hope you're not expecting—'

'If you want my opinion—' said Edith.

'We're paying if off week by week,' said Mark.

Then Sally phoned.

'I'm coming home, Mother.' She sounded subdued. 'Is that all right?'

'Darling, of course! That's marvellous! Mark's here, too. I'll come and fetch you.'

'No, don't bother, I can manage. Tim'll bring me.'

'Extra hands for the fete, dear,' said Aunt Fay. 'Who'd have thought it? Both children home; it will be just like old times!'

Edith buttoned her lips and raised her eyebrows so high that they were lost in her lilac curls as she turned to her son.

'Right!' said Hugh, clapping his hands together like a pistol shot. 'As soon as Sally has had her cake and her bath and whatever else you lay on for these prodigal returns, I'm seeing both children privately in the drawing room. It will most certainly not be just like old times, I can tell you! From now on I'm dealing with them and we'll have a little discipline and consideration for others around here. This house will cease to be a holiday home for tired waitresses, or a clearing station for drug addicts. It will now be run on my lines, you'll see!'

Sally said she had had enough, that was all. Who wants to

spend the summer – if there ever was a summer – in Bath, anyhow? She was fed up with the Bull's Eye, fed up with everything. She listened in silence to all her father had to say, showed little interest in her brother, escaped to her own room.

The evening paper reported the fining of Mark and Baz in one small paragraph on page four, below details of the inquest on Miss Zoe Zynskya, who had died of coronary arrest. Although alcohol, opiates and tricyclic anti-depressant drugs had been found in the body, a verdict of death by misadventure had been returned. Miss Zynskya had a cardiovascular condition, said the coroner, and such drugs were contra-indicated, but there was no evidence that she had planned to take her own life.

Connie read that through several times. The anti-depressants must have been Max's fairy pills. Contra-indicated with her heart disease. More so, probably, when taken with liberal doses of *eau de vie*. Might one add murder – conscious, premeditated murder – to the list against Max? She kept the paper from Sally, but knew that she must have heard all about it.

It wasn't until several days later, the eve of the Hallatrow Hall Garden Party, that Sally's reserve broke down. She and her mother had taken over the oven from Aunt Fay – three seed cakes stood like fortresses on the rack – and were making scones.

'Thanks for not nagging, Mother,' Sally said, not looking at her, scrubbing lard onto baking sheets. 'I couldn't bear to tell you before, but—'

'Darling, don't, if it's going to upset you. I've read about Zoe's inquest. It was in the paper.'

'Oh yes. I suppose it would be.' Sally pushed hair out of her eyes. 'But that's not all. That's not the lot, at all.' She thrust the trays away and sat down. 'You know they're doing Hell up, I think I told you? Well, I'm very dim-witted; pretty stupid, really. It's being turned into three nice rooms. Three nice rooms for us girls, with nice new double beds. How about that?'

Connie wasn't sure how she was supposed to react. Tim and that other boy, Adrian? A horrible thought – Max? Was Max after Sally? But he had his own house in St James's Square. It sounded quite unnecessary for Charles to go to such trouble to accommodate Sally with Tim. 'I don't understand,' she admitted.

'No, you wouldn't.' Sally laughed, but not unkindly. 'D'you want to know? Well, I'll tell you anyway. Just for your education. We've all got to grow up sometime, haven't we? Although it wasn't exactly put that way, it's a bright idea of Max's that we'd pick up randy males at Jupiter's, or more like, he'd arrange for his kinky chums – I see you're getting the picture. Great, isn't it?'

'I don't believe it!' With truth Connie could say that. It wasn't possible. She remembered glancing at the possibility of Max bringing his rich clients to the Bull's Eye to look over the waitresses, but that she had later dismissed as her usual over-anxiety. 'You don't mean a – a sort of – ?'

She had joked with Roger about Avon Street, had no difficulty finding words like brothel, bordello, seraglio, whorehouse, for the organised prostitution of the eighteenth century, but could not bring herself to utter any such term to her daughter, not even in jest. Some concepts are simply unthinkable in connection with one's children; shutters snap down in the mind and remove a whole vocabulary.

'That's it,' said Sally. 'A great new leisure industry! Well, not that new, I suppose. Honest – I'm not joking. Sharon caught on immediately, but then she would; she's very canny. Of course he didn't exactly say it in so many words – he implied we'd get our cut if we were good girls. It's a long-term plan, if you see what I mean. No force involved.'

'But are you sure? You could be misinterpreting it all, jumping to conclusions. What about Charles? It's his house, after all, and he seemed – well, he seemed to me quite a nice person.'

'Oh Charles is okay, he's really nice. He drifts and dreams, wouldn't hurt a fly, but he's completely under Max's thumb. They've been living together for quite a long time. Charles would do anything for Max.'

Connie stared at the scone mixture. If she didn't roll it out soon it would harden and crumble. And Aunt Fay would be back to decorate her cakes. 'Darling, finish those baking sheets, would you. We must get this lot into the oven.' That helped her brain to change gear, cleared away a whole clutter of misconceptions and left her quite blank to consider Max in this new light at another time. Tim, at least, was predictable. She could mention Tim. 'What's Tim doing? And what about Sharon and Amanda?'

Sally finished and arranged the trays at one end of the table. 'Sharon and Mandy are trying it out. They're not fussed; no one can force them, they're not slaves. And Mandy's got this terrible overdraft she daren't tell her parents about. They're just going to see how it goes. Tim's gone home for the moment, he's thinking of working in a garage for the summer – he likes that kind of thing. Oh, and Adrian – remember him? Believe it or not, he's moved into Max's house. How about that? That *really* surprised us. I mean, we'd no idea he was gay!'

'But I though you said – Max and Charles – I don't understand.'

'Poor old Mum!' Sally took over the scone cutter. 'Don't try, okay? It really doesn't matter. I only told you because you'd met him. Let's forget it, shall we? I can tell you, when I first heard about Max I nearly freaked. Charles – yes, of course, he's an absolute sweetie. But Max, well.'

What difference? Connie thought as she prowled the drawing

room straightening things on tables, tidying newspapers and books, pretending to be efficient, adult, unsurprised. After two hundred years, still the same male-dominated business enterprise with the same incentives of free lodgings, pretty clothes, pin money for vulnerable young girls. But at least today they could choose. Sally could choose, thank heaven! Had Amanda's overdraft driven her to accept Max's 'protection'?

* * * * * * *

In the drawing-room mirror Connie can see the shadows of a party, the card table and the Duchess and, against the light of the windows, Hugo plotting with M. Duclos. They are on their way now to interrogate Sir Roger, Sir Roger who has flown to Hampshire after an excessively passionate and heart-rending farewell to his lovely Polly. Swooning with love and longing Polly rests in Annie's room while the evil Frenchman batters at the doors of Widbrook and wreaks havoc in the house, extracting clues from the servants.

'That doxy –' Hugo curses Polly. 'When I return—'

'No. Attendez!' says Duclos, thoughtfully turning in his cold white hands a button bearing in the centre an impression of the ancient Crown of France surrounded by three *fleurs de lys*. 'She shall be useful to us, that 'demoiselle, Polly, I think. Sir Roger has gone with speed to Southampton, that much we know. We can assume then that the expeditionary forces sail to Brittany this week. That we suspected and that I will now confirm. Now all that is left to us is to await Sir Roger's return and exact no more than vengeance. But revenge is sweet, is it not? I have a great desire to ruin that young gentleman for the trouble he has caused. It would please me *énormément*! You, Mr Bryant, shall hold Mademoiselle

Polly prisoner until such a time as Sir Roger comes to rescue her. Then – oh then, we shall have our *amusement*!'

The Armadilla arrives at Quiberon Bay and on the 21st July, at night, the whole Emigrant Army is either killed, or wounded, or taken prisoner.

Chapter 20

By noon on July 21st trestle tables had been set up all over the top lawn at Hallatrow Hall.

'It's going to look like a battlefield by tonight,' said Edith from her vantage on the terrace where she would be in charge of the cake stall.

Lettice, her self-proposed assistant, pinned down the cloth with a plate at each corner and glanced at the sky. 'I don't mind a battle as long as the rain keeps off. A thunderstorm at say three-thirty will cause pandemonium! Can you imagine? I think Connie's very brave having only the pet show under cover.'

'As if the pets matter,' Edith sniffed. 'But personally I prefer to be outdoors. Let us pray.'

'Lovely weather, we're so lucky!' trilled Aunt Fay passing with a fireguard and a Bakelite wireless. 'I almost wish my White Elephants were to be out by the laurels, it's quite gloomy under the cedar tree. But Sally's helping me cheer it up. That old pink bedspread from the spare room looks lovely as a tablecloth and we're putting ragged robins and moon daisies in anything that will hold water. So pretty!'

'That's daft. No one will think of buying something full of flowers – they'll assume they are part of the décor. But it's your stall, dear.' Edith twitched her scarf back into place at the throat of her spanking grey-and-white costume. She had had her hair done, too, and was not at all happy with the wind gusting down the terrace. 'Lettice dear, I wonder if we should move a little further back, between the windows? Out of the draught, don't you know.'

Lettice surveyed the moss-covered stonework with its curtains of wisteria. 'The leaves are still rather wet,' she said. 'And I don't think you'd like to be right up amongst them.' The table had been moved three times already and took a lot of patience to balance on the worn flagstones.

Down in the spinney Mark had outlined a ring for his Variety Dog Show. Old Pony Club rosettes had been refurbished as prizes for the Most Obedient Puppy, the Best Trick, the Smartest Dog, the Dog Most Like its Owner, the Dog with the Waggiest/Longest/Curliest Tail, and the Most Appealing Eyes. He had sixteen entrants (forms on sale at the village store) and was proudest of his point-to-point course, a series of jumps to be taken by dog and owner checked by a stopwatch.

'Good boy!' Hugh was doing the rounds with secateurs and string in case any plant looked untidy. 'Like the jumps! Must get the Press down here to take a picture.'

He was secretly impressed by the ingenuity and sheer hard work his son had put into the project. Sally could be expected to make a success of her pet show, but he had been uncertain about the dogs. Mark had improved once he had something to do. All Mark needed was discipline and direction, and thank God he had taken over the children now. Even got the boy to shave, with the promise of teaching him to drive. Mark would be all right, if only he could keep him away from Connie. Humming 'It's a long way to Tipperary' he climbed the bank to the laurels and ran into Annie with a tray of seedlings in yoghurt pots.

'Tony has just dumped these,' she complained. 'I thought he and Ginger were doing plants. Really, he is the limit!'

'You look very nice,' said Hugh. 'Is that a new frock? Do you think you'll be warm enough?' He was appreciating her freckled arms, warm and brown like a new-laid egg. Everything about

Annie was wholesome, sparkling.

She fluttered pale ginger eyelashes, not coy or anything like that; she wasn't the sort to prink and preen and look at herself in the mirror. 'Listen *dear*, I haven't got the time for any of that now!' she laughed in her no-nonsense way. 'Who can we get to sell the plants? Connie and Emily and I will have our hands full with the teas.'

'Connie will find someone, don't worry.' He said it automatically, as one should. That was Connie's job, the wife's job, not his concern. In the same position Annie would have a list of stand-ins, but Connie did things differently, had no system, was blown about by fortune or misfortune. He could rely on Connie to be there and worrying about things, but she was usually worrying about the wrong things.

Lewis, too, was being his ineffectual self. As Secretary of the Social Committee the fete was really his baby, yet no one would think of asking his advice on anything. There he was now, scurrying about in Connie's wake with placards saying, 'Toilets', 'Plants', 'Way In', looking hot and bothered and willing. Not a leader of men, Hugh smiled to himself, snipping at the air with his secateurs; Lewis was incapable of controlling a dormouse. Really, Connie attracted the most pathetic little runts! That wet little Liberal was hanging around as well. It just showed how much these people cared for their own Parties; you wouldn't catch him pinning up flags at an Alliance 'do'. The best joke would be to persuade Benefield to sell raffle tickets – actually asking for money for Tory funds! He probably wouldn't see the point!

A scruffy little chap, too. Even Lewis wore a clean, pressed shirt with cufflinks and a tie. Benefield's was light blue (well, that was all right) but open-necked and rolled to the elbows like some navvy. He wouldn't be going home to change: Connie was scattering pasties and salad to all the workers now.

'Beer or cider?' he called from the kitchen door. 'Sally, take these round, will you? I don't want to disturb the teas in the playroom.'

'Doesn't it all look lovely?' Aunt Fay lowered herself with a grunt to one of the rugs they had spread on the top lawn. 'And just look at this brilliant sunshine! You've done wonders with the bunting, Mr Benefield. It all looks very festive.'

Roger made his wry smile and nibbled at Connie's pasty.

'Isn't Mrs B marvellous, feeding us all on such a day?' Lewis thought it rather bad manners to sit before their hostess joined them. He wasn't sure about Mr Benefield. Like Hugh he couldn't understand a chap who helped the fund-raising of the opposition. Annie was different. Although he suspected her motives she was, after all, a woman.

There they stood now, the two Hallatrow wives, silver and gold: his Annie all burnished, robust: Mrs B slender, pale and peering through her specs towards him. 'Come and join us!' he called. 'It's high time you two took a rest.' Mrs B looked grateful and floated across the terrace like an angel. Annie turned without any acknowledgement and stood with Mr B and Harman and Mark.

'I really didn't think you'd come,' Connie said to Roger once she had settled on the rug and sent Lewis to fetch the pitcher of cider. 'Into the lion's den, so to speak. Surrounded by blood-lusting Tories! Don't you think he's brave, Aunt Fay?'

Aunt Fay looked pink and surprised to be addressed while Roger replied quietly, 'How else was I to see you? You're so elusive nowadays. Can't we make some date, any date – lunch on Tuesday? Connie, please!'

'Here we go!' Lewis poured the cider as if it were nitric acid, carefully into the centre of each glass. 'Annie asked who's to do the plants? And won't Sally need help with the raffle?'

'Lettice, I thought. Wouldn't you buy a used raffle ticket off Lettice, Roger? She's very persuasive. But I hadn't thought about the plants – wasn't that to be Ginger and Tony?'

'Ginger and Tony are all tied up with Our Member – he's opening the show, don't forget.'

'I could sell plants,' said Roger, 'as long as you promise to show me how.'

At 3.30, as forecast by Lettice, the sky suddenly turned the colour of blackberry fool in great swollen dollops behind the Hall while the sunlight bleached the front of the building. When the blackberry overtook and engulfed the light, extinguishing it like a snuffer on a candle, a thunderclap shook the whole garden, held its breath for the count of twenty and was followed by a splitting of the heavens to unleash a cascade of water.

Shrieks and squeals rose from every corner of the garden amid the drumming of rain as children in cotton frocks and shorts and ankle socks hurtled across the open space followed almost as quickly by the heavier adults. Sandals squelched and slid on the wet grass, hair instantly plastered to wet faces, clothing changed colour and clung or flapped against bare legs. And almost immediately, as it seemed, the rift was closed, the purple mass stood off behind the lime trees and the sun dazzled from a high and empty sky.

'I don't believe it!' several gasped as they began to emerge from whatever shelter they had found.

Connie stood, dazed, by the laurels where she had dragged a young woman and her baby. A battlefield would have been no more frightening. She expected to see the lawn strewn with fallen bodies moaning for assistance, but the crowd was laughing, hysterical, nervous, relieved to discover they were still alive. Children were jumping and splashing in puddles on the terrace, a loose dog was charging up and down the lawn. Slowly, unwillingly, Connie focused on the tattered stalls. Roger's plants were scattered, the cake stall she could barely see for the host of helpers and sympathisers. She smiled at the woman and her bawling baby, offered her the kitchen to recuperate and then forced herself to search for the casualties.

Trapped behind the table of cakes, Edith had made no attempt to escape. Flattening herself against the drawing-room windows she had received the brunt of the downpour and she remained at her post still, in a state of shock, refusing all promptings to move. The lilac curls had uncoiled and hung Medusa-fashion over her cheeks, her eyes had run into dark pools and the cherry lips quivered and twittered, but she was not to be routed. Hugh was fetching Aunt Fay, but Sally pushed through and took her arm and guided her round the beaten plates of rock buns and shattered icing. 'Come on, Granny. That's it! We'll make a cuppa and tidy up. That's right. Round here.'

The crowd parted respectfully, awed to silence. Connie watched her daughter with love and pride. Sally could cope with anything, naturally, kindly, without fuss. Sally was worth a million experienced field nurses. On a battlefield Sally would rescue and console the wounded and the dying. Sally was all that Connie could wish, all she would like to have been herself. Edith was safe with Sally. She scrubbed the tears from her eyes and felt an arm consolingly around her.

'There, there, Mrs B!' Well, it had to be Lewis. Roger was observing them with his secret, pained smile.

'Now everybody!' Hugh was in his element restoring confidence, pulling them all together. 'That *was* a bolt from the blue and no mistake! But it looks fine now and we'll press on regardless. The fruit and plant stalls have had a good wash; the white elephants have not stampeded over there under the cedar tree;

there's the dog show well protected just down there in the spinney; pets snug in the stable block, and the ladies are about to serve us all with tea and home-made scones and cream round the corner there. A good cup of tea is what we need after all that! And don't forget the raffle – lovely prizes to be won!'

Connie bolted indoors to find Annie had already filled the urn and was pouring tea while Emily stood beside her with a box of coins.

'I've got it all sorted out, Mrs Bwy-ant.' Emily made her winsome, gap-toothed grin. 'You don't have to bother. 20p – *thank* you! Look at the heaps of money I've got already, though one lady only had a pound. She's coming back again when she's got some change, but I gave her a cup anyway.'

'I've told them to serve themselves with the scones,' said Annie, 'but it would help if someone—'

'Sorry,' said Connie and pushed her way to the end of the playroom. She had envisaged a simpler system, a tidier queue, with Emily on the scones, but she couldn't alter it now. Emily was too young to cope with the money. She prayed that someone was tidying the cake stall, selling raffle tickets, supervising the pets. Was Sally still with Edith? Annie would have checked, if it had been her responsibility. It was Annie who had asked what to charge for the tea – Connie hadn't thought about that – and who had suggested paying more to include the scones. ('I don't think that's fair,' Connie had said, 'in case they don't want one.' But now she wondered.) Annie didn't waste time wondering.

Through the kitchen window while she was washing the teacups Connie saw Roger helping Hugh carry tables from the garden. Again and again they crossed the yard, facing each other, held at table length from each other, weaving about on the wet cobblestones, occasionally cursing as they lost footing.

'Treacherous,' said Lettice beside her. 'These stones are really slippery after the rain. They shouldn't be hurrying. They could break their necks.'

When Connie half closed her eyes she could see the two men, Hugo and Sir Roger, separated by no more than a sword's length, parrying, lungeing, slipping on the cobbles. Soon Hugh must challenge Sir Roger and the best man must win.

As Roger slithered towards the Coach House, arched back at a manic angle, Hugh crashed his end of the table to the ground to steady himself and Roger laughed. Hugh made some remark and they danced on.

'Treacherous,' said Lettice. 'Shouldn't we go out and slow them down?'

Should we intervene? wondered Connie. Would Polly try and stop them? No, Polly would be excited by the fray. They must fight on to the death and then Polly will take the victor by the hand, cast a tear over the grave of the vanquished and, suitably decked in veils of black, ride away down the Hallatrow drive into the sunset.

'Are you all right?' asked Lettice. 'I bet you didn't hear a word I was saying! Really darling, you've got to stop this. Half the time I wonder if you're still with us.'

'I'm fine.' Connie scrubbed three plates to prove it. 'Of course I heard you, silly! Look, it's going to be a spectacular sunset after all.'

Lettice with her round pink hands clutching the teacloth, piling up tea plates, with her round pink face anxious, measuring, like a dish uptilted to catch any answer. But Connie would let nothing drop. No one would understand.

Would Hugo or Sir Roger win the duel? Was it up to her, who won? Was she in control of Polly's fate, or was Polly, like everyone else, free to dictate what happened?

As Roger left he said 'Tuesday?' so that she was forced to agree. By Tuesday she would have decided what to do about him. With both children home.

On Tuesday it rained, too.

'Is it always like this in England?' asked one of Connie's Americans, smartly draped in Aquascutum with a weatherproof deerstalker latched over her ears. 'It was rainin' in Edinboro. It was rainin' in York. And at Stratford upon Avon. And in London. We finally got wise and invested in these cute waterproofs when we were in London – isn't that just somethin'? And a real English brolly for Ed! Our best souvenir.'

'About time!' growled Ed, sniffing. 'How d'you folks manage to keep so healthy?'

'That's why, lover,' said his wife, tilting her face. 'It's great for the complexion. And just look at all those lovely green fields! When I think of the rates we pay back home to water our yard!'

'You have all been very courageous,' Connie told them as she returned her dripping band to the Abbey churchyard and pointed out the entrance to the Roman Baths. 'It's awful at this time of year to suggest you go indoors to dry out! I do hope the sun will shine for you tomorrow.'

Roger drove her to a pub overlooking the canal, where they sat in a window watching rain bounce on the water and a swan's nest. One swan floated up and down watching the towpath, the other sat alert and fussy over its brood.

'Very strict parents,' said Roger returning with glasses of wine. 'Very protective. Faithful for life, you know, and beyond. The one that's left usually pines to death. The animal kingdom – or the bird queendom? – is so delightfully uncomplicated. Either random coupling or fidelity. No superimposed codes of behaviour. No inhibiting concepts of honour and duty like us.'

'Do we? I mean, are we? Have we? Do they exist any more?' Connie willed him to say 'Yes – yes, mankind is honourable; that's what makes sense in this world of cruelty and vice; that's what makes some pattern out of the chaos; that's what matters. '

Instead he showed her his sad face. 'Marriage should only exist for procreation and the protection of the young, I believe. For the rest it's a destructive institution demanding unnatural restraints, a constant invasion of privacy. You've seen how difficult it is to survive it. Mankind needs his, or her, autonomy, grows to resent the enforced sharing of every nook and cranny. One grows out of that impetuous joy of living inside the other person very early on, I think. We all crave some personal airwave, some private space to dream in, to recharge. Most marriages don't allow for that.'

'Oh, I don't know…' The sharing, she thought, was the good part. It was the dead hanging around, not being noticed, not being cared about, that she couldn't stand. 'It's nice to be wanted. It's a nice feeling that someone wants and needs you.'

He looked at her as if she were a pathetic case. 'Maybe,' he said. 'I suppose we all see it differently. But it doesn't end up happy – you must admit that. When the passion begins to wane reason sets in. Reason wrecks love. Love's irrational. It's either totally blinding or it doesn't exist. Have you ever come across someone being rational and in love at the same time?'

'But there are lots of happily married people.' She wanted to ask if he had ever been blindly in love, but felt sure she would hit an embargo. He looked as if he had been, perhaps was, but it couldn't be with her or he would have made some show of it by now. And she couldn't be in love with him because she was behaving so rationally. She felt weary, exhausted by the effort of trying to understand him.

'Of course there are – happily married people.' He said it as if she had suggested people with crossed eyes, or pimples or broken arms. 'But I fear they have to make a lot of sacrifices.'

'Of course they do! Good heavens, life's full of sacrifices – it's not only marriage that's tricky, it's the whole of life. We all have to learn to compromise. What one lives *for* may be uncertain, how one lives is not.'

'Isn't it?'

'No it's not!' She felt suddenly bold, defiant. She hadn't thought about it before and feared that she sounded rather like her mother, but it seemed important. 'Of course not, silly! At least one has control over what one does.'

His smile implied that she didn't. 'Freedom of choice,' he said. 'I like that. Don't you suspect that you just might be driven by your hormones or some other impulse outside your control? Or perhaps that your morality is based on masochism or expediency? There's usually something devious and unconscious lurking behind every good honest honourable decision.'

'Don't say that!' She had been telling herself that her decision about Roger (had she made a decision? Hugh was always saying she was incapable of making a decision) was at the least honourable. Expedient? Masochistic? It was probably both. 'Would you say that being in love is simply a matter of hormones?'

'Well no, I wouldn't say that. But then I'm a romantic.'

She wondered now about that. He *looked* so romantic, so like Byron with his rumpled forelock, open shirt, sensuous mouth, but he had never behaved like a romantic with her. 'Are you?' she asked.

'Well, I think so!' He looked pained, rather hurt that she should question it. 'Reality is so drab, so miserable, one has to do something about it. I look on myself as a romantic decadent – it has a nice ring about it.'

He must be laughing at her. She turned her attention to the menu. 'Shall we have a sandwich or do you want something more filling?'

Now he was laughing. 'I can't accuse you of being a romantic! You always bring the subject back to something sensible. You're very good for me, dearie, you know.'

Last night she had rehearsed what she would say. They would be strolling finger-linked beside a stream, lying amongst moon daisies in a meadow, wandering through a beech wood dappled with sunlight. He would turn to her, about to declare his long-supressed ardour and she would raise a hand, perhaps press a finger gently to his lips. 'No,' she would murmur. 'Not a word. We both know. There is no need to speak.' And then, or later, she would say: 'My darling, this has become too important, too enjoyable, too total – and it must end before someone gets hurt.' Amazement, horror, pleas, tears. 'You cannot! You are breaking my heart!' etcetera.

But she would be strong. She would have the strength for both of them. He would admire her sense of honour and duty, applaud her for saying what he could not bring himself to say, for doing what he could not bear to do. He would draw strength from her moral conviction, would love her even more for her selfless courage.

'You're very good for me,' was the closest he had got to any declaration and she felt herself melting and quivering inside, knowing she must produce the *coup de grace* and end it all before it had really begun.

'We can't go on like this!' She wasn't sure she actually said it and looked to him for some reaction. They could not go on like this, she had decided. Nothing to do with masochism or expedients. If he had shown he cared, just a little, by word or deed; if he had kissed her, praised her, even commented on something about her other than her opinions or lack of them, she would have persevered. But their friendship seemed so remote, almost sterile, that it wasn't worth the conflict she felt every time they met. Every time she anticipated more, ran to meet him knowing that today they would break through the barriers of embargoes and lose themselves in a new world of lust and shared information – yes, love. But all he would do was talk about it. The balance between reason and erotic passion, romance vs realism, trying out pet theories on her as if she were a student or another chap propping up a bar, when all she wanted was for him to take her, take hold of her, hold her, cherish, ravish, love her. *That* was masochism.

'I think,' she said, aloud or again, 'we must stop meeting like this.'

'We can't go on meeting like this!' He struck a mock-tragic pose, fist to forehead. 'My dearest Connie! I'll get the food while you rewrite the script!'

She stared after him miserably. Didn't he care, at all?

'One ham 'n' salad, one cheese 'n' salad, and two refills.' He unstacked plates and glasses. 'Now, I'm listening. Why must we stop what? Have you tired of me so soon?'

'I wish you'd stop laughing at me,' she complained. 'I'm trying to be serious.'

'I'm not laughing,' he said. 'Just slowing you down. I've got the message, so you don't have to explain. We had a bargain, remember? I should have thought to add, no explanations. Forget I asked, will you? I'll leave you be, but remember I'm around if you get lonely. We were good for each other, don't you think? We shared something, you and I; we had our patch of sunlight, our little oasis. Don't you think?'

'Oh, we did! We do! … Will you mind?' She couldn't help asking, giving him one more chance.

'Mind?' he echoed. 'Of course I'll mind! What on earth did

you imagine, you little fool? *Mind!*' He looked put out, ruffled, misunderstood. 'I'd have thought—' he began, but decided against it and bit into his sandwich.

They both gazed out through the small leaded panes at the rain dancing on the canal, at a shaft of light spreading over a rape field.

'I thought we'd steered clear of moral pitfalls,' he said. He ate her sandwich, too. 'Conscience and all that. I thought it could work like this – no demands, no emotional blackmail. Strange.'

He drove her back to her car and she could think of nothing to say. Afterwards, inevitably, she remembered and wept as she thought of all she might have told him. She might have asked what he thought about parting; she might have explained her feelings; she might have mentioned love, thrown his theories back at him, talked of passion and suffering as if they had some meaning. What she had done was not masochistic or expedient, for duty or for revenge, as he was bound to assume. What she had done, she now realised, was to hope against hope that he would shout 'Nonsense!', stop her lips with kisses, silence her with action. Rape, at the very least. Some sign that he was human and she desirable; proof that she existed.

Chapter 21

Sir Roger remains in Hampshire for the summer. Some say he sailed with the ill-fated expedition to Brittany, some that he is hatching further plots with the Portland Whigs, some that his wife's health demands his presence on his estates near Winchester, that she is dying, has died. He sends no word to Polly. Hugo and M. Duclos loosen their hold on her and there is nothing to witness all summer long at Hallatrow Hall.

Talk of peace, talk of war, talk of invasion. Encouraged by anarchy in France, Pitt prepares to negotiate peace with the Convention in Paris while increased poverty and rising prices for every necessity of life lead to even more misery and riots up and down his country. The national debt has doubled, banks close, architects and builders in Bath are bankrupted midway through their elaborate expansion across the river. Local militia of 'loyal volunteers' are formed and marched about, spies are suspected everywhere. Into this autumn of distrust and discontent Sir Roger is rumoured to have returned to Widbrook.

* * * * * * *

Connie drifted through the summer watching over her children. At first she wrote long letters to Roger in her head continuing discussions they had had on riverbanks, walking in the Botanical Gardens, at picnics and in pubs. She could argue better when he wasn't there and found quite a lot to say, about love and reason in particular. She missed him, ached with memory. Such silly little things she remembered; there had been nothing momentous: the way he looked when he thought something clever or witty, the way he looked when he cared passionately about some injustice or some work of art, the way he looked, the way he looked. His head, his hands, at different angles in different moods, expressions guarded and, very occasionally, impulsive. She could turn up these pictures at will and they would also drop before her in free association with any sound, sight, smell. Everything reminded her of him now – trees, flowers, walks, water – reminded her of what she could have said or should have said, and made nonsense of her decision not to meet him. Masochism. She had blown this vacuum for herself. She had only herself to blame. He remained with her perhaps more closely bound than before, more real than before, as a spiritual companion with whom she could share every daily farce or frustration. But now quite out of reach.

Mark passed the time at home brewing beer in the playroom, training Legs, driving the car, but he spent most of the days at the squat and avoided any discussion of police monitoring, any discussion at all. He remained cut off from his family, like a sleepwalker in their midst, unresponsive. Meditation, he said; though Hugh said he didn't know the meaning of the word and even Connie thought that an excuse. Aunt Fay saw a foothold for Religion and pursued him with titbits of tracts.

Sally finally tired of Tim, pleasing both her parents. Of course Tim was sweet and would always be her bestest friend, but he was so like Mark, more of a brother really, rather childish in so many ways; he simply hadn't grown up. Connie and Hugh nodded and smiled their relief until it became clear that she had exchanged him for BJ newly returned from celebrating the summer solstice at Stonehenge. To BJ clung the glamour of action, persecution and honest dirt, and he was preparing to turn next winter's Sabbing into a theatrical production undreamed of anywhere in the country. Talk of media hype mingled with earthier jargon from the battlefield and Sally was beginning to enthuse about a press campaign against all cruelty.

'What this country needs ...' she would announce at breakfast. 'We must wake up the conscience of the whole nation. We will bring out the good qualities which are lying idle in every human being. We will make everyone care, really care ...'

'Twaddle!' growled Hugh. 'Sentimental bunk!'

BJ, she told her mother, was a saint, an inspiration. Everyone believed in him; he was a really marvellous person; she was madly in love with him; it was all just amazing that he loved her too, just amazing!

'Where is he living?' Connie asked with fearful visions of a return to the benders in pursuit of her second child.

'Oh, he's in the squat with the Sabs' office. We're making it all really comfortable for the winter – no way can they chuck us out.'

Connie didn't like the sound of 'us'.

Sally managed to fit in the teaching of Emily and Pickle when BJ was busy, and on sunny days Amanda and Sharon joined her to lie in the garden. No one mentioned Max or Hell and Connie felt she shouldn't enquire.

With the beginning of the autumn term came the long expected announcement of a general election and all parties went wild with delight; the Conservatives because the other parties were weak, ineffectual, useless and torn by internal wars, the Socialists because everyone was sick of the Tories' socially divisive policies and lack of any human quality, the Lib Dems because with both these parties at each other's throats they could easily slip through and gain all marginal seats. Everyone was confident, on and off the screen or platform, and looked forward to a most enjoyable month of campaigning.

Hugh's kitchen map leapt alive with coloured pins and tags to indicate different activities, from leaflet drops to personal visits, and he bought extra-large sheets of cartridge paper to record the results of all canvassing by town and village, cross-referenced in shades of political colour from true blue through yellow, green, orange, red. He was very proud of his rainbows.

'At a glance!' he told Connie. 'No need to read the details if you don't want to. Anything they've said which gives a clue can subtly alter the colour. You see here, this woman at 11 Broadoak Close for example. She says she's SDP, doesn't like Cameron's voice, thinks Miliband's too silly, but she has no idea of the Liberal policies and hasn't heard of Vince Cable! It's only David Steel she likes. Tony visited her and made mincemeat of it all. Kindly said that Steel is over and out now, and voting for him would accomplish nothing – the usual kind of thing. Her husband she says is Labour, but she's obviously the dominant partner and if Tony's done his job they could both join us. So we have a blue stroke with a fuzz of yellow and a bit of red at the other end, like this. They're the ones to watch, to follow up. At the end we'll pass over the straight blues and reds and concentrate on capturing these mixtures.'

'It's quite effective,' said Connie, 'but it would be prettier with a different red. Couldn't you make Labour Burnt Sienna? And the Greens less grassy? A bit more green would spice it up, too.'

'You're not taking this seriously,' he sighed. 'You're no use at all. Just tell me what conclusions you draw from this chart.'

'Rather a yellow blue, I'd say.'

'Right! And so?'

'Yellow and blue makes green.'

He glared at her. 'You just don't care, do you? You don't realise how much this matters. But I warn you, if They get in you'll get a nasty shock. Everything will go. Everything we believe in, everything we stand for.'

'Isn't that a bit dramatic? Come off it, the world will not come to an end and a lot of people will be happier, better off.'

Hugh stared for a moment in silence; his eyes had stopped darting about and had come to rest on heresy. 'I don't think you mean that,' he said very seriously. 'I know you are trying not to understand, but don't start parroting sentimental twaddle as well. It's people like you, without direction, who will ruin everything. If you can't discuss it sensibly just shut up. That's what we've got to contend with, wishy-washy ideals which mean nothing! You have no idea what's involved. My own wife! God – look what happens giving women the vote!'

For four weeks Hugh was either out canvassing or colouring charts with Annie. The children were told: if you want to pay more taxes and have your life controlled by the State, vote Labour; if you want to live on hot air, vote Liberal; if you want to pay lower taxes and be governed by a party which supports and encourages free enterprise and freedom for the individual, vote Conservative.

'Yes Dad,' they both said.

'You can choose,' he told them. 'It's your vote. Just think about it, that's all.'

'What's Mother doing?' they asked, for amusement.

'Your mother will vote Conservative, as she always has. She likes her little joke, she must have her little joke. She's got a rather warped sense of humour and she enjoys baiting me! But when it comes to the point – she knows which side her bread is buttered.'

Annie obviously knew about bread and butter and was more artistic than Hugh. Her rainbows glowed dutifully blue; she had found a much prettier crayon which managed to mop up the yellow and pleased everyone.

'There's no need,' she said, 'to call on *them*, or them, or them.'

Connie watched and listened and made no more little jokes. Politics, as she had always guessed, was a treacherous business. She felt sorry for Hugh, who didn't understand that. As all around her grew more fervid and more partisan, she longed for Sir Roger's return and the excuse to rejoin Polly. Somehow, as much as she willed it – screwing her eyes up tight or staring past herself deep into the mirror – he refused to be hurried home.

* * * * * * *

Distrust and unrest sweep the country; the landowners fear mobs and violence, the poor prepare to fight for their ultimate right of survival. As the radical movement grows and benefit societies are set up for the starving, even the idle rich are forced to notice that the country is divided, dangerously divided.

The lovely Polly still dreams of Sir Roger and knows that he will come for her soon. He is returned to Widbrook, she knows that, and is preparing her new home for her. Since the expedition to the Brittany coast was terminated – over 700 prisoners, most of them nobles and many of them former naval officers, were shot in their English uniforms for high treason – and the final royalist uprisings are being consistently repressed, Britain's active support for the Bourbon cause is over and national concern returns to protecting the island from invasion. M. Duclos is no longer particularly interested in troop movements and many local people have become suspicious that he is not the émigré he pretends to be. But he is still welcome at Hallatrow Hall, where he passes his time turning cards with the Duchess and ignoring the ladies of the night who surround him.

Polly's role in the household is unique. The Duchess has promised Sir Roger to protect his betrothed and refuses to allow Hugo to put her to work. Each evening Polly graces the drawing room in a becoming new gown, chats with the ladies and the gentlemen, helps pour the wine and then retires to her cot in Annie's room.

And finally, one day in late September, Sir Roger arrives to claim his bride. Early in the evening, the first of their guests, he strides into the drawing room to bow low over the Duchess' hand, nod to Hugo and then to stand and gaze at his sweetheart, who presents the most delightful picture of dignity and beauty in a carnation-coloured silk. He is transfixed, entranced, as he observes the pleasure lighten her eyes and a blushing glow rise in her cheeks. She runs to him, forgetting all dignity, throws herself into his arms, nestles against the coat of celestial blue whilst he kisses her with the utmost rapture.

Even the Duchess' lips twitch into a grimace which might be construed as amusement, though her son's do not. Wine is called for, and the lovebirds must drag their bodies and eyes from each other while Sir Roger compliments the Duchess on her good health and Annie on her good looks and Hugo on his good fortune in having secured Annie as a wife.

'And I, too, have my licence,' Sir Roger informs them all. 'My adored Polly and I will be married tomorrow!' His eyes tell her that it should be tonight, that he will die waiting for the morrow, that his passion for her is too impetuous for him to resist. 'And now, if you will excuse us, it is only right and fair that I should ask Mistress Polly in private for her agreement to this proposal.' He escorts her through the door and out onto the terrace.

There, in the shadow of the house and with the sky darkening down to a golden line of afterglow above the spinney, they can barely see the features of each other's face. Sir Roger's eyes shine with all the fires of inflamed nature as he traces with a finger her cheek, her throat, and caresses her naked shoulder. With burning sighs he draws her close into an embrace of boundless pleasure. And so they fail to hear footsteps on the flagstones approaching from the stables.

'You have caused me much trouble, M. Beauchamp.' Duclos's voice strikes from the shadows, startling them like the breath of a viper close to their faces. 'I expect you to oblige me with your presence this instant in the courtyard.'

'Now?' Sir Roger is still befuddled with lust. He has forgotten the sinister Frenchman and can think of no reason why he should be called out so intemperately. Besides, it is damned inconvenient. He can feel Polly's heart beating against his, her soft skin under his hand, and a rage of active delight inflames him. 'Tomorrow,' he murmurs. 'Have your seconds call on me tomorrow. Or the next day,' he adds, remembering the wedding plans.

'*A l'instant*!' Duclos insists. 'M. Bryant awaits us there. I suggest Mademoiselle returns herself to the other ladies.'

Polly clings to her idol's arm, distraught, implores him to ignore this stupid challenge, to leave with her without delay, to take her now to Widbrook where he can do with her whatever he will; but Sir Roger has returned from the threshold of paradise and knows that he has no alternative.

'Go in,' he bids her. 'I shall be with you shortly.'

'No, I will not leave you now!' She runs beside him as he sets off to follow Duclos.

In the stable yard stands Hugo with swords (a sword has not been a part of fashionable dress since Beau Nash banned them in the city of Bath half a century ago). He offers Sir Roger his choice.

'But it is dark!' poor Polly cries. 'It is too dark! You might be killed!'

The men laugh. Duclos and Sir Roger strip off their coats and their white shirts gleam in the uncertain darkness, gathering light as if they are phosphorescent. Sir Roger laughs again. 'The targets are quite clear, as you can see. I only hope, my dear fellow, that you know what you are about. In this light it may be difficult to avoid doing you some serious damage.'

'That,' hisses the Frenchman, 'you have already done me. Many of my compatriots have died because of your interference in our affairs. I will be revenged for them.' He draws his sword and makes arcs of light reflected from the lamps burning on the coach-house wall.

Sir Roger kisses Polly tenderly and leads her towards the house. 'Go in,' he repeats. 'By the time you have poured me some wine I shall be with you. Go now.'

But Polly remains under the archway. 'This is madness!' she moans.

No one heeds her. The duellists strike attitudes, salute each other, cross swords, and the stable yard rings with the clash of steel. Hugo stands impassive, a coat over each arm. Polly leans against the cold stone, faint with fear. Bright white squares dance before her as if performing a ballet, the white linen of an arm shooting straight to thrust, angling again to parry, back and forth above the shining cobbles. Sword blades and hilts flash a sharper, brighter light. The Frenchman curses and Polly's spirits rise, but the clash and scrape of metal continues. Someone grunts, it is impossible to tell who. Hugo steps aside as they prance towards him. One slips on the cobbles and the other holds back while he regains his feet. The dance continues, more like a sexual flirtation, building up through thrust and parry to its climax. Another slide and an Anglo-Saxon curse and the Frenchman pursues, arm raised and straight, one long white shimmering member pointed directly towards and into the falling, accommodating square.

'Aha!' an orgasmic groan.

Polly shrieks and rushes forward. One white shirt stands high and rectangular, withdrawn, the other is flung across the cobbles. The fallen shirt spreads and writhes as if in ecstasy. Hugo steps into the pool of light and peers down, then kneels to examine the body on the ground more closely. Polly sees the lamplight gleam on the high domed forehead of M. Duclos as he sheaths his weapon, and she falls swooning beside her lover.

The surgeon, when he arrives, pronounces Sir Roger not dead but mortally wounded. He may live for a few hours. They carry him to the drawing room where they lay him on the sofa and Polly bathes his wound before the surgeon binds it in an effort to stanch the blood. He lies like the dying Christ, a broken body, an arrangement of useless limbs. This is no time for tears; no time to give way to grief yet. Polly kneels at his side, the carnation-coloured silk crushed and stained with his blood, her cheeks marked with rivulets of tears as she studies him for the first and last time. No longer do their eyes meet to demand, to devour, impatient of social restraint, rapacious; no longer does his fancy rove unbounded over her charms. His eyes are dulled now and his mouth twists and labours to force out his final words. Hugo and M. Duclos stand over them, expressionless, waiting for the end.

Chapter 22

'If Hugh's going to be busy Telling,' said Lettice, 'all the more reason for you to come along to my election-night party. Don't be so middle-aged! You simply can't sit at home watching the results by yourself.'

'I had no intention of watching them in any state,' Connie laughed. 'After this last few weeks I'd rather watch my knickers going round in the washing machine. Or just go to bed. It's like New Year's Eve – everyone will be hysterically happy or miserably sad and repeating the same old formulae and drinking too much.'

'How can you? No one's ever miserable at my parties! If I promise there will be no 'Auld Lang Syne', will you come? You can have the car? Come on now, Hugh will go on to Tony and Ginger or the Fosters, you know that. You can be as Scrooge as you like, no one will mind. Sylvia Benefield, as you've probably heard, has escaped the whole process and fled to the South of France without so much as a postal vote.'

'Oh? How wicked of her!' And Roger? Connie hadn't seen him in the Abbey churchyard for several weeks and had even begun to fear that Max might have killed him.

'Well, it gives Roger a breather. She's so neurotic about him, poor chap, always checking up on him. The number of times she's phoned here, you wouldn't believe.'

'But why? Why doesn't she trust him? I'd have thought –' But it wasn't for her to defend Roger's fidelity simply because he had behaved blamelessly with her. 'Do you know if he has, um – ?'

'I'm sure you know as much about Roger as I do.' Lettice

sounded quite prim. 'Anyway, he'll be at my party. You're coming, aren't you?'

'Yes,' said Connie.

Election day began early at Hallatrow Hall. Aunt Fay was to be the first Teller, checking polling-card numbers as each voter arrived at the local infants' school. The responsibility thrilled her and she was dressed for breakfast in various shades of blue, not usually one of her favourite colours.

'You only have to write down the number,' Hugh told her for the umpteenth time. 'You're not allowed to ask them how they propose to vote, or say anything else, is that clear? If you say anything, someone might think you're canvassing and make trouble. In pen or biro, too. Last time some idiot scribbled in pencil and we couldn't read the numbers. Remember, you're the first cog in today's wheel. It's your numbers which will let us know later on who hasn't voted, so that we can round them up.'

Aunt Fay beamed. 'Yes, I've got both a fountain pen and a biro, just in case one runs out. Wish me luck now, children!' And she set out as though to tackle the Amazon basin.

Hugh left next in the car to start the ferrying of the lame, the halt, the sick and the old who had not had the foresight to arrange for a postal or a proxy vote.

'I asked for a chauffeuse – a woman!' complained one, eyeing him with suspicion.

'I thought it would be a bigger car,' said another. 'The Labour chappie has a Granada, I'll use him next time.'

'Which is the gentleman we're supporting, dear?' asked another. 'I'm afraid I can't see too well, would you come in with me and tick him off?'

Later Hugh joined Annie at the Campaign Room set up in Ginger and Tony's farmhouse, where she had arranged their rainbow charts along a line of tables. The rest of the Committee were all driving or telling; Annie was checking off the last batch of numbers against the electoral roll and then against their colour coding.

'It's going well,' she grinned up at him. 'This lovely weather makes all the difference, brings them all out early. Tony says we'll have a good idea of the result quite soon.'

'It's far too close for comfort,' Hugh groaned. 'And in Bath, too. The poll just now on the wireless was quite frightening. Anyone else need fetching?' He slumped into the dog's chair. 'Connie wants the car tonight to go junketing in Bath – I suppose you couldn't pick me up from the Bear at ten, could you? I'm on the last stint there and she says she can drop me at eight, so that's all right. If you don't mind.' He raised his head and gave her a brave smile.

'No, of course not. Do you want to look in on the counting after that? Tony's asked me if we'd like to go, as he's Recording Officer. And then I gather the plan is to come back here to watch on the box until dawn. I've packed Emily off with a friend for the night, so we're quite free.'

'Lovely,' he sighed, picking white terrier hairs off his suit. 'Is there a clothes brush around; just look at this!'

Lettice's house was festooned with yellow and orange balloons, Harman wore an orange cummerbund and Lettice herself was swathed in gold silk. 'Aren't we lucky,' she crowed as Connie arrived, 'not to be stuck with dreary old blue or that vulgar red! It's the only civilised party, you can tell.'

'What, your party?'

'Of course my party! I can see you're sitting on the fence, though that grey dress carries just a hint of green maybe?'

'Don't ever mention colours to me again,' Connie pleaded. 'Not any colour! We've been immersed in every shade of almost all of them for weeks.' She had arrived late, having enjoyed driving around the lanes after dropping Hugh at the Bear, restless to see Roger again but in no hurry to seal her fate. Roger was balancing a glass and a plate and listening to a pretty young woman with an expensive tan and bleached blonde hair.

'You're way behind us all,' said Lettice, leading her to a table of cold food while Harman produced a very dark Scotch, 'or have you already been celebrating?'

'No, why?' But she felt as if she had been, sparkling, witty, warm. And several unfamiliar men seemed to think so, too. They laughed at what she said and kept their eyes fixed on hers. It was a lovely party.

All too soon they settled to the serious business of watching the predictions, the computer, the election results. Connie sat on the floor where she could lean against an arm of the overstuffed sofa and quite by chance Roger perched just above her. While the television boomed on about statistics and swings, and MPs of every hue pontificated about each other's drawbacks, Connie leaned back as intended and Roger stroked the back of her neck – at least, she assumed that was what he was doing. He might, she considered as she pretended to listen to yet another distortion of the unemployment figures, merely have been scratching his thigh or removing dust from his trousers, rather slowly. When, finally, she had to turn her head to check, he was smiling down at her as he did in all her best dreams. And she smiled back like a conspirator, not wanting to be caught by Lettice, who had been behaving rather like a Head Girl recently and would very likely tell on her.

'Let's go,' he whispered. 'I can't take much more of this false confidence. I'd rather hear the facts tomorrow.'

They slipped out during a startling gain (or loss) in the Midlands and stood in the alley remarking on the stars and an almost full moon, the silhouettes of 'real Georgian chimneys' and a yowling cat.

'Do you think it's one of Lettice's?' Connie stumbled over the sibilants and giggled and wondered how she could be drunk. 'Should we ring the doorbell for it?'

'No,' said Roger. 'Let it ring its own doorbell. Will you walk with me to the Crescent or shall we drive? Sylvia's in France, you know.'

'I know,' she said, and as they passed her car he took hold of her hand.

Once inside his flat he seemed uncertain what to do with her. With glasses of whisky they stood admiring a church candlestick Sylvia had converted into a lamp, and when they could think of nothing more to say about it Connie gulped her drink and looked towards the bedroom door. He must have some plan.

'There's a television in the bedroom,' he said, following her eye.

'That's very sensible,' she said. 'They look so unattractive in a living room.' And then she noticed one beside her. 'More comfortable in bed, anyway. Though I suppose you fall asleep too easily.'

'I don't,' he said. 'Do you want to see some more results?'

'I'd love to,' she said politely.

He refilled their glasses and she held them while he switched on a bedside lamp and the television without its sound, folded the lime-green bedcover into three and hung it over the back of a chair. The curtains, swagged and draped and tasselled, looked like a fixture to Connie and he left them alone.

'Would you like to undress in the bathroom?' he asked.

The bathroom continued green and white out of the bedroom, more like a garden, full of plants ramping high and trailing, doubled in reflection from several walls of mirror. The glass was so angled that Connie could see all views of herself without turning. She watched her grey dress slip down to a puddle at her ankles, raised her arms, pushed up her hair and studied her back in dimensions she had never seen before. From behind she could have been any body, quite unrecognisable, with or without glasses. She pirouetted around, wiggling her hips, and began to laugh. Thank heaven no one could see her! On the door hung Sylvia's pale silk dressing gown. Not to shock Roger she put it on, then swapped it for a bath towel. She didn't want to be taken for Sylvia. How would a proper seductress emerge? She opened the door, still laughing.

Roger was in bed with the sheet pulled up to his armpits, studying her as if she were a picture in an exhibition. 'Yes, that suits you. A little looser down the back so that it hangs in folds; that's right! You're good in green; it affects your eyes.'

His first comment on her appearance. Affected her eyes how? But laughter had shed some of her inhibitions and she found it quite easy to skip across the carpet and into the bed, dropping the green towel at the last minute. Roger had been courteously watching the television until she was well under the sheet but now he took her hand and squeezed it.

'This is nice,' he said. 'Don't you think? Much nicer than crowded like cattle at Lettice's. We've just won Northampton; that's quite a surprise.'

She leaned across him for her drink and mechanically he said 'Sorry' and reached for his own. The sheet slipped and they left it at waist level. While she sipped the whisky, facing Miliband and his losing or winning grimace, she saw with the outer edge of her vision his pale flesh against hers, his luminous skin, ripples of rib and muscle, quite unlike Hugh's hairy chest. She placed her empty glass carefully beside the lamp feeling warm and affectionate, and snuggled her cheek against his silken shoulder. With that point of contact to control any reaction – like a doctor's reassuring grip on a tourniquet – she touched his chest with one finger and then slid her hand up and across to his other shoulder. All sensation seemed drawn to her fingertips as she recorded the texture of his skin. He shivered and looked towards the window.

'Don't you feel rather exposed,' she said, 'with no curtains to draw? I know it's only a garden, but I'd still feel overlooked somehow. Even at home, way up on the first floor, I like the enclosed feel of drawn curtains. Except, of course, some summer evenings ...'

She wished she hadn't mentioned home; he appeared startled, unhappy, and made an obvious effort to distract her:

'She wears silk pyjamas
In summer when it's hot;
She wears her woollen nightie
In winter when it's not
But sometimes in the spring time
And sometimes in the fall,
She creeps between the linen sheets
With nothing on at all!'

Connie had already heard that, as a child, recited by her father with a lot of rolling of eyes and waggling of eyebrows, and had only been surprised that the girl had wanted to wear pyjamas in summer. Unless she was camping. Another one had been 'Vio-late me in vio-let time in the vile-est way that you know…' Which made her think of an old aunt who always carried crystallised violet petals in a small tin. Somehow it seemed rather near the bone to tell Roger that tonight.

'Do you usually wear pyjamas?' she asked, rolling onto her stomach so that she could see his face more clearly, and to blot out a harangue by Cameron.

Roger propped himself up on an elbow, glanced again at the window, and then captured her roving hand. 'There's something I must tell you,' he began, but was interrupted by a crash in the garden. He held her still, for the first time encircling her with his arms, trapping her head beneath his chin. 'Don't move!' he whispered.

She listened to the beating of his heart and heard footsteps on a gravel path, then the distant creak and bang of a door, the back door to the kitchen, a sound she had heard before. Then a tuneless whistling and movement in the drawing room next door.

'Roger old boy?'

Connie fought her way out of Roger's arms and sat up, staring at him sprawled on the pillows. 'That's Max!'

'I know.' He lowered his eyelids as if exhausted, but his voice was strong. 'I was going to tell you. I've been meaning to tell you. But I was hoping—'

'What is Max doing here?' She knew it was no social visit at this hour, even on election night; besides, he must have seen them through the window. A hand of ice seemed to touch the back of her neck and she shuddered. 'Why has he come in? He must know Sylvia's not here.'

Roger opened his eyes and studied her. They heard a clink of glass next door and a squirt of a soda siphon.

'He's expecting you.' Connie fitted another piece to the puzzle, or created another gap. Max is here in Roger's flat, by his own key. Max knows that Sylvia is away, therefore he has come to visit Roger. Max knows that Roger is in bed but he is settling down in the next room, therefore he expects Roger to join him. Why? 'But he must have seen that I'm here. Is he going to wait for you?' Why?

'Yes.' Roger pulled a dressing gown from the floor and wriggled into it. 'There's no point in beating about the bush, dear Connie, my very dear Connie. I had hoped – a lot of things – mainly, that it wouldn't come to this, that I wouldn't have to explain it to you. But.' He slotted a silk tie at the waist of the dressing gown and tied it, and turned to face her again. 'Max and I have been lovers, off and on, for many years. More off than on, actually, but it's on at present. I thought he would be too busy with the election tonight. I had no idea he'd come over, you must believe that.'

Connie had been kneeling on the bed watching his movements like a well-trained hound, wide-eyed, quite intelligent. It was not, after all, very surprising. She could have guessed it, should have guessed it. Max, after all, was at the bottom of everything. Max was the blight of her life. She blinked at Roger very slowly, as if a slice of darkness would reset the whole machine, change the record, put back the clock, but he remained sitting on the edge of the bed, fishing for his slippers, in crimson tussore that did not suit his pallid complexion. For a second she pictured Zoe in her crimson room, another of Max's works.

'You must believe me,' Roger pleaded. 'I wouldn't hurt you like that.'

Like what? Her head buzzed. Bees in the head. She climbed down off the bed to look for her clothes, tried to look through the window, tried to imagine looking in at the shaded light by the inactive bed, the blue-white light from the ever-active television. Political activity. More gains, more losses. Your gain, my loss. Green-white light in the bathroom led her to a crumpled dress and a kaleidoscope of images as she dragged stockings up her legs, the petticoat down over her head – wriggle, wriggle. She stared at the reflections, unamused, pushed up her hair and let it flop.

Roger waited on the bed with hound-sad eyes. He had switched off the television now and the light in the room had mellowed. She wished she could escape without seeing Max, without having to open her mouth, or that she could say something clever or conclusive. Roger was waiting for something.

'It's late, I must dash,' she said. 'Or I'll turn into a pumpkin.' That reminded her of Sally. What was Sally doing? Max and Hell. Max and Sally. The bees were at it again, buzzing so that she hardly knew where she was or where she was going.

In the next room the only light encircled Sylvia's church candlestick, shining down from under its silken shade to dazzle on a mahogany commode. All other furniture crouched in shadow. On the distant sofa sat Max, recognisable only by the shape of his head and an insolent position she remembered well. Somehow without willing it her hand grasped the candlestick, wrenched it high into an explosion of darkness and hurled it towards the sofa.

And then she was able to leave with dignity, not running, guided as if by magic across the room and through the hall and through the door and clattering along the curve of the Crescent, down streets under patches of light and patches of dark, like a homing pigeon to her car. And the car winged her home without any assistance, stopped under the portico light, let her out, let her in.

Only one o'clock showed on the oven panel in the kitchen. Only one o'clock after so much, after what seemed like a lifetime. The night is young! Celebrate with brandy! She filled a mug with Remy Martin, sniffed it and transferred it inaccurately into a champagne glass.

'Cheers!' It tasted hot, spiced with pepper.

She carried it with care but a trail of drips all the way to her favourite chair in the drawing room. At the mirror she paused to gaze into the room. She could just see the sofa in its underwater reflection, and something, someone, lying there, dying there. The death of the heart! She giggled and zigzagged her way back to the sofa and sank to her knees trying to keep the glass level. Always on her knees! Sir Roger would be dead by morning. Max would be dead by morning. They would all be dead by morning.

****

Sir Roger dies spectacularly.

Polly knows all about heads being chopped, lopped in the *Place de la Revolution*; the scaffold, the drums, the basket, the bounce, the involuntary twitches of the severed body. She had seen death and blood at a distance, in a crowd, impersonally, but is forced now to share this personal death with Sir Roger's enemies. As he chokes his farewell, his face contorted and grey with pain, eyes rolling upwards like so many religious paintings, fingers tightening in her grasp, the surgeon adds more bandages to stem the flow of blood and Duclos and Hugo turn away.

At the last moment Sir Roger manages to groan the one word, 'Kill!', rearing up to stare directly from her to Duclos and back again. All his strength flows into that command and then he seems to sigh and slip and his head rolls sideways until his cheek rests against Polly's bosom. The surgeon steps forward to feel the pulse and close the eyes and signals the two men to follow him from the room, and Polly is left with the body of her lover and the end of all her dreams.

For a long while she kneels there cradling his head to her breast, weeping silently. Then she rises and in a storm of grief staggers about the room searching for a weapon. All that remains for her to do is to obey Sir Roger's last wish. All that she can find is a silver candlestick which she grabs as she stumbles to the door.

The men return after an interval; first the surgeon, who hurries to check the sofa's burden, then Hugo noticing blood on the carpet and concerned for the sofa's brocade covering, and last M. Duclos. As the Frenchman enters, Polly raises the candlestick high and dashes it to his skull.

* * * * * * *

When Hugh returned home with the Fosters, the Conservatives had won and it was nearly five in the morning.

'A close run thing,' he kept repeating while he twisted the wrong key in the kitchen door. 'Too close for comfort. Bloody close!'

He could hear the clatter of Sheba's claws as she padded across the kitchen tiles, and Legs making her grunt-growl.

'All the bloody lights on, too!' Eventually the right key turned up and the door surprised him by opening itself. 'Bloody magic! Down, you bloody dogs!'

Working his way from switch to switch he followed his wife's route to the drawing room to find her asleep against the sofa. It seemed better not to waste time going all the way upstairs to bed. If she had taken over the sofa he would have her chair. But it took ages to find a comfortable position and in the end he chose the floor.

When daylight flooded the room, another bright and beautiful autumn dawn, the first thing Connie saw as she awoke was Hugh stretched across the hearthrug. She blinked, but he lay there still. And again.

Hugo dead? But she had killed the other one, M. Duclos! Hadn't she? Who was dead? No one on the sofa, no trace of blood. They had taken Sir Roger away! Why hadn't they taken her away? Murderess. Just wait till they found out! But it didn't matter any more, nothing mattered any more. Now that Sir Roger had died, gone away, left her, nothing could ever matter again. It didn't matter, really, whether she had killed M. Duclos or Hugo. They both deserved to die.

She got up with difficulty; one leg was fast asleep, without any feeling, just like her head. On the side table lay the silver candlestick she had used on M. Duclos – or was it Hugo? She picked it up and limped to the hearthrug where she gazed with distaste at Hugo's dead body. Why had no one removed it? Annie would be most upset. And where had they taken Sir Roger?

In the mirror her appearance shocked her. Hair all rumpled, uncombed, uncurled, a strange grey shroud instead of that delightful carnation-coloured silk; and so old, hag-like! How could any man have loved that face? She peered more closely, hoping to surprise herself with a view of Sir Roger riding past the windows, to one side, striding through the door, to the other. But she knew that wasn't possible. She would never see Sir Roger again.

Unutterable grief overwhelmed her and she had to clutch at the mantelpiece to stop herself from falling. As she did so, the candlestick slipped and struck the glass and when she next looked the whole room was distorted, crazed. Her strange old head was now comfortingly unrecognisable, merely an eye here, another one there, half a mouth; and the greenish underwater room was broken up by vivid silver snakes.

'Thank heaven!' she shouted. 'It's done! It's all over!'